A Crime in the Land of 7,000 Islands

A CRIME IN THE LAND OF 7,000 ISLANDS
ZEPHANIAH SOLE

THE **BLACK SPRING**
PRESS GROUP

First published in 2023
Published by Eyewear Publishing Limited (BSPG)
The Black Spring Press Group
Maida Vale, London W9
United Kingdom

Cover art Andrew Magee

The author has requested the publisher use American spelling
and grammar wherever possible in this edition

Trigger warning: contains themes of crimes against minors

ISBN-13 978-1-913606-48-0

For my Mother

PROLOGUE

SPRING 2010

> *Always remember daughter, Warriors do not apologize.*
>
> *Warriors hold themselves accountable for the consequences of their decisions.*
>
> *So now that the time is right, I will tell you that story of the things you must know.*

There exists a land which takes the crossing of several oceans to reach: a land of many, many islands. Seven thousand in fact, clustered together in the blue and green of reef and sea. In this land, on one island, in one province of this island, there is a village. The Villagers are poor but they work hard. They help each other. They have Faith.

One day, a rich man came to this village. He was a foreigner, an outsider, from a strange and faraway place, so we shall call him what the Villagers called him in their Language – *Tagagawas*. And Tagagawas was an odd fellow. His voice lacked the joy in the wind from which our breath rises and returns. And he walked upon the earth as if he believed he were bigger than the whole world. But he shared his wealth with the Villagers. He bought them food. He bought them clothes. And the Villagers slowly grew to trust him.

Tagagawas enjoyed the company of the village's children. He spoiled them with the trinkets and toys they would otherwise not possess. He took them on excursions, fed them well, gave them the space to play and be carefree. And when he returned the children to their homes in the evenings, they'd stay up all night, remembering their wonderful treks with Tagagawas, who put dreams in their heads of a bigger, better world than the small and poor village that set before them each dawn.

But one evening, the children did not return home. The Villagers searched frantically. Luckily, they found them at a nearby waterfall. The Villagers were relieved. The children were quiet. Tagagawas was nowhere to be seen. The Villagers returned home with their children, and as the days wore on, it became more and more apparent that something was not right. Tagagawas had disappeared. And the children had changed. Something had gone missing from their eyes.

You see, my love, Tagagawas had stolen their Innocence.

The Villagers could do nothing. There were warriors who walked about, charged with the Villagers' protection, but those warriors were often corrupt, and the Villagers did not trust them. So, the Villagers buried their tears and chose not to seek the Justice they lacked the power to demand.

Tagagawas meanwhile, had returned to his own land, where he, starving for something he could never have, stole the Innocence of yet another child. But a small group of warriors in his land learned of this and their hearts burned with hatred for such evil. They conducted an inquiry into the actions of Tagagawas and in doing so, shed light on his further offenses. They learned he had shamelessly done the same in that faraway place – The Land of 7,000 Islands.

How could the warriors help the Villagers in this remote land? It was no easy task to travel there. Finding this village would require a journey fraught with numerous obstacles. Who amongst them would even be willing to go?

One warrior stayed silent. This warrior was known to have suffered many defeats of late. She had a strange and faraway look in her eyes. Many believed this look to be the sickness that consumes a good many warriors: a sickness of the heart that turns compassion in on itself, shutting off a warrior's natural love for the world. But a few believed this look to be the beginning of wisdom. Perhaps it could have gone either way: sickness, or wisdom.

Perhaps this warrior understood that, which is why she agreed to be the one to travel to The Land of 7,000 Islands.

And so, this warrior woke one morning, faced the rising sun, knelt, and said a prayer. Not for herself, but for the children who had been wronged by Tagagawas. She asked the heavens to use her thoroughly; use her as an angel; use her as a demon; use her however she needed to be used to help her do her best. Her very best. And with that, she organized her abode, packed her belongings, stepped outside her door, and began a journey - the completion of which would leave things never to be the same again.

"How do I know these things?" you ask. That is a good question.

I know these things because I *was* that warrior.

The one they call Ikigai.

This is my tale.

CHAPTER 1

FALL 2021

Ikigai Johnson, my mother, disappeared seven years ago.

She was last seen off the coast of Mambajao by Mickey Sheptinsky, her lover, who said she'd been rowing. Rowing and laughing. I'm not sure I believe his account. Mom didn't laugh often. The best you could hope for was a slow, cautious smile that, even then, was tinged with a deep weariness. She *did* laugh when she told stories. I remember them all. Especially the very last one she told me eleven years ago, the one that wasn't just a story. The one that made me grow up.

Like all tales, it was a truth conveyed with many lies. Lies that were warm and well-intentioned, spun from moonlight and boiled milk for the mind of a child. But at 23-years-old, I'm a woman now, and I still need to understand the full importance of that tale; the tale that broke me; the tale that tore my guts out. It's not done with me: it isn't over. Mom's body was never found, but her story, darting like a shadow just beyond my peripheral vision, has teased me to chase it, teased me to understand it further.

I need the facts. I need the reality behind the myth Mom created. And the first cold, hard, and heavy fact is that the story did not start with my mother. It started with her friend, Geri Bradford: the Amazon.

That's why I take a Personal Day off my regular night shift and meet Geri at the Portland Police Bureau's East Precinct. She's a lieutenant now, running a high-speed, low-drag, interagency narcotics task force. After I smile with my eyes at the receptionist — it's hard to smile with these masks on — I badge my way through the access-controlled entrance, navigate the maze of disorganized and mostly empty cubicles, and stand at Geri's office door. She peers over the rim of her old woman glasses and grins.

"Junior," Geri calls, and reaches for the mask on her desk with her huge hands. "You want me to wear…?"

I step into her office and shut the door, taking my own mask off. "I'm vaccinated."

"Good," she says as I run smack into a Geri Bradford bear hug. "Means I can give you one of these."

I always marvel at how gentle she is for such a strong person. She lets me go and I wish she'd held me a little longer. I look at her face and take it all in. It's been a while. After Mom left those eleven years ago, Geri's been a second mother to me. I still get a kick out of her steel-blue eyes, like a wolf's. They never miss a thing. She grabs my left arm and pulls up my sleeve. "New?" she asks.

I pull my sleeve up further, letting her see the whole piece. "Finished it last week."

Geri looks at the lily tattooed on my inner forearm. Stalk and leaves trail away from petals, wrapping down to my outer wrist, over the back of my hand, then narrow into that spot on my ring finger covered by a platinum band. Geri purses her lips and tears up. She's sensitive.

She sits behind her desktop computer and clicks her mouse. "Took forever and a day to find," she says. "Got buried deep in Records at Main." I step behind her and peer over her shoulder. A frozen image from a video file lingers on her screen: two blurry figures, one much larger than the other. She touches my forearm and asks, "You sure?" I nod. "Can't bring myself to feel wrong about this," she says. "Given the totality… but it ever comes out I showed you this? I mean, I can fall on my sword Junior, I got twenty-nine years in. This is long adjudicated. It'd just be easier if…"

"Hey," I cut her off. "This is me."

Geri nods and squeezes my hand. I grab the other chair in her office, pull it up to hers, and sit. She clicks her mouse. The two blurs jump into focus and come to life. The larger one is Geri, twelve years younger, six feet tall, several pounds heavier than she is now. She's lost a bit of muscle as she's aged. Her hair's dyed platinum blonde, not the dusky light brown with strands of gray I see now. She still looks like the collegiate heptathlete she used to be: gorgeous but intimidating. And she knows it. That's why she speaks very gently, very softly, to the other figure, short, thin and crumpled in the chair directly next to hers, whose wilted dark brown hair falls over paper thin pale skin.

A knot ties itself in my throat.

Geri explains to me these are the cases where it's hardest to stay professional: the ones where you look at a child and see yourself staring back, trembling and afraid. The girl in the video, her eyes are the exact same color as Geri's. But whereas Geri's had taken on the piercing look of a huntress, the girl's had taken on the spacey look of someone retreating from reality.

Geri plays the video:

"I'm gonna ask you something easy. Ready?" Geri said. The girl nodded without looking up from the coloring book she was working away at with the crayon in her hand. Geri continued, "The sky, is it purple?"

The girl looked at Geri, confused. "No," the girl said, "it's blue."

"Alright," Geri went on. "Now, how are you with math?"

The girl answered with a voice made of broken glass. "Not good."

"That's okay," Geri said. "I've got another easy one for you."

"Okay."

"If I told you two plus two equals five, what would you say?"

"It's four. I'm not that bad at it."

"Well, there you go." With that, Geri established the girl could discern between true and false statements. "And how old are you now?"

"Ten."

"Ten! What grade are you in?"

"Six. Sixth grade. I was skipped."

"Look at that. What do you like to do? You know, outside of school."

"Um, I like, um, I like soccer. I play soccer a lot."

"Oh, I love soccer. I used to play when I was your age too."

"Yeah, I play on a team."

"Which position?"

"Forward. I'm not very good though."

"That's a tough spot. Lots of pressure."

"Yeah, it's kind of hard. And I mess up sometimes."

"You'll get better." Geri took an almost imperceptible breath. It was taking all her concentration to simultaneously build rapport and direct the conversation where it needed to go. "Do you play soccer every day?"

"Just, um, Mondays, Wednesdays, Fridays. Saturdays we... we'll have a game."

"Busy schedule. What about Tuesdays and Thursdays when you don't have soccer?"

The girl went mute and stared off into space. Then she returned to her coloring book, humming and rocking her body. She was withdrawing. Geri needed to pull her back in. "Did you win your last soccer game?"

"Uh-huh. I didn't play much though. I didn't score any points. There's this girl on the team, she's so good. She got two of... two goals. She's so fast."

"Do you hang out with this girl?"

"I don't think she likes me."

"Have you talked to her?"

"Nuh-uh."

"Well, how do you know she doesn't like you? Maybe you guys can practice extra together. Like on the days you don't have normal practice."

"But then we'd… It'd have to be Tuesday… or Thursday," the girl said, rocking again. Geri watched her, weighing whether to push or let the girl come to it herself. Geri opted to wait. Silence. Then the girl kept going. "But Tuesdays and Thursdays, I have… um… I have after-school."

"What do you do after-school?"

"Just, like, reading, and math. I hate math. I always have lots of questions."

"Who helps you after-school?"

"Mr. um…" she said, rocking again. "My teacher, Mr. Campbell."

"Does Mr. Campbell help you with your questions?"

"Uh-huh," she said, still rocking, but engaged.

Geri pressed. "When Mr. Campbell helps you, are there other kids in the class with you?"

"At first, yeah. But I always have so many questions. And, um, he can't get to everyone. So, after the other kids leave, I'll stay, like, I'll stay later and he'll help me."

"And what's that like?"

"He'll, um, help me. With fractions and decimals and stuff."

"How is Mr. Campbell when he explains things?"

"I don't know."

Geri rephrased the question. "What's it like, for you, when you are with Mr. Campbell and he's explaining things?"

"Um, it was fine. At first. But then, I don't know."

"What was it like for you then?"

"I don't know, he'd um…"

Silence. Geri waited.

"He'd kiss me. Before I'd leave. He'd kiss me," the girl said in a broken-glass whisper.

"Where would Mr. Campbell kiss you?"

"Like, on my head. And that was okay. But then he was… he'd, um, kiss me on the cheek. And that was, I don't know. Then he'd kiss my mouth. And I didn't like that. But he said don't tell anyone or I'd get in trouble and he wouldn't help me anymore. And I didn't understand."

"What did you not understand?"

"I don't know… I didn't want to get in trouble. And I didn't want to fail. And… And… Um, he kept doing it. Then he… um, he kept saying…" The girl muttered, too low for the audio to pick up.

Geri couldn't lose her now. She leaned forward and said gently, "Can you tell me what you just said? Can you say it again, a little louder?"

The girl stared at the floor, disconnected from the words retching from her throat.

"He kept saying he liked it tight, and I didn't want to get in trouble and he said it felt good and I didn't want to fail. I didn't want to get in trouble…"

I focus on the knot in my throat and tell myself to get used to its presence. It's not going to untie itself anytime soon. But I will not stop. Mom taught me that. When you decide upon a course of action, you keep going. Do not let the pangs in your chest stop you. Do not let the knots in your throat stop you. Do not stop. Ever. Geri freezes the video and peers over her glasses, "You okay, Sweety?"

I don't acknowledge the question and ask my own instead. "What happened next?"

Geri sighs. "Well, the most important part of the rest of this interview is me establishing with her that when she says *it* she is, in fact, referring to her vagina."

I fight back tears.

"And," she continues, "establishing that when she says that he said, 'it felt good wrapped around him', she is referring to his penetration of her vagina by his penis. Which was more complicated to unambiguously establish than one would think, because jackass Mr. Campbell liked to play games and use a cute little word for his penis."

Do not stop. Ever. I grit my teeth. "Then what?"

"Well." Geri leans back in her chair. "I remember it was raining."

FALL 2009

Of course it was raining. This was Portland: the west coast one –
where it rains, on average, a hundred days a year. At least it's not as
bad as Seattle.

Geri had to keep the defogger running on high that morning.
Her plain-clothes vehicle was an old Buick and it was a bit clunky,
to say the least. Her vision was 20/20 back then, but the windshield
kept fogging up from the rain and the chill and she needed to keep
those huntress eyes on the Toyota Camry she was tailing. Some
idiot had cut her off and now there were two vehicles between her
and the Camry, so she had to stay sharp. She put her windshield
wipers on a higher speed and held her car radio up to her chin.
"Two for cover, signaling left turn at the red ball. Clown in front
of me's moving slow as fuck. Who's north on the double niner?"

The radio talked back. "How slow, generally speaking,
does fuck move? 'Cuz my wife tells me my fuck moves too fast."

Another voice crackled in. "Vinnie, I have offered my services
to your wife to no avail. I think she may actually like you."

"Nah, Sarge," Vinnie said. "She's just waiting for me to get
vested. Then she'll leave and take half."

Geri shook her head. She loved working with these guys.
Normally, she'd join the banter, but not today. Not on this one.
"Focus boys," she told them.

"Geri, you on the 4-2 Charlie?" the Sergeant asked.

"Affirm," Geri replied.

"I'm coming up north from below."

"Red ball is now green."

"Got him."

Geri didn't care that Sarge had eyes on the Camry. She wanted
it herself. Bad. She honked the slow-moving sedan in front of her
and drove up close to its bumper. The driver waved his open hand

out of the window to signal a *What the hell?* But he moved forward and out of Geri's way and that's all that mattered. She hit the left turn on the 99 West and sped up when she saw the Sergeant's Dodge Charger tailing the Camry about a half mile ahead. Geri caught up to them and got back on the radio. "Sarge, Fred Meyer parking lot's right there. It's still too early to be open."

Sarge answered, "You are authorized Detective Bradford. We will follow your lead."

"Vinnie, pull him over," Geri said. Vinnie shouted a static filled, "Woo hoo!" Then Geri grabbed her radio and said, "Search Team, we're executing the arrest."

Geri let Vinnie catch up and pass her. He was driving the marked unit. He drove up behind the Camry, flashed his red and blues, and got on his horn. "Pull into the parking lot," his amplified voice commanded.

The driver of the Camry obliged. Vinnie, Geri, and the Sergeant followed. The grocery store parking lot was empty, save the tweaked-out meth-head stumbling away from a cliché late model Chrysler Sebring. A teener level deal had just gone down, but Geri barely registered it. At that moment, she was not there to stop more junkies in Portland from getting high. The Chrysler, wisely, left the parking lot, fast.

It was a textbook car stop. Vinnie squealed up and slammed his car to a stop, perpendicular to the front of the Camry. Geri and Sarge drove up behind on its left and right rear bumpers respectively, trapping it. Sarge and Vinnie jumped out of their cars and crouched beside their engine blocks. They drew down, training their Glocks on the driver's side of the Camry. Geri stayed in her vehicle and checked their angles, making sure Sarge and Vinnie wouldn't hit each other if someone had to squeeze the trigger. She got on her own horn and issued commands. "Evan Campbell. Turn. Your engine. Off."

The driver of the Camry obliged. Geri continued, "Unbuckle your seat belt. Roll your driver side window all the way down. Throw your keys on the hood of your car." The driver did so. "Unlock your driver side door. Stick your hands out the driver side window. Keep them out." Nothing. Geri repeated herself, calm but firm. Still nothing.

Geri stepped out of her vehicle and drew her weapon. She trained it on the Camry. She made eye contact with Sarge then stalked forward, toward the driver. Sarge moved in parallel to the passenger side. They checked the rear passenger seats as they crept past: empty. In dynamic situations like these, you could miss something in those rear seats. Geri reached the driver's side window and glared at her subject. "Evan Campbell," she said. "Slowly, stick your hands out of your window."

Evan did so, mumbling, "What's this? What is this?"

He was pasty and frail and wearing a sweater at least two sizes too big. This chump was milk toast and that's what put Geri on edge. Hardened bangers and motorcycling outlaws knew the score – they knew to lawyer up, do their time and wait patiently to get back out on the street and back into the game. Chumps like this, watching their carefully constructed facade of respectable citizenship come clattering down, were bound to do anything. "Is your door unlocked?" Geri asked. Evan nodded. "Open your door from the outside and step out of your vehicle." Evan blinked. "Step out of your vehicle, Evan," Geri repeated, her Glock 17 still trained on him. Evan pulled his hands back into his car. "Keep your hands out of the window!" Geri barked.

Then the chump went and did that anything he was bound to do and dove for the passenger seat.

Four minutes prior to that hairy situation, when Geri said into her radio, "Search Team, we're executing the arrest," there was a stack of six officers waiting at Evan Campbell's apartment complex in Southwest Portland for that verbal cue to go forth and rock and roll. They lined up outside Evan's second floor apartment. The big guy at the front of the stack, Detective Nate Schwinn, shouted, "Police! Search warrant!" He waited a moment. Then Nate swung a thirty-pound ram. One hit and the door frame splintered and the door swung open. Nate dropped the ram and moved to the back of the stack. Everyone else paused in motion, letting the opened door breathe. Nate called out again. "Police! Search Warrant!" Another moment of hang time. Then they made entry and cleared Evan's 636 square foot one-bedroom apartment, slowly and meticulously. None of this slam-bang shit you see in the movies. No less than two officers per room. Check the corners. Open the closets. Look for those hiding spots.

Slow.

Meticulous.

The apartment was empty. No surprise there. But, given the context of the search, something caught Nate's eye: an open laptop on a small desk in Evan's bedroom. "Let's get on that," Nate said to one of his colleagues, and approached the laptop carrying a go-bag. Nate grazed a thick finger over the laptop's cursor pad and the screen lit up. "Lucked out. Still powered on," Nate said, and produced two USB wires, a write-protector device, and a solid-state portable drive. Nate touched the cursor pad again, clicked open the Task Manager, checked Running Processes, and shook his head.

"He's got encryption all up in this box," Nate said. "I'm gonna have to do a live data capture. You let me know if you see any other computers, cameras, phones, anything, please." Nate connected a USB wire to the open laptop and held up his portable radio. "Geri, Nate, residence cleared. We're searching now. How y'all doing?"

Geri heard Nate's voice over her radio, but at that moment she was a bit preoccupied. Evan was leaning on his passenger seat, hiding his hands with his body. Geri and her team were in a pickle. They didn't have probable cause to shoot. But they didn't want to risk going hands on with the guy until they had a better idea of what he was doing. Then Geri got a quick glance. "He's holding something!" she shouted. "Hands, Evan! Drop what you're holding and show me your hands!"

Luckily, Sarge had a better view from the passenger side window. "It's a phone!" he shouted.

"Fuck this," Geri muttered. "Cover me," she said, louder. She holstered her weapon and pulled open the driver side door. Vinnie shifted his angle at the front of the Camry, keeping Geri out of his line of fire. She leaned in, grabbed Evan by his hair with her right hand and pulled. Hard. "Drop the phone, Evan!" Evan screamed in pain, but held on, fumbling with his smartphone. Geri snaked her left hand to his jaw and gripped it, twisting his head toward her. She set her left foot on the floor of the driver seat and pulled. Harder. Evan could only resist for a second. He dropped the phone on the passenger seat. His body followed his head as Geri pulled him out of the car and directed him, face first, into the pavement. Still holding his head, she straddled his back, lifted her weight up off her feet and pushed most of her 170 pounds into her hands, squeezing Evan's head into the concrete. Evan screamed again. Vinnie kept his weapon trained on him. Sarge ran over, handcuffs ready, and grabbed Evan's wrists.

Back in Evan's apartment, an officer approached Nate, who stood over the laptop. The officer asked, "How's it going?"

Nate smiled and fought back the urge to do a happy dance. "Box is still on, so we can decrypt in motion. Stupid ass left everything open, even his email."

The officer smiled back. "In like Schwinn."

"You know it."

But Nate's delight was cut short by the brief appearance of a command prompt window before the screen went black. "Shit," Nate said, inspecting the laptop. "Spoke too soon. Motherfucker just powered off on its own."

A few hours later, Geri watched Evan Campbell pick a piece of lint off his too-large sweater and look around the interview room. He probably expected harsh fluorescent light bouncing off a clean steel table and dirty linoleum tiles. What he got was a plush sofa in a lamp-lit, off-white colored office. If it had a TV, it would have felt like a living room. There was no two-way mirror, but Geri had set a digital recorder on the Ikea-brand footrest before them and explained it was on. Geri and Nate sat in low plastic chairs in extremely close proximity to Evan, making him visibly uneasy. But besides that, he was perfectly comfortable. Geri even took his cuffs off.

The three of them started off talking about the weather. This led to a prolonged discussion, mostly on the part of Evan, regarding how much it hurt when Geri face planted him in the parking lot. See, Evan explained, the rain made the concrete slick. So his face slid when he hit the ground, tearing his skin up even more. He had the bruising and bleeding to show for it. Geri softly apologized and inquired as to whether he needed anything to alleviate his discomfort.

Evan replied, in an almost stoic way, that he thought he was okay. The discussion then led to his family life, the funeral of his recently deceased mother, and how hard it was for him to get up in the morning. Nate teared up at this and shared the recent passing of his brother. Geri sat back as the two commiserated about the difficulties of moving on with life. During this commiseration, Nate smoothly inserted the reading of Evan's Miranda rights, as if it were a minor digression. Evan signed the form Nate put before him, waiving his rights. Then, after about forty-five minutes of them circling around topics that ranged from favorite breweries to the Portland Trailblazers, to all the Californians who insisted on moving to Oregon, Evan himself jumped the gun and said, "I think, uh, you know, my students? Those kids? They get me up in the morning. I can tell you that."

Geri prodded, carefully. "Gotta have something to live for: a purpose, right?"

"Right," said Evan. "A purpose. You get it. I mean, I get to change their lives. I get to guide them."

"Absolutely," said Geri. "It's a, uh, it's an honorable…"

"Honorable."

"An honorable responsibility. Why math? Why not English, social studies, gym?"

"Because," Evan snickered, "I suck at math." The three of them shared a laugh. Evan explained, "I never got it in school. Never. But I stuck to it, right? Studied it in college, got C's mostly. Then one day, everything opened up. It wasn't a bright light going off. It was more like something got removed from my eyes, to see the light that was already there. Then you see the world, the whole world, the equations between everyone, the variables that shift our perspectives."

"That's insightful," Geri said, in an admiring tone.

"I needed to share that," Evan said. "I needed to make sure everyone had access to that. It starts young."

"It does," Geri said. Evan smiled. Geri exchanged a glance with Nate, who nodded. This was the perfect moment to go for the confession. Geri moved her chair even closer to Evan. She lowered her voice even further. "We need to talk about why you're here."

"Yes, Detective," he said, lowering his voice as well. "Why are we…?"

Geri cut him off. "I need you to listen to me right now. I need you to hear this."

"I am listening Detective. I am. I just don't understand…"

Geri talked over him. "This is important and this is going to make everything very clear." Evan leaned back on the sofa. Geri leaned forward to stay close to him. "I don't think you're a bad guy, Evan…"

"I hope not. I'm not. Why would…?"

"I think you're a good guy who really loves those kids, who really wants to help them see the world the way you do. All the magic you see since that thing got lifted from your eyes. But I think you went a little too far with that love. I don't think you meant to. I don't think you ever, ever, intended to hurt anyone."

Evan froze. Geri pressed. "Evan, I need you to talk about what happened after school with…" Geri let her sentence dangle.

Silence.

"With…?" Evan asked.

"You know who," Geri said. "And I need you to talk about what happened, because this is your chance. Right here. To explain to us, just us, in this room right here, right now, so we get your perspective. So we understand what happened. Before this whole thing gets out of control and you're made out to be some kind of monster when that's not what you are."

Evan took a deep breath. Geri pushed. "Talk to us. Tell us what happened."

Evan adjusted his glasses and rubbed his hands over his face. "I… I wouldn't know. I mean, where to start."

"Okay," Geri said, putting her hand on his knee. "That's okay. Let's start simple. You were running your after-school class. The kids had left. Except for one. Let's start there. Who stayed behind?"

Evan made eye contact with Geri. Geri returned his gaze, wolf eyes bearing down on her prey. "We've got your phone. We've got your laptop. We've got everything. This is your chance."

"Yeah," Evan smirked, fighting back laughter. "Have fun with that." He adjusted his glasses again and blinked. "I don't want to talk to you anymore, you know, without a lawyer."

★★★

"…you know, without a lawyer."

I listen to the voice on the old digital recording and a weighted, sludgy thing burrows itself into my gut. Geri clicks the recording off. "That's how that went down. He toyed with us. Strung us along. Revoked his waiver and invoked his right to counsel."

"You had his phone and his computer and…" I remind her.

Geri chuckles. "I was bluffing. We knew nothing at that point."

"At that point," I repeat.

"At that point," Geri says and smiles. "A few days later is when things got really interesting."

★★★

After the interview Geri sat in her cubicle, depressed. The minor female victim's testimony was convincing. Geri's ears had been trained to pick up on things that would clinch an alleged victim's credibility, or lack thereof: little things. Like things a child would say that a child would not normally know; in this case, the girl's recollection that Evan said he liked how tight her vagina was. Geri wasn't naive, she knew kids could be surprisingly perverted. But this girl was ten, and she gave the impression that she was very naive. Either way, it wasn't enough to put Evan in jail.

So, when Nate Schwinn peered over Geri's cubicle and grinned at her, she grinned right back. "Hey handsome," she said. Geri liked Nate. A lot. He was the only man she would even consider dating. She didn't care that he was shorter than her. His complexion was perfect. A warm, even brown — not the pasty paleness she was used to seeing in a town where it's rainy and overcast most of the year. Also, she really had a thing for tech geeks. Too bad he was married.

"You crack that computer for me?" Geri asked.

Nate shook his head, sheepishly avoiding her flirtatious gaze. "Sort of."

They took a walk down the hall to the elevators, and traveled up three flights of the Portland Police Bureau Central Precinct's downtown building. Geri followed Nate past framed wall photos of police gear, weapons and smiling officers – none of which Geri paid attention to. She was marveling instead at Nate's shoulders. She followed him into his forensic examination room, shivering as he closed the door behind them. "Sorry it's so cold," he said and pointed to all the computer servers in the room. "Gotta keep the temperature on these babies down." Geri smirked as three different inappropriate jokes pertaining to babies ran through her mind. "What's so funny?" Nate asked innocently.

"Nothing," Geri shook her head, "Whatchagot?"

Nate sat at his work desk, put on latex gloves, and beckoned Geri to look over his perfectly muscled shoulder. "Homeboy's phone," Nate said and held up Evan's smartphone. "Heard you almost pulled his head off making him drop this."

Now it was Geri's turn to be sheepish. "I didn't…"

"You did and it's good you did," Nate scrolled through the phone's screen. "He didn't get a chance to turn it off. If he had, I wouldn't have cracked it."

"Anything good?" Geri asked.

"Not in and of itself, but check what he was doing when you were tearing his face off."

"I was executing an arrest with officer safety in mind."

"Remember that for the civil case you know the asshole's gonna try for. Anyways, look."

Geri peered at the screen. "He sent an email? To himself? Why?"

"Look at the content," Nate said.

"Just a bunch of code."

"That's a batch script."

"Okay?"

Nate put the phone down, grabbed a laptop and opened it. The screen was black. "This was the laptop in Mr. Campbell's living room."

"The one that mysteriously shut off on its own?"

"Homeboy had his email open on this laptop, follow? He emailed himself that batch script to shut this laptop down."

Geri shook her head, comprehending. "Damn."

"Soon as I looked at this laptop, I knew it had encryption programs running. Once he shut it down…"

"Now the whole thing's encrypted. We're not getting in." Geri rubbed her temples. "Gotta figure some other way to nail him."

"I wouldn't give up on the computer yet," Nate said. "I was able to pull some stuff while it was powered on. Open files he hadn't saved yet."

"Involving our victim?"

"Nope."

"That helps us how?"

"I don't know how it helps us, but I wouldn't give up on it yet. This one bothers me." Nate accessed the digital forensic workstation on his desktop computer, pulled up a list of files and clicked on one. It opened.

A photo appeared.

Geri stared at the photo. She fought back a shiver. "Now, who in the world is that?"

"I was hoping you knew," Nate said. "This ain't some picture he pulled online."

"You think he took this picture?" Geri asked.

"I do. Check the metadata." He pulled up the metadata file. JPEG Exif. Meta info. Camera model. "See?" Nate said. "He took this picture." Nate pointed to Evan's phone. "With this phone."

"Is the original picture on the phone?"

"He must have deleted it. I'm not seeing it in any of the recovered files from the phone."

"What about other metadata? Can't you tell *where* he took the picture? When?"

"Dude's no dummy. When he transferred it to the laptop he scrubbed date, time and geolocation data."

"You can do that?"

"You can."

"Damn," Geri said again, gazing at the picture. This time she couldn't fight the shiver. The picture was of a girl.

The girl, like the victim who started this case, couldn't have been older than ten. She was squatting on the ground in what looked like a suggestive pose. The kind of pose you'll see grown women perform in pornography: legs splayed open, back arched, arm resting on a grubby wall beside her for balance. It looked like the girl was in an alley, the ground half concrete and half dirt, enclosed by walls of metal and cardboard.

Nate's voice cracked. "I know we do a lot of these, but this one bothers me."

"I know," Geri said gently. "It bothers me too." Geri stared at the photo, taking in the details. She'd seen worse. The girl was in a disturbing pose, but she was fully clothed, so they weren't going to get Evan Campbell on a Possessing Sexually Explicit Images of Minors charge. But the shivers kept running up and down Geri's spine, and it was obvious Nate felt it too. Geri tried to figure out what it was, what bothered her so much. She looked at the girl again. The girl was a deep, sun-tanned brown, with long, straight, jet black hair and dark eyes. But then Geri looked, not at the girl's eyes, but into them. And for a second, Geri felt lost. Lost in whatever pool those eyes had come from; whatever pool they were drowning in. The girl's mouth was closed with a faint, forced, close-lipped smile. But her eyes, were they pleading? No, they were more intense. Were they were enraged? Yes, but that wasn't it either. Then Geri saw it.

The girl's eyes were screaming.

★★★

Geri gets up from her seat and moves her arms around, dispersing the energy of the memory.

"Never heard something so loud without actually hearing it," she says. "Nate was good, he was *so* good." She sits back down. "But he'd cracked as much as he could from the computer and the phone. It wasn't easy for us to admit, but we needed help." Geri chuckles. "And by us, I mean me. Nate was humble, he was the one who said it." She loses her train of thought.

I bring her back. "Said what?"

Geri smiles. "That we needed to take it to Ikigai."

CHAPTER 2

FALL 2009

It is often said when you hate something, take a step back. Examine this hatred. Find what it is in yourself you truly hate.

When I was eleven, I hated water. It wasn't until much later in life I came to understand I hated water because, at eleven years old, water governed everything about me. Everything, in all ways, felt wet. When I was upset, I cried. Hard. I was always sweaty, clammy, smelly. I had to start wearing deodorant. I hadn't got my period yet, but my body knew what my mind didn't. Subtle aches and pains below my tummy told me, in a knowing way, that change was coming.

I felt gross and two things didn't help my emotional and bodily sensations of consistent, unceasing, uncomfortable wetness. One, we lived in Portland, where the rain never, ever stopped. (I promised myself when I turned eighteen I was moving to California.) And two, the boys in school had recently taken to making fun of my name. My mother, I believed at the time, was both stubborn and lacking in creativity. Stubborn, in not allowing my father to choose my name. ("Ah, so you were the one who carried her for nine months," she reportedly stated as she brushed off his input.) Lacking in creativity, in that she simply chose to name me after herself: Ikigai. Of course, it was predestined that the boys in school would call me 'Icky'.

However, unlike my mother, I was filled to the brim with creative inclination. I came to a staggeringly elegant solution to the dilemma of finding a way not to be referred to as Ikigai, yet in a manner that paid respect to my mother. (I still respected her, even when I hated her.) When this answer came to mind, I proudly stood up during roll call in sixth grade homeroom as Ms. Broner called out, "Ikigai Warner," and I announced for all to hear, "I prefer to be called…"

Wait for it.

"Junior!" I grinned and sat back down.

My brilliance was hella tight. And it commanded respect. None of the boys even laughed. (Probably because they didn't care.) My teachers quickly fell in line with my fiery will and only referred to me as Junior from that point forward. (Likely because they too had run out of shits to give.) And the best part was my mother, Ikigai Johnson – the dragon lady herself, acquiesced to the genius of her progeny and agreed with nary the slightest whimper of protestation, to calling me Junior. (I later learned she liked calling me Junior. It gave her the answer to her own problem, which, when formulated as a question, was: how can I break out of the habit of calling my child 'you'?)

★★★

"You," she said that to me that morning on the river. (She was still working on it.) My eleven-year-old shoulders screamed in pain. I pulled my double-bladed paddle through the water and twisted my neck, trying to look at her sitting behind me in the tandem inflatable kayak.

"It's Junior," I whimpered.

"Don't face me," she snapped. "Face the east. What do we do in the morning?"

There we were again, surrounded by water. This time it was the Willamette River, which was the case every morning I slept over at her condo. Dad was so much easier to live with. I would have rolled my eyes at her question, but they were still too tired from being shocked out of slumber at four am. "We get up," I answered.

She splashed water on me with her paddle, on purpose. I cringed. "Then what?" she asked.

"We face the rising sun," I answered, and wished that the inflatable kayak would get a puncture so I could just be done with it all.

"Then what do we do, Junior?" she said, gently this time. Or maybe I just heard it as gently because she didn't call me *you*.

I perked up. "We do our best," I said, "our very best."

"Good, baby," she smiled. Even though she was sitting behind me, I could tell she'd smiled. I loved her approval. It made me feel like freshly baked cookies, with white chocolate and macadamia nuts. "Two hundred yards," she said, ruining the moment. "Go get it."

Hot, wet tears returned. "I hate you," I whispered.

"I heard that," she said. "Move! Before I push us further back."

I laid down my paddle, jumped out of the kayak into the cold, morning river, and swam to shore.

Later, back in her condo, she towel-dried me when I got out of the shower. "I can dry myself. Dad doesn't dry me."

"Hm," she grunted. When she and Dad got divorced, she was the one who moved out of their house. She bought a little one-bedroom condo in a Portland suburb called Lake Oswego. It was small and cheap and she loved it because it was right on the lake. It was also a short walk from a little beach on the Willamette River. So, she was always near the water she, unlike me, loved so much. She lived alone, she always ate out, and she could paddle with her inflatable kayak, in lake or river, whenever she pleased. The only thing she didn't like, she would say, was that she got to spend only half her week with me.

"Ow!" I proclaimed. She was inspecting me again. This was a constant thing with her, always poking and prodding, checking everywhere on my body – under my arms, between my legs.

She pushed her finger into a bruise on my left hip. "Mo-om!" I squealed. "Come on!"

"How'd you get that?" she asked.

"During scrimmage. God, it's just a bruise."

"How did you get it?" she asked again.

"I ran into the forward. It was an accident." (It wasn't, I body-checked the shit out of that kid.)

"Playing rough again?"

"No." I tried to change the subject. "Come watch practice later?" I said and mustered the cutest face I could.

"Put cute-face away. Do I look like your father?" Shit. Cute-face backfired. She was pissed. She finished drying my hair, muttering, "Going to have to repeat myself again."

Now I was annoyed. I pushed back. "It's just part of the game. I got the goal."

Mom closed her eyes, took a breath, and forced herself to speak very, very patiently. "You did not have to body-check your teammate."

"I didn't body…"

"Stop it," she cut me off. (How did she even know I body-checked the kid?) "Why would you do that?" she asked. "Because you were better than her? Because you were stronger?" I stayed quiet and kept my eyes on the gray square tiles of the bathroom floor. She took another breath. "Do you remember the story of the Arrogant Tree?"

"Yes, Mom," I said respectfully but with a tinge of impatience. She'd only been telling me that story since I was, like, six. She wrapped the towel around me. "Sit," she said. "Clearly you still don't get the point."

I did as I was told and sat on the bathroom floor, leaning my back against the wall.

"If you can hold yourself in the silent space of this coming dawn," she began as she had always begun her stories, the timbre of her voice changing to a pitch that placed me in a state of near hypnosis. "You will see, my love, that one day, you will be strong and tall. There was a tree once, who also grew strong and tall..."

This Tree bloomed a canopy of green leaves and succulent fruit on its thick trunk with sturdy roots, and as such, was very proud of itself and all it had accomplished. Then it came to pass one day, a gaunt, tired man, approached the Tree.

"My dear," he addressed the Tree. "I have been working all day in the sun in those fields nearby. Would you mind terribly if I sat beneath your lovely leaves, to partake in the shade you offer? Only briefly, I promise."

"And who are you to call me *dear*?" the Tree haughtily responded. "The growth of this canopy, the shade it provides, this is my doing. Who are you to partake in the joys of my success? If you are so weak that your labors have tired you such, that is your problem. Please, move along."

The man, wordless with shock, stared open-mouthed at the Tree, then sadly bowed his head and walked away.

You see, what the man knew, that the Tree did not, was that the man was not just any man. He was a Farmer. And many, many years ago, he spotted a seed on the ground, struggling to reach its full potential. The man covered this seed with rich soil. Watered it when the rains did not come. Nurtured it. Until it sprouted and expanded roots and grew into that very same Tree. It broke the Farmer's heart that the seed he had cared for had grown into such a snide creature, and he never visited the Tree again.

Years passed and the Tree grew more fruit and it was happy. One day, a tall, broad woman walked by and approached the Tree. "Hello, friend!" she said jovially. "I am famished from so much of my training. Would you grant me the sweetness of one of your fruits? I only need one. Just to keep my strength up for the rest of the day."

"Friend?" the Tree replied. "I know not who you are, woman. As for my fruit, did you grow them from your limbs? Of course not. If you are so weak you cannot handle the demands of your training on your own, that is your problem. Move along."

The woman gritted her teeth and furrowed her brow and forced herself not to curse at the Tree. Muttering to herself, she stalked angrily away.

You see, what the woman knew, that the Tree did not, was that she was not just any woman. She was a Warrior. And many years ago, when the Tree was but a sapling, struggling to shoot out of the ground, Invaders attacked and tried to take the very land the Tree was growing on. The Warrior remembered this Tree, for she had told her cohorts to fight for it; to fight to protect that struggling Tree on their land; to protect its right to strive and grow and become. A right it would never have if the Invaders won. It broke the Warrior's heart that the sapling she had fought for had grown into such an arrogant creature, and she never visited the Tree again.

Time moved on, and the Tree's leaves fell. They did not grow back as quickly, and the Tree's fruit fell to the ground and did not grow back at all. One day, a slender, soft-spoken man walked by and approached the Tree. He was very gentle and very excited at the same time. "You are so lovely!" he exclaimed. "With your drooping canopy and your nest of fallen fruit about your trunk and roots. I would like to sit here and gaze upon you and paint your likeness. Would you grant me your permission to do so?"

"Absolutely not," the Tree said tiredly. "You had nothing to do with this canopy, with this fruit, with the growth and the becoming of all that I am. What right have you to copy my likeness? Go away."

This hurt the man deeply. For as I'm sure you can guess, he was not just any man, but an Artist. And what this man knew, that the Tree did not… Actually, this Artist didn't really have anything to do with the growth of the Tree. Artists don't really have much to do with the growth of anything. They just draw pretty pictures and write thoughtful things.

Regardless, it was very mean of the Tree, and the Artist, being such a sensitive person, ran away crying. Like a baby.

More years passed. The fruit that fell to the ground rotted. The leaves that fell grew back no longer. The Tree was getting old. One day, an Invader snuck over to the field in which the Tree was planted. "Hmm," the Invader said to the Tree. "You are going to die. Better to chop you up now before your wood is too decayed to be of use."

"Oh, no," the Tree muttered. And mutter was all the Tree could do. For the Tree had driven the Warrior away many years ago, and now there was no one to defend it. The Invader hacked the Tree to pieces and carried off the wood, leaving behind the seeds that came forth from the decomposed fruit on the ground. But the Tree had driven away the Farmer, so there was no one to care for those seeds. They never sprouted, and the Tree had no offspring. The Invader had hacked the Tree so thoroughly, not even a stump remained. The seeds were blown away by the wind and eaten by mice and crows. It was as if the Tree had never existed. The strength and beauty of what it once was, did not matter. For the Tree had also driven away the Artist. And now no one would ever know, or be inspired by, the Tree's former glory.

"So why are we strong, Junior?"

"So we can help the weak," I mumbled, having gone through this before.

"And why do we help the weak?" she said.

"To learn that they may not be so weak."

"And?"

"And that we may not be so strong."

Mom nodded. She was done with her inspection and her lessons for the morning. I asked again, and made only a half-cute-face this time, "Watch me practice later?"

She stood me up. "You know I will. You don't have to ask."

"I dunno," I said, taking advantage of her shift in mood. "Maybe you're gonna be busy doing crazy, awesome, FBI stuff."

Mom smiled. That slow, weary smile. "Momma doesn't work that kind of stuff anymore."

★★★

Geri puts a huge, booted foot up on her office desk and wiggles it. "Man, this ankle's been jacked up," she says. "Getting old, Junior."

"Glucosamine helps," I say.

Geri laughs. That big, hearty laugh. "Glucosamine helps old age?" I smile. "You know what I mean."

"So, anyways," she says. "Nate was good, but Ikigai was better. And Nate never made bones about that. 'Let's take it to her,' he said, which was a bit of an issue for me."

"Why?" I ask. Geri chuckles.

"Fine. I'll take it to her," Geri said to Nate, unable to look any longer at the photo of the girl with the screaming eyes. "But you're coming with me. She and I do not get along."

"She ain't that bad," Nate said.

"She *is* that bad. Crabbiest bitch I've ever met. And you know she fucking hates me, since…" Geri trailed off. "You know…"

Nate nodded. "I know. I'll call the RCFL."

That was how, a few days later, Geri and Nate found themselves in the Lloyd District area of Northeast Portland. They drove by Holladay Park, observing the mix of 30-something year-old mothers jogging with their strollers; 20-something year-old slackers begging for change; and any-something year-old junkies fiending for a hit. They circled around the park, looped back to Northeast Lloyd Boulevard, and drove into the garage of the building that housed the Northwest Regional Computer Forensics Laboratory.

They found the elevators and, on the top floor, exited into a hallway that wasn't drab, but was exceedingly plain. They followed the signs that pointed to the RCFL, found an innocuous door, and pressed a buzzer. A cheery, female voice with an accent greeted them. "How can I help you?"

Geri responded. "Schwinn and Bradford to see Special Agent Johnson." She put such emphasis on *Special Agent* the receptionist behind the door likely heard the rolling of her eyes. A buzz was followed by a loud click. Geri and Nate pulled open the door and walked up to the face behind a glass pane that belonged to the cheery voice. "That's a pretty accent," Geri said and smiled at the receptionist. "British?"

The receptionist smiled back. "New Zealand, actually."

"Aw, you're a Kiwi."

"You got it."

"Didn't think the FBI would hire someone from New Zealand."

"I'm with Washington County Sheriff's."

"How's that work?"

"We're all a mixture here: FBI, state, local."

"There must be a story behind how you ended up here. Want to chat about it over coffee sometime?" The receptionist smiled and held up her ring finger. The princess cut diamond glittered.

Geri chuckled. "I'm guessing that's the story."

The receptionist nodded. Nate fought back a laugh. They signed in. The receptionist pushed a button behind the glass pane. Another loud click and Geri and Nate were able to open a second door. "Take a right and she ought to be two doors down," the receptionist said. Geri and Nate smiled and waved as if they were about to embark on a long journey.

"I need to visit New Zealand," Geri told Nate as they entered and walked down the hall. They found the office they needed. They stood at its open door and peering inside, saw a short, wiry, dark skinned woman with thick, wavy hair and very photogenic cheekbones packing her purse, shoving a protein bar down her throat, and texting on her mobile phone.

"Ikigai!" Nate proclaimed. "What's goin' on, sister?"

Ikigai froze mid-text, looked up from her phone, swallowed a chunk of protein bar, and stared the two of them down. "Nate," she said slowly, "just because both our fathers were Black does not mean they were the same man."

"Wow," Geri said. "Okay, we were just hoping you could help us with this."

"What's *this*?" Ikigai asked and returned to her texting.

"This," Geri said and held up a one-terabyte external hard drive.

"You fill out the request form?" Ikigai asked.

"Yup," Geri said.

"That a working copy?"

"Of course," Nate said. "Original's back in my lab."

Without a word, Ikigai walked toward them at top speed. Nate was easily twice Ikigai's size, and Geri was even taller. Yet, they both parted like that famous sea as Ikigai zipped past them and left her office. "Leave it on my desk," she said as she walked away, down the hall.

"When do you think…?" Geri said.

"When I get to it," Ikigai replied, disappearing around the corner.

"But…"

They heard the clicks of a door opening and closing reverberate throughout the hall. Ikigai was gone. "Seriously?" Geri looked at Nate imploringly.

"She'll get to it," Nate said.

"Yeah, when? Barely three in the afternoon, her day's already over?"

"She'll get it done. I'll touch base with her in a few."

"Wish I had those working hours."

★★★

What Geri did not know, was that Mom was rushing out of her office for a very good reason. She didn't want to break the promise she made to watch a certain little someone's soccer practice. She only had to drive five miles north to get to Columbia Park, but traffic was getting worse and worse those days, and she didn't want to miss anything. That's why she left work early, texted her ex-husband (aka Dad) that she was on her way, inhaled that protein bar, and fought the traffic heading up to North Portland. She got to the park and made a beeline for the field. But what she encountered when she arrived would make any mother a bit concerned, to say the least.

There was me. Sitting on the sidelines. Bawling my eyes out.

Dad had his hand on my shoulder, but not exactly in a comforting way. Coach Fritz was explaining everything to him. Mom walked up to us.

"Hi, Ms. Warner," Coach greeted my mother.

"Ms. Johnson," she corrected him and crouched next to me, forcing me to make eye contact through my tears. "Can you please," she said to me, "take a deep breath and tell me what's going on?"

"Ikigai," Dad said. "Coach Fritz was explaining..."

"Greg, I'd like to hear it from her first."

"She's upset right now," Dad said. "Maybe we..."

Mom raised a hand to silence him and kept her attention on me. "What is going on?"

"He said I can't play anymore on the team!" I blubbered through snot and tears.

"Why is that?" she asked.

Silence.

"Why is that, Junior?"

"She was fighting with another girl," Coach Fritz said. Mom did not acknowledge him. "Why were you fighting?" she asked.

"She hit me first!" I screamed.

"We can't tolerate that: physical fighting," Coach said.

Mom stood up and faced Coach. "Got it," she said. "You removed the other girl from the team as well?"

"The other girl... I don't understand." Coach stalled.

Mom turned to Dad, "Greg, am I not being loud enough here?" She turned back to Coach and raised her voice. "So. You. Removed..."

"Ikigai, come on," Dad pleaded.

"The other girl. From the team?" she said to Coach Fritz.

"I hear you just fine." Coach said.

"Did you or did you not?" Mom said.

"I did not."

"Why not?"

"We didn't feel..."

"Who's we? And what did this we not feel?"

"I did not feel…"

"Whatever you felt, did you get the facts? Why were they fighting?"

"Let him finish," Dad said.

Mom ignored Dad, continuing at Coach. "How did the fight start?"

"The girls were punching each other before…"

"So why has Junior been removed and the other girl has not?"

"I don't, I didn't think the other girl… given her…"

"Given her what?"

"Given her demeanor, I don't think she started the fight."

Mom smiled like a hungry tiger eyeing food. "Are you saying Junior's demeanor is what led you to believe she started the fight?"

"Ikigai," Dad broke in, stronger this time. "Let's come over here, let's talk for a second."

Mom still ignored him and glared at Coach. "You are *not* removing Junior from the team. She has to sit out this practice, she has to sit out the next game, that's fine. She shouldn't be fighting. But you're making judgment calls based on what you perceive to be the demeanor of what, ten and eleven year-old girls? And one of them just so happens to be the only girl of color on this team?"

"Woah, time out." Coach Fritz held up his hands. "This is not about that."

"What's *that*?"

"I don't need to stand here and be accused of *that*."

"What's *that*?" Mom repeated. "I haven't accused you of anything."

Coach took a breath. He was outclassed in this fight and he knew it. He needed to extricate himself and still save face. "I can keep Junior on the team if she sits out this practice. But she cannot fight again. She fights again, I'm sorry, I'll have to take her off."

Mom squinted her eyes. "Fair enough," she said, grabbed my hand, and beckoned to my father. "Let's have that family discussion now."

Mom and Dad stared each other down. Dad was a good six foot four, and if you went to the *B* section of the dictionary and scrolled your finger down to *big-goofy-white-dude*, well, you get the joke. Given my mother's diminutive stature, they would have been a humorous sight if they didn't genuinely look like they were ready to murder each other. And Mom always had her gun on her, so I was a little concerned this could be the day.

There weren't a lot of physical demonstrations of anger. No shouting or flurrying of hands, no pointing of fingers. We were at the side entrance of the field, where I waited in Dad's parked car as they talked on the sidewalk. I rolled down the window and heard every word. They didn't want to attract attention from the people strolling by so they, externally speaking at least, kept it civil. Yet, each word they spoke, however calm, was a feint, a strike, or a riposte.

"Thank you. For having my back." Mom attempted to draw first blood.

"I'm not going to back you up when you're being unreasonable."

"What is unreasonable about asking a man to provide reason as to why he was going to remove our child from the team?"

"You wouldn't even let him talk. You just went off into your angry power-woman mode. Not cool."

The problem here was, Dad was the drunken master of domestic squabbling. He looked and talked like he was mellow and carefree, but each cut he made was subtle and dangerous. He knew that last remark would throw Mom off her stance and make her lose form.

"Not cool? Because I didn't let him talk bullshit?" she said, trying her best not to shout. "Because I forced him to talk about the real issue at hand?"

"Right," Dad cut in. He had her now. "He's a racist. Everyone's a racist. It's always been like this with you."

That was it. "Fuck you, Greg," Mom said, and with her loss of control came her loss of the battle. "Fuck you. I want to talk to her before you go."

"Nope, no way," Dad said, still calm. "Look at you. You're angry, you're cursing. No."

"The hell do you mean *no*?"

"Ikigai, she's had enough for one day. It's my night, I have custody now."

"I want to get to the bottom of this," Mom said. "I see you over there listening," she called out to me without taking her eyes off Dad. "I *will* get to the bottom of this."

I slunk deeper into the car seat.

"See? Absolutely not!" Dad said. "You expect her, after the day she's had, to deal with you and your anger? This is what she's seeing when she's with you? And it's a surprise she's fighting?"

Mom balled her hands into fists. He'd won. At this point she could be silent, or she could speak and be labeled an angry woman, out of control. Her only way out was to speak, but not from her heart; to speak, but not from her gut; to speak, but to paste a calm, emotionless veneer over her words. Then, to present those words, drained and dry, to her ex-husband in a palatable, passionless format. Mom, however, did not have this tool in her arsenal. She did not have this ability. So, she stayed quiet and looked off to the distance with burning eyes.

I didn't like taking sides during these arguments. I would have been perfectly happy continuing to be Switzerland, but Dad just had to deliver a finishing blow. He'd won, he should have shown mercy, but he didn't. What bothered me most was he used me

as the hydrogen bomb. "She keeps seeing you like this, Ikigai…
I mean, what, you want her to have your childhood?"

Mom's face crumpled. She quickly turned and walked away.
Something inside me cracked. I almost jumped out of the car to
run after her, but Dad was already getting into the driver's seat and
silently turning on the engine. I stayed quiet. I looked at the back
of his head as he put his seatbelt on. Hot, wet tears welled up in my
eyes again, and I felt something acid and poisonous in my chest.
I often said I hated my mother. But at least I said it. Sometimes I
even screamed it. Right at her. And Mom would take my hatred.
She'd hold it up for me to look at. She'd pound it into submission,
stretch it, dye it, weave it into a blanket, or a story.

"You alright, buddy?" Dad said wearily.

"Yeah," I responded, just as tired. I wasn't alright. At that
moment, I hated him. And it was a hatred I would never say out
loud.

★★★

According to Geri, she received a phone call from my mother later
that very night. Which means Mom would have returned to her
office after that fight with Dad. What people did not understand
about Ikigai Johnson was how hard she worked. She worked until
she broke, and then she worked some more. Work to her was the
salve for all illnesses. You were tired — work harder. You were sick
— work more. You were broken-hearted — go to work. And if you
worked yourself to death, well, in Mom's mind, that was a damn
good way to go.

She would have driven back to the RCFL and parked her car.
It would have been after hours. Mom worked longer hours than
most. She just worked them at odd intervals to make sure anything
involving my schedule took priority. As a result, by all external

appearances, she often took off early or arrived late. Many had the perception she was barely in the office and didn't really do much of anything. But my mother was never one to care what others thought about her.

No one would have been around. I imagine she felt perfectly comfortable talking to herself as she paced around her office. I imagine her words bouncing off the walls, were something to the effect of, "No Greg, I'm not making this racism up in my head." Or, "You better wake up. You didn't wake up for me when we were married, but your daughter is getting older, so you better wake up for her." Or maybe, just maybe, it was, "Please, Greg. Why can't you see me? Why couldn't you ever just see me?"

I don't know exactly what she would have said, I wasn't there. I do know she would have slammed her purse on her desk, sat at her computer workstation and powered it on. She would have rummaged through case files, not to find anything, just to burn off some energy. She would have conducted administrative tasks she needed to catch up on. Then, at some point, her eyes would have fallen on the one-terabyte hard drive left behind earlier by PPB Detectives Geri Bradford and Nate Schwinn.

She would have taken a SATA cord and connected it to her workstation. She would have interacted with the user inter-face that pulled up files and folders on her workstation's screen. She would have taken a preliminary glance at the live data capture saved within those files and folders. Eventually, she would have found and opened that picture – the one of the little brown girl, with the screaming eyes, posing in a way most little girls wouldn't know how to pose.

These were the hardest ones: the ones where you look at a child and see yourself staring back, trembling and afraid.

Mom would have forced down her disgust. She'd seen worse. But something was different about this one. And, just to make sure it was exceedingly and unambiguously clear to her that this one *was* different, I'm pretty sure that's when the Emperor's Ghost would have appeared.

The Emperor's Ghost appeared in different forms to my mother, depending on the situation. I don't believe, at that moment, she would have perceived him as a man, for he had no guidance to offer. He probably appeared as a little boy, crumpled and squatting in the corner of Mom's office, crying. She would have ignored him. She could do nothing for him. But maybe, she could do something for this girl.

Mom always carried something with her, something she never showed me. She carried it in the inside pocket of her coats and jackets, as close to her heart as possible. Mom would have touched her fingers to this thing and looked in the little girl's eyes. The screaming from those eyes would have been a rock that struck the base of Mom's spine. A spark would have flown from this strike, sent lightning up her back and combustion to her brain. The reaction would have been too much. Mom's eyes would have burned until she too wanted to scream. That's when she would have picked up the phone on her desk, looked at the paperwork left behind by Detectives Bradford and Schwinn, found a number and dialed it.

A groggy voice on the other end, "Bradford."

"It's Ikigai. I'm looking at your data capture."

"My annoyance at being woken up is now erased by my utter elation at hearing you actually give a shit."

"You want to give me a little background on this case?"

"Ikigai, it would be my pleasure."

Mom would have looked at the picture while listening to Geri. She would have touched her fingers to the thing in her jacket's inside pocket, and felt her eyes grow hotter. And hotter.

CHAPTER 3

Geri burst into the office of Multnomah County Deputy District Attorney, Robert Martel. "This is taking too damn long," she announced. Martel peered from behind his desk — over the wall of files and paperwork that had accumulated around his space like a coral reef; each court order, motion, and counter motion, adding another layer or direction. Geri looked around. "You gotta tidy this place up."

"Hello to you to too, Bradford," Martel said. "Nice to see you. Do come in. How's the girlfriend?"

"Gone." Geri sat down. "Didn't want to commit to a cop."

"She didn't want to stop smoking weed?"

"Hey, legislature's been talking about legalizing it."

"Didn't want to stop smoking weed," Martel concluded and stood up from his desk.

Martel was a cop himself before he got his law degree at Lewis and Clark, and he still looked the part. Fit and athletic though he was well into his fifties at that point, he was clean cut, clean shaven, and he always wore his personal firearm on his hip. His eyes and ears, like Geri's, didn't miss a thing. "Common story in this here Rip City," he said. "Sorry to hear. How may I be of service?"

"I want to proffer Evan Campbell."

"Think that could be premature, maybe?"

"It's time to bring some pressure."

"I thought the FBI was helping."

"They've had the computer and phone we seized from him for two weeks now."

"And nothing?"

"Far as I'm aware. The examiner isn't, she's not very, communicative."

"Ikigai?" Martel asked. Geri nodded. "She's good," Martel said. "Hard-charger."

"That rep comes from how she used to be," Geri said. "You know, before…"

"You think she's a burnout now?"

Geri shrugged. "We're not getting anything from the computer or the phone. We've got… As it is now, this case is built only on the testimony of one girl."

"You believe her?"

"I do. But we've got nothing hard. No communications. No texts, calls, emails. No pictures." Geri pursed her lips.

"I hear ya," Martel said, letting out a deep breath. "Well ma'am, let's try to entice this bastard with a plea deal."

In the late hours, in the quiet of her lab, when everyone else had gone home and thought she had done the same, my mother would have stared at the photo of the girl with the screaming eyes and wrestled with the problem before her. The world these days, she would have thought, had been reduced to ones and zeros. On or off. Yes or no. She'd even heard her male colleagues rate women on a binary scale. Apparently, they no longer found it necessary to objectify a woman on a scale of one to ten. Now it was even simpler: is she a one or a zero? Would you fuck her or not?

But the ones and zeros could never account for the states of existence not yet determined by observation or interaction. This was why my mother, when she was in college, preferred quantum mechanics to computer science. But computer science got her a job right out of school – allowing her to waste no time racking up the years of full-time employment she needed to qualify for a position with the FBI. Becoming a Special Agent was always her goal. It was not a popular decision among her peers. She had joined the Bureau in 1993. This was only one year after the Rodney King

Trial on the west coast and two years after the Crown Heights Riots in her hometown of Brooklyn on the east. This was before the political pendulum swung back the other way when the Twin Towers fell in zero-one. People, at least people my mother hung around, were not happy with law enforcement. But Mom never cared what other people thought. She kept her own counsel. And as she told me once when I was in my teens, she'd hoped she could make things better from the inside.

Now there she was, sixteen years on the job and burned out from having not made anything better at all, given her colleagues' comfortability with rating women in a binary manner. But she couldn't stop staring at the photo of the girl with the screaming eyes. A girl who couldn't have been older than ten. One-zero. How would that girl get rated? What would her number be? And what happens to the number of a girl in the past tense? What digit represents not would you fuck her, but *did* you fuck her? What digits represent you fucked her and she didn't want to fuck you, she was so young she didn't even have the capacity to think about fucking you? One for you? Zero for her? Would one-zero suffice?

One-zero. But she needed proof. She needed hard evidence. A picture of a girl fully clothed was not going to cut it. A queasy feeling in her gut when she looked at that picture was not going to sway a jury and, even if it did, the decision could be overturned on appeal. Where the hell was this picture taken anyway?

Mom would have turned those problems over and over in her head. She probably didn't see the Emperor's Ghost then. But she likely heard him, in the back of her mind, mewing those pathetic tears. She would have broken down the ones and zeros of the image file before her. Looked for something she had not yet seen. Angry, that in order to solve this, she too had to reduce this girl to binary code.

Unless.

The cries of the Emperor's Ghost would have gotten louder, turning into a high-pitched whine at the base of her skull that let her know she was on the right track. Unless, unless. Unless there was a relationship between the ones and zeros of the picture and the ones and zeros of the other, apparently benign, unsaved files on Evan's laptop that were pulled during Detective Nate Schwinn's live data capture. For example, it was rather odd that one of the word documents from Evan's laptop looked like a grocery shopping list: sparkling water, granola, almond milk, zucchini, hibiscus tea. Mom would have squinted at that list and wondered, who writes a grocery list on their laptop?

And did this asshole really eat zucchini?

★★★

Geri faced Evan Campbell again. This time the lawyers were present. Everyone sat at a conference room table in the Multnomah County District Attorney's office downtown. Geri and Martel were on one side, Evan and his defense attorney, Zach Weddle, on the other. Geri smiled politely at Evan then visualized grabbing him by the hair again and pulling him across the table.

"No rush, Zach," Martel said to Weddle, who read through the paperwork.

Weddle didn't look up. "I'm not rushing."

Geri stared at Zach Weddle and paid close attention. Weddle used to work as a state prosecutor. Then he switched sides. That prior experience made him a dangerous opponent.

"It's kind of boilerplate," Martel gestured to the paperwork Weddle was looking over and smiled. "You did 'em plenty in the good old days."

"They're not that old and they weren't that good," Weddle told him. "Also, I'm confused. What's the benefit here for the state?"

"Backlog, friend. You're right, those days weren't that old, so you remember how overwhelmed we are here. Let's clear this out of the system."

"You're reducing this to a misdemeanor?"

"Class A. He'll still do a year."

"The state's accusing my client of raping a ten-year old girl and now finds *one year* a satisfactory sentence? Because of backlog?"

"He'll have to register as a sex offender too Zach, you know that."

Weddle faced Evan, exchanged a glance, then turned back to Martel. "I need a few minutes with my client, if that's okay."

★★★

"If I put that girl on the stand, she'll fall apart," Geri says and raps her knuckles against her desk. "That's what Weddle said. Leaned over real close to Evan when we were leaving the room, right? And that's what he said, 'She'll fall apart.' Guy wasn't stupid. He pretended he was saying it in confidence, but he did it on purpose. He made sure we heard him."

"Ballsy," I say.

"Smart," Geri says. "Weddle knew what he was doing. He put doubt in our minds. He put doubt in my mind. What if the kid was lying? What if she was just angry Evan kept failing her at math and wanted to get back at him? Or she was being abused, but by someone else: mother's boyfriend, uncle, family friend, next door neighbor, but not her math teacher, not Evan Campbell. Was her memory sticking things together, conflating events? These things happen, especially with young kids. We know this."

My voice forces its way past the knot in my throat. "You thought she was..."

"No." Geri's voice gets softer. "I always believed her. We just didn't have the evidence. We didn't have proof beyond all reasonable doubt. That's what Weddle was showing us. If he could so easily put doubt in our minds, what was he going to do with a jury?"

I let out a pent-up breath. Do I really want to keep digging all this up?

Don't stop, I hear Mom's voice in the back of my head. Do not stop. Ever.

"What happened next?" I ask.

★★★

"Son of a bitch refused the plea deal," Geri said, leaning against a wall in Ikigai's office.

Ikigai didn't bother looking up from her forensic workstation. "Not everyone's going to roll over and expose their belly just because you show up."

"Anything in those electronics?" Geri asked.

"Nothing that will help your case."

"There's gotta be something."

"There's a grocery list and a disturbing picture of a little Asian girl."

Geri rubbed her eyes. "What does that mean?"

"I don't know. I'm still figuring it out." Ikigai stood up and put her coat on.

"You're taking off?"

Ikigai ignored the question.

"Ikigai, we're going to trial. It could be as early as next month."

Ikigai glared at Geri. "You jumped the gun going after a plea deal. You should have waited. Don't put that on me."

Geri backed down. "I just want to know what's in there."

"So do I. I think he might be using stego."

"We paleontologists now?"

Ikigai cocked an eyebrow, confused.

"Stegosaurus?" Geri asked with a grin.

Ikigai didn't crack a smile. "Steganography. I think he hid something in that image file, encoded. I think that shopping list is related."

"That's promising."

"It is," Ikigai said, grabbed her purse, and bolted out of the office without another word.

Geri, finding herself alone again, looked around the office for a pillow she could scream into. In doing so, her eyes fell on Ikigai's workstation, and gravitated toward a yellow post-it note on the screen, on which Ikigai had written: "Zucchini?"

"Huh," Geri grunted. She pulled out her smartphone, typed an email and sent it to Ikigai.

★★★

"I am so utterly disappointed in you right now." Mom glared at me across the restaurant table. She pulled another plate off the sushi conveyor belt that ran next to us, salmon sashimi, her favorite. She poked at it with her chopsticks and fought to keep her voice even. I stared at my shrimp nigiri, picking apart the bed of rice and avoiding eye contact.

As she'd promised two weeks ago, she did get to the bottom of my incident with the other girl on my team. The first week after the incident, when I stayed at her condo, she never brought it up. This made me believe she'd forgotten all about it, which was her intention. The following week, she elicited information day by day, in a calm, roundabout manner, stalking the truth with patience and tenacity. Was there anyone else I did not get along with on the team? Who *did* I get along with? Why didn't I get along with the girl I'd fought with? And I, being an eleven-year-old with a short memory span who loved to talk about what she believed was her oh-so-interesting social life, totally fell for it. I spilled the beans without even realizing it. The truth came out. And she was pissed.

"Every parent sits there and tells their child, 'I raised you to be a leader not a follower,'" she said and swallowed a piece of salmon. "But that's crap, because you can't lead all the time. The trick is to learn when to lead, when to follow, and if you choose to follow, how to follow intelligently. Do you understand what I'm saying to you?"

I nodded, fighting back tears. Mom continued. "That's what I've always tried to teach you. And clearly, I have failed. Because following a group of spoiled little…"

"*Jon-son-san, zembu ikagadesu ka?*" the waitress interrupted.

"*Hai,*" my mother replied and bowed her head slightly. "*Subete daijoubu desu.*"

It was for two reasons I hoped the waitress would hang around and chat with my mother as she often did. One, it would have provided a respite from the verbal beatdown I was receiving. Two, I loved hearing my mother speak Japanese. But the waitress picked up on the fact that this was not a good time, politely bowed, and hurried away.

"Following a bunch of spoiled little white girls into bullying another girl because she's a bit different…" Mom's voice rasped with barely contained disgust. She took a breath and regained her composure. "That is not intelligent following, Ikigai."

When she said my name, my real name, it wasn't just disappointment I heard. It was pain. I'd hurt her, deeply. And she didn't deserve that, especially given what I'd seen Dad do to her recently. I couldn't hold the tears back anymore. "I'm sorry," I blubbered.

"I don't want your apologies," she snapped. "I want your accountability. You're not crying because you feel sorry. You're crying because you feel something else. Is that the case?" I nodded, wiping snot from my face. "Then say that," she said. "Say what you actually feel." I stared at the table, unable to make the words come out of my mouth. "Such a big, bad, bully," she said. "So strong and so tough. And you can't even say what we both know you feel. What is this girl's name?"

Silence.

My mother looked at me, incredulous. "You don't even know! You body-check her in practice, taunt her with the other girls because, why? She's weird and talks to herself? So what? I talk to myself all the time. Then she stands up for herself, gives you a well-deserved slap in the face, which probably didn't hurt, because you're the biggest kid on the team, and instead of being mature and recognizing you deserved it, you beat the snot out of her." Mom threw her chopsticks on the table. "And you don't even know…"

She took another breath and forced me to make eye contact. "I don't need to say anything else. You know exactly what you need to do. Just remember, Ikigai, warriors don't apologize. We can do nothing with apologies. They're useless. But we can always work with what we truly feel."

Mom would have gone back to work the next day and taken her anger out on the problem before her. Between me, her ex-husband, and a case she couldn't crack, whose solution she knew was staring her right in the face, she was dealing with quite a bit.

There was an image file of a little brown girl in an alley and there was a word file with a grocery list.

Since Mom suspected the image file was steganographic, she definitely would have deployed one of the software tools on her workstation to try and decrypt it. The tool would have bounced back an interface requesting a password. The Emperor's Ghost would have whined again at the base of her skull. She didn't know the password. But the interface's request for one would have confirmed there was indeed data encrypted and hidden within the ones and zeros of the little brown girl and her screaming eyes.

Now, what the hell was the password? *Zucchini* was probably her first guess. Between sparkling water, granola, almond milk, and hibiscus tea, *zucchini* just stood out. But no, that wouldn't have worked. Evan hadn't made it that easy. He was smarter than that. But Mom would have known she could figure it out. She would have kept hacking at the problem.

Or at least, that's what I think. I could be wrong. Perhaps she had no idea whether or not she could figure it out. Perhaps she only kept plugging away because it was a good distraction from a daughter she was disappointed with, and an ex-husband who was so cruel he weaponized her own childhood against her.

I do know from old case notes Geri shares with me these twelve years later that Mom tried breaking the word *zucchini* down to the ones and zeros of its ASCII representation and typed those digits into the password request. She got nothing. Then she tried different variations of text words from the shopping list and different variations of their binary representation, all of which had been to no avail.

Then she would have remembered her phone. It had gone off with a buzz, signaling an email, the day before, while she was driving up to the Northeast part of Portland to pick me up from school. She would have remembered she'd checked her phone while she was driving and seen that the email was from Geri.

She didn't open it at the time, probably because she didn't want to risk being distracted. The last thing she needed was to get into an accident. Then it probably slipped her mind afterwards as she was too busy burying my face in the dung of my failure as a human being while we ate conveyor belt sushi.

Regardless, she would have finally checked her phone while she was at work and read the email from Detective Geri Bradford. That email said: *Zucchini? According to the victim, that's the word he used for his penis.*

At this juncture, the first of Mom's thoughts would have traveled from gut to brain, zigzagged its way up nerve endings, passed the calm hum between chest and throat, and leapt around the horrific whine of the Emperor's Ghost at the base of her skull. This thought would have been: *Yeah, no shit.*

The second thought, directly succeeding the first, traveled the same neural pathway but in reverse, and would have been: *I already tried everything with 'zucchini' and the file it's in. That doesn't work.*

But the third thought would have been different. The third thought, spurred by Geri's email, would have traveled from spine to fingers, dashed up triceps and shoulders, lingered with the hum below her throat, then found itself translated by her voice as she blurted out loud to no one in particular: *Well, what word did the girl use . . . ?*

She would have ceased talking to herself mid-sentence. Not because she thought she shouldn't – she very much liked talking to herself. It was how she best solved problems. Rather, it was because the question was important, and Mom needed to check something else first.

She would have looked closer at the word file; at its metadata, and the metadata of the links and shortcuts pointing to it. That's when she saw it. The creation and last modified times of the file. Now she could ask her question. Mom responded to Geri's email: *He created this word file days before your search but changed it only hours before you arrested him. I've got an idea. What word did the girl use for her vagina?*

A few minutes later, her phone buzzed with Geri's response and Mom probably did her best not to bash her head against the wall when she read it: *Good question. Unfortunately, I don't know.*

★★★

When Geri responded to Ikigai's question over email she was running late to a meeting at Martel's office. She wasn't late because she got called out on another case, or because of traffic, or because she'd come down with a case of food poisoning from the catfish pho she ate the night before at her favorite Vietnamese restaurant. If any of those things had occurred, they would not have stopped Geri. She was never late to a meeting she didn't want to be late to. Another call out? It'll have to wait. Traffic? She was still a damn good runner. Food poisoning? Suck it up. No. Geri was late to this meeting because she just didn't want to be there. She knew what was coming.

She walked into Martel's office as he was in the middle of his conversation with the woman. The woman did not have the same penetrating blue eyes as her daughter, but she had that same pale, paper-thin skin and that same general countenance of frailty – heightened by the facial scabs and rotten teeth that aged the woman well beyond her thirty years. The woman was clearly a continuous user of meth. Geri really did not want to be there.

"Ms. Phelps, are you absolutely sure?" Martel asked the woman, not looking at Geri.

Ms. Phelps' words spilled out of her mouth in a way that made them sound as if they didn't come out in the same order in which they were spoken. "We just... You know. For trying. Thank you. But, we gotta move on."

Geri and Martel exchanged a look. Geri felt sick. So sick she would rather have had food poisoning. "We can..." Geri started weakly, knowing anything she said wouldn't matter. "There's still evidence we're going through."

Ms. Phelps looked at the floor. "She would have to testify. In front of a jury? Some lawyer picking her apart? My baby can't do that."

Geri and Martel stayed silent. They could tell that as frail as the woman looked, she'd been in and out of the system and knew the score.

"I just," Ms. Phelps broke the silence, "want her out of that school. Away from him."

"I can make some calls to the other school districts," Martel said quietly, defeated. "We'll help however we can."

Ms. Phelps nodded, blinked, muttered a, "Thank you," and stood up to leave. She awkwardly smiled at Geri as she headed for the door.

"Hey, uh," Geri said. "I'm so sorry to ask you this. It's something, a little detail, something I didn't ask your daughter when I spoke with her."

Ms. Phelps waited for the question.

"I'm sorry. I know this is all… I can only imagine…"

"It's okay," Ms. Phelps whispered. "What do you need?"

Geri let out a sigh. "Your daughter, what did she call her…? Did she, or you, did she have a word she liked to use for her vagina?"

Later, after Ms. Phelps had left, Geri sat in Martel's office and fiddled with her smartphone. "Why'd you ask that question, Bradford?" Martel asked.

Geri didn't look up from her phone. "Ikigai wanted to know."

"That who you're emailing now?"

Geri nodded.

Martel continued. "Ikigai hasn't found anything in the

electronics. And that girl and her family are broken in more ways than one."

Geri looked up from her phone, more tired than angry. "So that's it?"

"Yeah," Martel said. "That's it."

Geri looked at the draft email she had written thus far: *I found out just now. The girl called it her petal.* Geri thumbed a few more sentences: *As in flower petal. Of course she called it that. It doesn't matter now. We were just told she doesn't want to testify. The state is dropping the charges. I think I will go home and drink now. A lot.*

Geri tapped the send icon and silently walked out of Martel's office.

★★★

I wonder if Evan Campbell smiled when the guards at the Inverness Jail in Northeast Portland escorted him to the outtake area. How well did he contain what I'm sure was his absolute delight, when they gave him the clothes and belongings he had on him when he was arrested? His jeans. His too large sweater. Did he clap; did he jump up and down and giggle like a gleeful super-villain when they left him alone to change out of his orange jumpsuit?

I like to see that in my mind, but that's probably not what happened. The reality is, practical affairs of daily existence would have immediately taken over as priorities. He wouldn't have had time to celebrate.

Sure, the jail staff gave him his clothes, but his phone was seized as evidence and was being searched by my mother. He couldn't call or text anyone, and Uber wasn't a thing yet anyway. Even if he could get back to his apartment, it wouldn't matter. The jail staff had returned his apartment keys, but they couldn't return the apartment itself; after its door had been busted open, a search warrant executed upon it, and its tenant arrested, its landlord would have affected a no-cause eviction. The landlord would have called the emergency number on Evan's initial rental application (his mother, who had passed away), and receiving no response, would have repaired the damage, rented the apartment to someone else, then designated Evan's property as abandoned and tossed it all in a dumpster.

So, for me at least, there is some slight consolation in knowing Evan was in dire straits when he walked out of Inverness Jail. But it's only slight. Evan Campbell was highly adaptable. His recently deceased mother's house was still on the market. He likely walked to it from Inverness Jail. He then promptly withdrew it from sale and moved in himself.

Shelter: check.

He still had his bank accounts, and his wallet and bank cards would have been returned to him.

Money: check.

Since he had money, he could go and retrieve his vehicle, the Camry that was towed when he was arrested and had to leave it behind in the grocery store parking lot.

Transportation: check.

Now he needed to get his job back, which would have been a process, but since the charges were dropped, the school would continue its own "investigation". In the meantime, it legally had to keep him in its employ. Evan Campbell was good to go.

There is one thing he would have been worried about though. After he bought a new phone, he would have called up the Portland Police Bureau's Main Office, pressed a few voice prompted numbers, got in touch with a human being, explained his situation, and asked a very pointed question: when am I going to get my phone and computer back?

Luckily, it would still be a few more days before Evan got

released and asked this question. Prior to his release, Geri had paid another visit to Mom's office.

★★★

"Tenacity your middle name, huh?" Geri asked, surprised to see Ikigai still working on Evan's laptop.

Ikigai didn't look up from her work. "That's what it says on my birth certificate."

"We gotta give this stuff back to him."

"Right now?"

"He's going to be released. He'll want his stuff back."

"I don't care what he wants. Has the state formally dropped the charges?"

"They will tomorrow."

"Then the authority of your warrant is still valid."

"This case fucked me up Ikigai. I don't want to drag it out."

"I don't care what you want either," Ikigai snapped. She wasn't getting much sleep lately. Staring into the little brown girl's eyes night after night was getting to her. "There's something here. There's one more thing I want to try. Let me try it."

"Try what?"

"I'll explain if it works," Ikigai said.

"Fine," Geri said and stormed away. "Charges are getting dropped tomorrow though."

One more night. Mom would have had one more night to stare into the pools of the little brown girl's eyes. She probably would have been talking to herself by now. Or talking to the little girl, talking to the Emperor's Ghost, talking to anything in the room she felt would listen. Talking to the grocery list, as she made slight alterations over and over again.

Sparkling water. Granola. Petal. Almond milk. Zucchini. Hibiscus tea.

Sparkling water. Petal. Granola. Almond milk. Zucchini. Hibiscus tea.

Petal. Sparkling water. Granola. Almond milk. Zucchini. Hibiscus tea.

"One more night to figure out what you're trying to tell me," she would have whispered to the girl, pulled up a DOS prompt with each permutation and typed: *FCIV -md5 -sha1c:\windows\users\Ikigai\Shopping List*

Rejected.

Rejected.

Rejected.

None of the permutations worked, for either hash type. Then, desperate, she tried one last thing.

Sparkling water. Granola. Almond milk. Petal. Hibiscus tea.

Then she entered: *FCIV -md5 -sha1 c:\windows\users\Ikigai\Shopping List*

The DOS command spit out the MD5 hash of the altered shopping list: *ab7e078e94f08070c41f1485f8d2a16a,* and the SHA-1 hash: *e6aeod956ca3c75ec3fdca30bobfa917b7779e13.*

Mom typed the grocery list's plain text into the password request interface of her steganography decryption tool.

Rejected.

She typed the MD5 hash of the list into the password request interface.

Rejected.

She typed the SHA-1 hash.

And the image file decoded.

Mom's hands shook. Okay, it decoded. That didn't mean anything. There could be nothing in the now visible files. There could be nothing.

Geri's smartphone rang. She woke up, looked at the screen and saw 'Special Agent Icky' on the caller ID. She answered. "It's damn near midnight."

"I cracked it." Ikigai's voice came over Geri's phone sharp and clear. "Did you hear me?"

"Yeah, yeah, I heard you. What did you…?"

"First thing in the morning. You need to get everyone together. Everyone."

★★★

Meanwhile, back in my eleven-year-old life, I had amends to make.

A light drizzle had started as Dad dropped me off at the soccer field. I remember because I was hoping it would turn into a full downpour. Then practice would get canceled, and I wouldn't have to confront the source of my anxiety. I also remember Dad took off as soon as he dropped me, saying he'd be back at the end of practice. That was another cause of aggravation. I understood he had things to do, but he'd said he would stay and watch. Mom was different: when she said something, she did it.

A group of my teammates had crowded together near the benches off the field, whispering and giggling. Coach Fritz must have been off somewhere, distracted with getting practice organized. I walked toward my teammates, my ears picking up on the nasty pulses of hatred they spoke into the damp air.

"So weird," I heard one of them say.

"No one wants you here," said another.

I couldn't see the target of their poison. I didn't need to. I knew who they were talking to. I jogged toward them.

"What's going on?" I asked. My heart made my voice tremble. There were four of my teammates, standing over her, looking down on her. She sat on a bench, quiet and helpless, blinking those pale blue eyes. I joined the group and my heart broke when I saw her bow her head and shrink further into herself at the sight of me. At first, that made me want to cry and hide my face forever. Then I became enraged – mostly at myself. Why had I helped these girls hurt her?

The leader of the pack (I can't remember her name, I do remember she was blonde though, with little pigtails) said, "Weirdo's talking to herself again. Mess her up, Junior!" I watched their victim, once my victim, tremble at the mention of my name. She was so afraid. I'd never hated myself more.

So, I grabbed little Ms. Pigtail by her pigtails. She screamed in pain and the other girls watched me with these dumb, confused looks on their faces. They thought I was one of them. I needed to make it very clear that I was not. Not anymore. And never again.

"Leave her alone," I hissed in Pigtail's ear.

Another girl piped up. "Junior, you fight again you're off the team."

"So what," I said, not letting go of little Ms. Pigtail.

"What is wrong with you?" Pigtail screeched.

I let Pigtail go and shoved her to the ground. "You bother her again and I'm gonna hurt you. Like, here, in the real world. Not online."

Little Ms. Pigtail stood up, shocked, and led the pack away from me and their victim.

Their victim was confused too. She sat, frozen like a deer, at the scene that had just unfolded before her. When I turned my attention to her she flinched and hyperventilated, not taking her eyes off me. I sat next to her.

She muttered something under her breath. I couldn't make out what she was saying. She looked at me with those eyes, waiting for what was coming next. She tried to catch her breath. I put my hand on her back and patted, awkwardly. Her breath slowed and she looked at me with that wide-eyed stare. She was so helpless. I didn't know what to say. I was about to tell her how sorry I was. Then I remembered what my mother had told me. Neither I, nor this girl, could do anything with my apologies. They were useless. But we could do something with what I truly felt.

I looked at her squarely and forced myself to finally say it out loud. "I am ashamed."

My lips quivered. I wiped my face with my sleeve.

Her own face creased, still trying to comprehend what was happening. Then she spoke, in a voice that sounded like broken glass. "Me too."

It was my turn to be confused. "But you don't have anything to be ashamed of." She muttered something unintelligible again. I leaned toward her and said, "I don't even know your name." Her eyes lit up.

She moved a brown wisp of hair from her face. She told me her name. And when she said it, it seemed so simple, so obvious. Of course that was her name. I should have known her name simply by looking at her; simply by paying attention to her; simply by listening to her voice.

She put her head on my shoulder. Her head was so light. It felt like a feather had landed on me, or a butterfly. I felt her sigh as she finally relaxed, before she sat up again. The two of us looked out at the field, the light drizzle dampening our hair and faces. Without realizing it, our hands had come closer together, our pinkies touching. We didn't say anything else. We didn't need to.

And that's how me and Lily became best friends.

★★★

The best thing about being a kid is how easy it is to find your soulmates. When you get older, the layers take over: layers of pain, disappointment, and disillusion; layers of roles and responsibilities; reputations; expectations – that grow into a thick shell until it's not warm, sloppy, egg yolk people interacting with each other anymore. It's just their shells, touching gingerly, bouncing off, and mostly scraping.

But if they scrape long enough against each other, little chunks start to fall away.

Geri's shell was getting scraped big time as she listened to Ikigai during that case coordination meeting between the Portland Police Bureau and the Portland Division of the FBI. Everyone sat in a conference room at the District of Oregon's United States Attorney's office. The room was decked out in antique looking mahogany furniture. A blown up, enhanced image of the little brown girl was projected on the overhead screen. Geri couldn't look at the girl. She looked out the window at the picture-perfect view of downtown Portland: the West Hills rolling and green and dotted with trees and houses over a city whose few skyscrapers are only about forty stories high. Portland was such a beautiful place, she thought, why in the world did some of its people do such horrible things?

Detective Nate Schwinn was there, hanging on every word of Ikigai's presentation. Also present were DDA Robert Martel, Assistant US Attorney Diane Appelo, the Chief of the Violent Crimes Unit for Oregon's US Attorney's Office, and Brent Oberley, the Supervisory Special Agent for the FBI - Portland Division's Violent Crimes against Children Squad.

"Should have checked for stego," Nate shook his head. "Was right in front of me."

"It wasn't easy to see," Ikigai said, standing in front of the room, underneath the projected picture of the girl. "And getting it open was a process. Long story short, the simplest thing is always the solution. I had to replace the word *zucchini* with the word *petal*.

Evan took that shopping list and SHA-1 hashed it. That hash was the password that decoded the files hidden in the photo of this girl."

That was when the first chunk of Geri's shell fell away. "Amazing," she said.

SSA Brent Oberley chimed in. "That is, wow, that is good work."

Ikigai's shell was still intact. She was swayed just as much by flattery as she was by criticism. She knew what she had done. She ignored the compliments and continued. "He hid quite a few files in this encoded picture." Everyone watched her move the cursor on the overhead screen which projected the image from her laptop. The cursor pulled up files Ikigai explained as she opened. "More images," she said, as a photo of two young boys, playing in the pool of a waterfall, and another photo of a teenage boy standing on a dirt road, appeared on the screen.

AUSA Appelo spoke up. Her voice was iron. "I see no evidence of any crime in these pictures."

"Not on their own," Ikigai agreed, then clicked the cursor and pulled up text files on the screen. "He also encoded these Facebook chats." Ikigai showed them samples of the chat conversations. Words and phrases popped up before the group's eyes in all their wondrous vulgarity:

I'll pay you 1000 pesos to suck me off.

You know I like it so tight.

I'll be in the barangay next week.

"Before we keep going down this track," Martel said, "does anything in there help our state case?"

"Nope," Ikigai said.

"You've got nothing related to the minor female victim here in Oregon," Appelo said. "You've got pictures of some kids in what's likely another country, and some perverted Facebook chats. Creepy, but not illegal. Those chats could be with consenting adults."

"I believe these chats were with the children in the photos," Ikigai said.

"And that would be a reasonable suspicion," Appelo replied. "But reasonable suspicion a conviction does not make. With what we've got, we couldn't federally indict or arrest him."

"Of course not," Ikigai replied. "There's still work to do. Say someone goes and tracks down these kids. Interviews them. Proves it's them in the chats. Gets their direct testimony of what he did to them…"

"That's, uh, that's Child Sex Tourism if they're in another country," ssa Oberley said. "That's our federal violation."

"Okay," Appelo said. "Do we know what country they're in?"

"Pesos," Ikigai said. "Barangay?" She let out a deep breath. "He's been traveling to the…" Ikigai's voice broke off and she tried to use an intake of air to squelch the pain of the burning in her eyes. "He's been traveling to the Philippines to have sex with these children. Someone needs to go there. Someone needs to find these kids."

Geri admired the flame in human form that stood before her. It was nice to be reminded of where Special Agent Ikigai Johnson's reputation came from.

A few hours after that meeting, Mom met me at Dad's house. I was surprised to see her. It was Dad's day, not hers. She arrived at the house and she and Dad immediately went into the kitchen. I couldn't make out what they were saying, they kept their voices down, but they were fighting again. Dad said something about her priorities. Then I heard him say, "Do what you gotta do." Mom exited the kitchen, met me in the living room and asked if I wanted to ride my bicycle.

I loved riding my bicycle, but it was embarrassing. As athletic as I was, the bicycle was a challenge that I, for some reason, had yet to overcome. At eleven years old, I still needed training wheels. It was fun nonetheless. Especially since it was autumn and the streets of my Northeast Portland neighborhood were overrun with crunchy leaves, golden brown, orange and red. I rode my bike through the crunch and the color as Mom directed me to try and balance the bike without letting either of the uneven training wheels touch the ground.

"I talked to that girl," I said, rode up to Mom and stopped, catching my breath. "We're friends now. And I told the other girls to leave her alone. They won't bother her anymore."

Mom kissed me on the forehead. "I'm proud of you, baby."

Something was wrong. She wasn't normally this affectionate. "What's going on?" I asked.

"You're always so perceptive," she said, looking me in the eye. "I need to talk to you about something."

During that case coordination meeting, after everyone had absorbed the revelations of Ikigai's hard work, they immediately went into planning mode.

"Rob," Appelo said to Martel, "I thought you were cross-designated as a DDA and an AUSA."

"Haven't used that designation in a while," Martel replied.

"Should be easy to reinstate you," Appelo told him. "If you want to prosecute this on the federal side, I figure you'd be the best choice. You already have intimate knowledge of the case."

"Absolutely," Martel said. "We couldn't get him on the state charges. But now, yeah, this gives us a shot."

Appelo faced SSA Oberley. "Can the FBI send Ikigai to the Philippines?"

"Woah," Ikigai said, her voice a thunder crack that froze everyone in place. "I can't just up and go to the Philippines. I said *someone* needs to go, I didn't say that someone was me. And I work out of the RCFL, I'm not on VCAC anymore."

Silence.

"She's right, she's not on my squad," Oberley finally admitted. "Problem is, the rest of my guys are swamped. And we'd need money from headquarters, the field office couldn't fund this trip."

"There's that B in the FBI," Nate muttered. "Say it kids: bureaucracy."

Oberley smiled. "The B in PPB means the same thing, Nate. Does PPB have the funds to send someone to the Philippines?"

"Wouldn't matter if it did," Geri said, protective of Nate. "This is federal now. It's not in our purview."

"Hey," Oberley said, not wanting to alienate them. "I know this case means a lot to you guys, I'm not trying to add obstacles. We want to keep working with you on this."

Appelo cut in. "Then here's what it comes down to: do you all want to pursue this, or not?"

Everyone nodded. Except Ikigai, who remained immobile. She saw where this was heading, and she was not prepared for it.

Appelo continued. "Then we have two issues. We need a federal agent to go to the Philippines and track down these children, and we need the funding to send that agent there. Brent, would it help if I got in touch with DOJ-Main? Asked them to chip in for the costs on the back end?"

"Yeah, it would," Oberley said, getting what he was angling for in the first place. "That would make it easier for me to sell HQ on providing funds."

"Then all we need is an agent willing to go there," Appelo said, and everyone looked at Ikigai, whose face hardened.

"I figured out everything you need to keep moving forward," Ikigai spoke slowly, looking at Oberley. "And no one on VCAC can go? If this is done right, it's going to take months. I can't leave my life for months."

"They're tapped Ikigai. Cases, trials, you used to be with us, you know how it is."

"Oh, I know exactly how it is," Ikigai said. "That's why I transferred off the squad."

"And here they are, sucking you right back in," Nate joked, trying to lighten the mood. Everyone laughed, awkwardly. Everyone but Ikigai.

Then Geri stood and held Ikigai's gaze.

"Ikigai," Geri started, softly. "Everything you did was amazing, but it doesn't help the state case. And it sounds like we don't have enough, yet, to arrest him on federal charges. Not until we find those kids. Am I right?" With her question she faced Appelo, who nodded in the affirmative. "Okay?" Geri said, facing Ikigai. "That means we have to drop the state charges and release him – today. Evan Campbell will be back on the street – today. What do you think he's going to do?"

"I know what he's going to do," Ikigai whispered.

"He's going to do this again," Geri said it anyway. "He will. He *will* hurt more kids." Ikigai and Geri made eye contact, and Geri saw a pain in Ikigai's eyes she had only seen once before. "I know this is hard," Geri went on. "And me, Nate, and everyone will do everything we can from here to help. But, please, we need you."

Ikigai looked out the window, past the view of the West Hills. "Let me…" she said, "can you people give me a day? To think about it?"

"If Campbell is going to be out of custody, we can't wait," Appelo told her. "We need an answer by tomorrow."

That was why, after that meeting, Mom had met me at Dad's house. She kept looking me in the eye as I stood over my bike and the autumn leaves fell all around us. "I've been asked to travel somewhere to work on a case for a while."

"How long would you have to go for?" I asked.

"A few months," she said, shaking her head. "Three or four, probably."

"That's a long time." I picked off a dried red leaf that landed on my shoulder and held it in my hands. I kept my eyes on it to avoid looking at my mother. I was not happy about this.

"I'm not going to go if you don't want me to," Mom said.

I brightened and dropped the leaf.

"I want us to make this decision together," Mom continued. "You know, like a family."

"Decision made then," I laughed. "You can't go."

Mom smiled wearily. "You need to know more facts before you can make that decision."

"Fine. What are the facts? Where do you have to go?"

"The Philippines."

"Where's that?"

"Very far away. In Asia."

"Will you see Grandma's family there?"

"Your grandmother was from Japan, you know that."

"Why do you have to go?"

"I have to…" She was choosing her words carefully now. "I have to help some people who were hurt. And try to make sure that the person who hurt them can't do it again."

"You always talk like that about your cases."

"Like what?"

"I don't know."

"Like what? Tell me," she urged.

"You don't say what's really going on. You talk around stuff."

"You're right. It's hard to explain right now. It'll be easier when you're older."

"I'm old enough."

"Not yet sweety."

"But someone hurt these people?" I asked.

"Yes."

"And if you don't go, they'll hurt more people?"

"I believe so, yes."

I breathed in the crisp fall air. "Why do people hurt other people?"

"That's a good question, baby. It depends. At the end of the day, to me at least, it doesn't really matter why. What matters is…"

"What matters is, they're stopped." I completed her sentence. And I said it in a way that was so strong and so sure, I surprised myself when it came out of my mouth. I think it surprised my mother too. She nodded quietly.

"Okay," I said simply.

"Okay?" Mom asked.

"You can go. But I have one condition."

"Anything," she said, and I knew she meant it.

"You have to tell me about it. Right now. The case. No more talking around things."

Mom hesitated, thinking of an angle to negotiate on.

"You said anything," I reminded her. "That's my condition. I want to know."

"That's a fair condition," she agreed slowly. "How about I explain everything when I come back? When it's all said and done."

I thought about it. "Okay," I relented. "But you have to promise."

"I give you my word," she said. "When I come back, I will tell you the whole story."

Mom wrapped me into a tight hug, the golden brown, red and orange leaves fluttering about us. "I'm sorry I have to leave you for so long," she said.

Then I said something back in that strong and sure voice that surprised me again. My mother heard me say it, and that was the first time I saw her cry. It was also one of the few times I really heard her laugh.

★★★

"When am I going to get my phone and computer back?" Evan Campbell asked the voice on the other end of his new mobile phone, bought quick and cheap with cash and a pay-as-you-go subscription. The voice on the other end told him to go to the Portland Police Bureau's Central Precinct downtown. So, he did. He entered the steel gray, yet somehow friendly-looking building. He walked up to the crusty yet genial individual sitting behind a grimy bulletproof glass window, who listened to Evan's explanation then politely told him, "Hold on."

Evan did, for about fifteen minutes, until he found himself looking up again at Detective Geri Bradford. "Mr. Campbell," she said quietly. "I'm real sorry, but we have to hold on to those electronics a little longer." Then she handed him a small stack of papers. Evan looked at the pages and immediately noticed the words *Search and Seizure Warrant*.

"How is the search not done?" he said. "The charges were dropped."

"The state charges were dropped. The state search warrant is done," Geri explained then pointed to the words *United States District Court* at the top of the warrant. Evan scanned the pages further and noticed something else at the bottom of one: a signature. It belonged to none other than FBI Special Agent Ikigai Johnson.

"This is federal now?" he asked.

"This is a federal search and seizure warrant for your electronics," Geri said.

"What is...? Why?" Evan asked.

Geri responded, calm and professional, "If you like, I can keep you posted on the status of the search. What's the best way to contact you?"

My mother would not have got much sleep the night before she left.

She would have been up all night, partaking in what she loved to call *the Sacred Art of Documentation* – writing the affidavit that supported the federal warrant to hold on to and further search Evan Campbell's laptop and phone – then convincing a judge to wake up late and sign it because she was leaving the country the following morning.

Her lack of sleep would not have stopped her from getting up early and paddling her inflatable kayak onto the Willamette River. She would have watched the rising sun. She would have thought of how Geri unexpectedly picked her up in a bear hug when she told Geri, "I'll do it." My mother refrained from any reciprocity of emotion and said to Geri sternly, "You and Schwinn are boots on the ground here. You keep your eyes on Campbell and we communicate everything to each other. Everything."

Geri held up her smartphone and said, "That's what this baby's for. I got your back, every step of the way." Mom simply nodded. At that point in her life, she'd heard many an individual say they had her back: ex-colleagues; ex-supervisors; ex-husband. Disappointingly, they were all full of shit. The extent of Geri's sincerity had yet to be determined.

After her morning paddle, Mom would have returned to her condo and made sure the stove was off; made sure the refrigerator was shut; made sure the windows were locked and the thermostat was set to fifty-seven degrees, so the pipes wouldn't freeze once winter arrived. She would have packed light and thrown everything into a medium sized gym bag. The day before, she'd touched base over the phone with the FBI Assistant Legal Attaché stationed in Manila, an agent named Mickey Sheptinsky. Mickey was blunt and brief. Mom didn't enjoy his curtness, but at least he'd informed her it was very hot in the Philippines and she wouldn't need much. So, she packed a few easy-dry workout clothes, a lot of clean underwear, toiletries, a toothbrush, and the three things she needed to never forget: her gun, her badge and the thing she always carried that she never showed me.

She would have thought of me as she closed the door behind her. She would have thought of the words I'd told her, in the strong, sure voice that surprised her. The words that made her laugh and cry at the same time after she said she was sorry for leaving me.

"Don't apologize," I'd told her. "Warriors don't apologize."

She would have locked her door, gritted her teeth, slung her packed bag over her shoulder and headed for the airport. She would have leaned fully into the thick, humid emotion of the moment: a feeling that hung around her body rather than coming from inside her, a feeling that manifested itself from the clear, bold act of embarking on adventure.

It was time to meet the Great Crane of the West.

CHAPTER 4

"Ikigai Johnson," I read to Geri. "April 20, 1968, to November 12, 2021. Headstrong and tenacious, with a willpower second to none, Ikigai defined herself by her service to others. She graduated from New York University in 1990, having studied Physics and Computer Science. A few years later, wanting to place her skills in service to her nation, she joined the Federal Bureau of Investigation, in whose employ she remained as a Special Agent for the rest of her life. Ikigai is survived and greatly missed by her daughter, Ikigai Warner. A celebration of life and cremation will…"

"It's nice," Geri says, cutting me off. "Short, straight, to the point. Just like your mom." I nod. "What's with the cremation?" she asks. I stay silent. "I thought you never found her body," Geri presses. I still don't respond. "Then, unlike your mother, it's a bit inaccurate."

"Mom was inaccurate when she needed to be," I say.

"Yes, she was," Geri agrees, and cocks an eyebrow. "How did she tell you about this case? Maybe it's your turn to talk."

I look toward the ceiling and reach back into memory.

SPRING 2010

"How do you know these things?" I asked Mom and sat up in the bed she'd set up for me in her living room, my back against the frame for support.

Mom replied in that hypnotic voice, "How do I know these things, you ask. That is a good question. I know these things because I *was* that warrior. The one they call Ikigai. This is my tale."

She sat at the foot of my bed facing me, legs tucked beneath her, heels under her backside. Her hands were on her knees. She sat up straight without any back support. It had been months since she'd returned from the Philippines. She was finally keeping her promise to tell me about the case.

"Now that this day has come," she asked, "are you sure you are ready?"

If I'd nodded any harder, my head would have fallen off.

"Very well." She folded a small hand towel and laid it neatly beside her. She took a paper fan, opened it briefly to reveal the crane drawn upon it, closed it, then laid it on the towel. "Before I continue, I must warn you. This will not be an easy story to hear. It takes bravery to follow. It takes courage to listen."

That's when it hit me: her posture, the fan, the towel. She hadn't told me the story of her case yet because she'd spent the past few months deciding how to do so. Her warning was serious. This was not going to be just another story. Despite the tinge of fear in my chest, I returned her gaze, my eyes imploring her to continue.

"Do you understand what I am saying to you?" she said in an almost whisper. "Telling a story is no different than preparing for war."

I nodded again.

My mother opened the fan, held the image of the crane before her face, and began:

"It was the Great Crane of the West who had posed for Ikigai the Warrior the first of her many challenges…"

You see, in addition to the satchel whose strap she gripped, there were three things Ikigai made sure to carry on her person as she left her home. These three items were indispensable. They were the artifacts of her strength and her very identity.

The first was her Weapon, carried at all times upon her hip.

The Weapon was more than the sum of its parts. Its blade was a physical embodiment of what existed beneath the flesh of her appearance. Ikigai's blade was her very soul – its gleaming steel reflecting the true intentions of those with whom she spoke, revealing when those intentions were evil, and razing this evil to the ground if it threatened the safety of the sacred, the fragile, or the blessed.

But her Weapon was useless without something deeper. Something deeper bestowed by and borrowed from the sacred, the fragile, and the blessed, which had charged Ikigai, as it charges all warriors, with the responsibility for its very protection. This deeper thing was her Authority, smelted directly into the gold of a badge she made sure to carry always beside her Weapon.

Now, the third thing she carried was harder to define. The best word she had ever heard to describe it was her own namesake, Ikigai, which in the Language of her Mothers meant: The Reason for Which You Wake Up in the Morning. But that would take too long to say over and over again. So, we will refer to it simply as her Purpose.

The Land of 7,000 Islands was very far away and it took the crossing of many oceans to reach. Travel by sea would take too long. Ikigai needed to travel by air. Given that she had never been blessed with the power of flight, she needed to employ the services of a Great Crane of the West.

Ikigai did not like this. The Great Cranes were an irritable bunch, and they took advantage of the high demand for their services – often over-charging or carrying too many travelers at once. There were frequent and unpredictable delays in their service as well, but Ikigai had no choice.

And so, with her Weapon, her Authority, and her Purpose, Ikigai reached the shore from which the Great Cranes launched into the air, carrying those who had hired them for transport to lands far and wide. She determined the specific Crane who would carry her and approached him directly.

"Stand in line with the rest of the passengers," the Crane said dismissively in a booming voice. Ikigai stood her ground. The Crane was as large as a building, and when he moved his wings even slightly, torrents of air forced people to grip their belongings tighter so they would not be blown away.

"I need your audience," Ikigai insisted. "I must inform you that I am a warrior, and as such, I will be carrying my weapon as I travel upon your back."

The feathers of the Crane's red crown, stark against his black neck and white body, bristled. "And what exactly are you a warrior of, little gnat? For what lost cause do you fight?"

Ikigai stepped closer and shouted, partly so the Crane could hear her better, but mostly because she was just annoyed. "I fight for Justice and Righteousness, arrogant Crane. My cause is never lost."

The Crane laughed, a haughty laugh. The bellows of his giggles forced the crowd of waiting passengers to cover their ears. "And what will you do, little gnat, if you fail?"

In Ikigai's younger days, she would have laughed at the Crane in return. She would have told him that she could not fail. But now, in her older years, with the taint of experience on her shoulders, she hesitated. For she had known failure, and she was very aware she could make its acquaintance once more. So, Ikigai replied simply, "I will get up in the morning. I will face the rising sun. And I will do my best. My very best."

"I suppose, at the end of the day," the Crane said, his voice softening, "that is all a warrior can do. I just wonder how effective your best will be without your Weapon."

Ikigai narrowed her eyes, instinctively moving her hand toward her sword.

"You are traveling to The Land of 7,000 Islands, are you not?"

the Crane asked and Ikigai nodded. "That is a foreign land, little gnat. You are not allowed to take your Weapon there."

"It is an inviolable rule, giant worm-eater," Ikigai shouted. "I can never be separated from my Weapon."

"Then you can never be transported to The Land of 7,000 Islands," the Crane said, and beckoned for the waiting passengers to climb upon his back.

Geri's laughter reverberates throughout her office. "That's how she told it to you?"

"Was there any truth to any of that?" I ask, cracking up as well.

"That's pretty much what happened," Geri says, catching her breath. "She got into a fight with the airline attendant. Your mom was so used to carrying her gun everywhere, it slipped her mind she couldn't take it outside the country. She tell you how she resolved that?"

"You were the Amazon," I say.

Geri laughs again. "The Amazon?"

Luckily, Ikigai had a compatriot in her homeland: a woman warrior, tall and broad like a statuesque creature of myth. We will call her the Amazon. At Ikigai's request, the Amazon rushed to meet her at the Pacific Northwestern shore from which the Cranes departed.

"This better be good," the Amazon said, jogging up to Ikigai. "I was in the middle of tracking Tagagawas."

Ikigai handed the Amazon her Weapon without a word.

"Seriously?" the Amazon said as she took it. "You know you can't take your Weapon to foreign lands."

Ikigai, short-tempered, responded, "Treat my blade as your own. I trust only you with it. And make sure you continue to track Tagagawas while I'm gone."

"I gave you my word," the Amazon replied. Ikigai nodded, then turned back to the Crane. "Are you happy now?" Ikigai shouted.

The Crane blinked and said, "Little gnat, I will be happy when I can retire, collect my pension, and focus solely on the construction of my symphonies. Are you coming or not?"

"Wonderful," Ikigai said to the Amazon and rolled her eyes. "This one's an artist."

The Amazon shook her head as Ikigai climbed onto the Crane. "Safe travels, Ikigai."

"I will find a way to communicate with you when I arrive," Ikigai said and waved.

Geri can't stop laughing. "Great! I'm a creature of myth. I had to fight through traffic, meet her at the airport before the plane took off, grab her gun, drop it off at the FBI office, then fight traffic again to get to a judge. I almost missed my appointment."

"Another warrant?"

"Yup, pen register and ping on Evan's new cell. The one he stupidly gave me the number of when I gave him a copy of the federal warrant. I had your mom's back. I was going to keep track of exactly what that shithead was doing. Anyways. Keep going."

Ikigai was not pleased with having been forced to leave her Weapon behind. Nor was she particularly ecstatic at the lack of space in the long, slender carriage fastened along the Crane's spine. The carriage fit neatly between the Crane's enormous wings, and it contained too many seats for its narrow size, into which the passengers squeezed their bodies.

Small favors can do wonders on a trek of this magnitude however, and the Crane, tickled by Ikigai's nerve, allowed her to sit at the front of his carriage. The flight was long and boring. Pestering Ikigai would keep him awake.

"What brings you on this journey, little warrior?" the Crane asked.

"It's a long story."

"We have nothing but time."

Ikigai peered over the huge wings of the Crane and thought about how different clouds appeared when moving through them instead of watching them from afar. From a distance, clouds were whole and self-contained. Moving through them, they were just a mess of fog.

"You should worry less about my journey and more about yours," Ikigai said. "How can you see through these clouds?"

"I don't need to," said the Crane. "It's much like listening to a musical composition you've never heard before. You don't know the song, but if you relax and don't think about it, you'll always know the next note to be played. The trick is to listen and keep moving forward. The world will take care of the rest. The song will be played."

Ikigai thought this was the stupidest thing she'd ever heard.

Regardless, she continued to engage with the Crane. "Someone from my homeland hurt people in The Land of 7,000 Islands. I am going there to help set things right."

"And you call me arrogant!" the Crane bellowed. "What if there is nothing you can offer that would be of use to the people to whom you travel? What if they don't want your help?"

This gave Ikigai pause. She had no answer.

The Crane laughed. "Your heart is good, little warrior, but you still have much to learn. The world will teach it to you. One way or another, the world teaches us all."

Time passed. The sensation of dense, wet heat that quieted the background noise in Ikigai's mind, grew stronger. Then there was descent; through the clouds of fog; through the air reflecting the unavoidable blue of sea and sky; through the scent of strange spices and marine life that wafted towards the passengers as they approached The Land of 7,000 Islands.

The Crane flew lower but didn't touch the ground. Not yet. Ikigai looked below as they flew over the numerous islands. Some separated by broad, bold seas with currents of rage, others by the quiet trickles of peaceful tributaries. There were big islands that looked like porcupines with buildings jutting forth like quills of concrete and steel; and there were small islands that looked like precious little emeralds, lush and green, with the promise of life. Ikigai looked at these smaller, greener islands, and marveled at their perfection. She pointed at one.

"Can we land there, giant worm-eater? Just briefly?" she asked the Crane.

"That is the Island of the Keepers of the Key," the Crane said.

"And?"

The Crane simply grunted, dipped one of his wings, and flew toward the shore of one of the porcupine islands. "No, little warrior," he said. "We will land on the Island of the Capital."

Ikigai had been sitting in the carriage on the back of the Crane for over a day. When they finally landed and she stood, she needed to let the blood return to her legs. "Best of luck to you," the Crane said. "And remember, you need not carry a sword to be a sword."

Ikigai was tired and rather annoyed with the condescending Crane and his second-rate philosophy. But he had done his duty and provided the service she requested. She bowed respectfully to the Great Crane of the West, climbed off his back, and they parted ways.

Ikigai adjusted the strap of her satchel, looked about, and tried not to feel overwhelmed. The Island of the Capital was a cacophony of sense and sound: the scent of stagnant water from shore; the wet heat on her skin; the drivers of mule-drawn carriages haggling for payment with passengers; and so many people arguing, selling, laughing and shouting. But there was a quietude to it all, an undercurrent of silence, as if she were listening to the world through earmuffs. Ikigai heard the island's people first. Then she saw them. She became disoriented.

"You Ikigai?" a voice called out behind her. She turned and faced a mule-drawn carriage from which two men stepped forth. One of these men approached Ikigai. His pale skin and wet-dog hair set him apart from the denizens of the capital. His speech identified him as one from Ikigai's homeland. "Ikigai?" he asked again.

"You Mickey?" she responded.

"You have identification?"

"Do you?"

The two warriors eyed each other and slowly drew their hands to their pockets to produce their badges of Authority. Upon seeing they carried the same badge, they let their guards down somewhat. The man smiled and put out his hand. "Mickey the Expatriate," he informed her, and Ikigai cautiously shook it. Mickey towered over her and his grip was strong. Having no desire to be one-upped, she put a good amount of strength into her handshake. Mickey, not expecting this, tried not to flinch, then beckoned to his companion.

Mickey's companion appeared to be a native of The Land of 7,000 Islands. "This is Hari," Mickey told her. "He's a local warrior. Me and this guy, we've been working together a long time." Hari and Ikigai nodded at each other and, for a moment, their movements were mirror reflections. Mickey the Expatriate noticed this and laughed. "Yeah, that's why I asked for identification," he said. "You, uh, don't fit the description they gave me."

"What description was that?" Ikigai asked.

"They told me you were a descendant of The Cradle of Humanity."

Ikigai considered whether to be offended or not. Mickey the Expatriate's voice was like mineral water, light and bubbly.

Though he sported a full-grown beard, his mannerisms were like that of a boy: a happy little boy. No, Ikigai concluded, as she measured and weighed his character, this warrior was not racist. He was just stupid.

"Are you not human?" she asked.

"Last I checked, I think so? Yes, definitely, yes. No, wait! You asked if I was not human. So no, I am not, not human."

"Then you would be just as much a descendant from The Cradle of Humanity as I."

Mickey laughed like a child, and Ikigai found herself fighting back a smile. "Point taken ma'am," he responded. "I just didn't expect you to look so much like the people here."

That's when Ikigai realized why she was so disoriented upon the sight of the denizens of the island. It was the first time in her life she found herself in a land where she looked like everyone else.

"Well, I am also a descendant of The Land of the Rising Sun," Ikigai informed him.

"Ah," Mickey replied with a smile. Hari the Local Warrior kept his eye on Ikigai, silent and unmoving. "So why are you here?" Mickey asked.

"You know why I'm here."

"Yeah, I know why you were sent here. I know what your mission is." The tone of his voice changed unexpectedly. The mineral water was gone, evaporated, leaving only the gravel of a dry riverbed in his throat. "Why are you," he said, pointing at Ikigai with his index finger, "and no one else but you," he continued, and pointed at the earth beneath their feet, "here."

Ikigai cocked her head, considering how best to respond. This Mickey the Expatriate may not have been as foolish as he appeared. A familiar high-pitched whine turned on at the base of Ikigai's skull, and she knew exactly why she was there, but that was not something she should tell them.

"You should tell us," Hari the Local Warrior spoke, as if he had heard Ikigai's thoughts, and this raised the hair on her arms. The Local Warrior's voice was the voice of his land, halting and rolling as if the words hopped on each island before they reached Ikigai's ears. "If you do not," Hari spoke again, "we cannot work with you."

Ikigai hesitated. They would think her crazy if she told them what caused the high-pitched whine at the base of her skull, what came forth when she encountered evidence of Tagagawas' crimes. No, she could not tell them that. She would give them a surface level answer.

"No surface level answers," said Mickey the Expatriate, the mineral water returning to his voice. These two were strange. And the strangeness stopped the thing between her brain and her mouth from creating words.

The Expatriate and the Local Warrior exchanged a look and a shrug and turned their backs on Ikigai. "Where are you going?" she demanded.

"To our inn," Mickey said, as they entered their carriage. "Let us know when you're ready to join us." The carriage driver spurred the mule, and they left Ikigai on the road, alone and perplexed. She watched their carriage as it was swallowed by the multitudes of denizens.

(And at this point, I felt my mother's lips on my forehead. I could no longer keep my eyes open. I was flying through a mess of cloudy fog, over the blueness of deep sea.)

While my mother carried forth on her grand adventure, Evan Campbell would have walked through the rain without an umbrella. He would have entered a small, six-story, downtown Portland office building made quaint by its preservation of early 20th century detail: exposed brick; functional vintage candlestick telephones. Evan entered a 1920s Otis elevator, manually shut its gate, and ascended to the boutique litigation offices of the Weddle Law Group LLC on the third floor.

I have no idea what was said between Evan Campbell and Zach Weddle. It would have been a privileged conversation no one, except them, would ever have access to. But perhaps Evan Campbell appeared at Zach Weddle's door, the long length of his shadow splicing Weddle's small office into triangular thirds, (I see this in stark black and white, no shades of gray) while white droplets of water rolled from Evan's black hair and splashed on the checkered floor as he approached Zach Weddle and asked in a monochromatic voice, "Why am I here?"

I imagine Weddle said nothing, then shoved a stack of papers across his desk. Evan would have picked them up, thumbed through them and said, "Damn."

"You got lucky with the timing," Weddle would have said. "They handed over Discovery when they thought they were going to charge you state-side. When they dropped the state case I didn't bother finishing my review. Then they went federal, so I took a second pass at it. That was in there, smartly buried under mounds of administrative bullshit. Detective Nathan Schwinn's report of a live data capture."

Evan would have held a page, a hard copy image, of a little girl: a little girl squatting in an alley with black hair and black screaming eyes. "I didn't send the batch script quick enough," Evan would have muttered. "This all they got?"

"That's what they found prior to their preparation for the state case, which they dropped. Being that a federal search and seizure warrant was subsequently executed, and we won't know what they've found on that search until they press federal charges, I'm advising you to use your common sense and assume the feds already found something."

"Common sense deployed," Evan would have said. "Thanks."

Evan would have stalked out of the office, headed back down the Otis elevator, and stepped out into the prickling needles of white rain nicking the city. He would have stepped under an awning and pulled out his cell phone.

Then he would have typed a text message.

As for myself, I was in school, daydreaming and sad. Lily had disappeared. She stopped showing up to soccer practice after our altercation with the other girls, now my enemies, who I'd antagonized for the protection of someone who didn't even stick around.

When Coach Fritz mentioned to the team that Lily was not returning, Ms. Pigtail and her pack of little hyenas intelligently exploited this to full advantage. Ms. Pigtail cried to Coach that I had pulled her hair and threatened to harm her. True, but conveyed out of context. The other girls, acting as witnesses, corroborated her report. When I was confronted by Coach before my father, I tried to explain through tearful shrieks that I was defending Lily. Of course, Lily, now gone, couldn't verify my side of the story. And, as my explanation tumbled forth, I knew it didn't sound credible. I *had* bullied Lily before. Then she left the team. Now Pigtail was claiming she was my next victim. I wouldn't have believed me either. I was defeated. The pack of hyenas had won.

"Mr. Warner, we discussed this," Coach said. "We agreed. She fought again. I can't keep her on the team." Dad didn't stick up for me. Mom would have.

So, I sat in class and missed soccer and missed Lily and missed my mother and daydreamed. I daydreamed about all the things I would have done with my new friend Lily. We would have stayed after practice and I would have helped her work on dribbling the ball, especially her cuts. (She kind of sucked.) We would

have ridden our bikes through the crunchy red, orange and brown
leaves and had sleepovers and stayed up all night to talk.

But Lily was gone. I was off the soccer team. Mom was in the
Philippines. At least I'd done the right thing when I stood up for
Lily. Mom always told me doing the right thing was often the
hardest thing in the world. She should have also told me it was
often the loneliest.

So every time I saw my mother after her return from the Philippines, I'd fight to not blink when I looked at her face. I didn't want
to miss a thing.

She sat again at the foot of my bed, fluttering the fan with the
image of the crane. "You fell asleep so quickly last night. Where
were we?"

"Mickey and Hari, those assholes left you behind, I can't believe
they did that!"

"Language, Junior."

But Ikigai could not believe it either.

She was furious. If those sons of dogs wanted to know why she
was there she would tell them. Let their judgments be damned.

("Language, Mom," I said.

"That's not a curse," she replied. "Damned is a real word."

"Then I can say it in school?" I asked. "Like, I can tell my
teachers, I care not what you think of my homework foolish fools!
Let your judgments be damned!")

If those aggravating men wanted to know why Ikigai was there
she would tell them. Let their judgments be ignored with the
greatest of irritation.

Ikigai hired the driver of the first mule-drawn carriage that
passed her way and demanded he take her to the inn of Mickey the
Expatriate. This made no sense to the driver. He knew very little

of Ikigai's language and hadn't the slightest idea what a 'mickey-expatriate' was. But he did know Ikigai's word 'inn' and promptly took her to the closest one. Upon arriving, Ikigai demanded the Innkeeper call for Mickey, to no avail. It was not the right inn.

Ikigai then decided she would visit every inn on the Island of the Capital until she found Mickey and gave him a good-sized chunk of her mind. Through broken words and motions, she recruited the carriage driver to aid her on this task, to which he had no objection. If this silly foreigner insisted on paying him to drive her all about the Capital, well, getting paid was getting paid. This assignment could provide rice for his family for months.

As they drove around, Ikigai took in more of her surroundings. Swarms of people and carriages milled about on streets and sidewalks in a chaotic fashion that stoked wonder as to how there weren't more accidents. It was not uncommon to see a carriage contain more people than it was designed to transport – scores of sun-browned denizens sitting in, on top of, or hanging off the sides of, a carriage as it ambled by. The air was thick and humid, but not oppressive. It filled Ikigai's lungs and had the effect of settling her thoughts. It helped her focus on her task: to find Mickey the Expatriate. After she and the driver attempted to locate him at inn number seven, the driver began to understand that Ikigai was a foreign warrior looking for another of her kind, so he narrowed their search to inns where such people would likely reside.

It took two more attempts. When Ikigai entered the ninth inn, the sun had set and she was tired. She approached the Innkeeper, about to demand for the ninth time that Mickey be called, when she heard a voice behind her. "You found it!"

Ikigai took a deep breath, thanked her driver, tipped him well, for which he was highly grateful, and saw him off. Then she wheeled toward the source of that bubbly mineral water voice and seethed. "Yes. Thank you for telling me where it was."

"They did warn me you were on the sarcastic side," said Mickey the Expatriate who lounged on a sofa in the inn's welcome area.

"They didn't warn me you were a piece of excrement."

"Hostile too!"

"Why did you leave me behind?"

"Needed to see if you could handle it." Mickey stood and the gravel in his throat returned. "You think running around the Capital looking for me while you're tired from a long journey across the oceans is tough? Wait until we start navigating seven thousand islands to look for the people you're here to find. I need to know if you're the quitting type because if you are, it's best I call home right now and tell them to send you back."

Ikigai straightened her spine and gritted her teeth and returned the intensity in Mickey's stare. "And at what point did you hear me complain about anything being tough? Looking for you wasn't tough. It was a waste of time. Time better spent looking for the children whose Innocence Tagagawas stole. And on that, I will never give up."

Mickey stroked his beard. "We'll see. Now why are you here?"

"I told you. I am here to find the children whose Innocence…"

"Why are you here, Ikigai?"

Ikigai bit her lip. "I see a ghost." She controlled the tremor in her voice. "The ghost of an Emperor. When my purpose is righteous, he appears, sometimes as a grown man, sometimes as a small, crying boy. If you think I'm crazy, so be it. There's your answer."

Mickey furrowed his brow. "Do you see him now?"

"No, but I hear him. When I'm on the right path, he whines at the base of my skull."

Silence. Then Mickey spoke, his tone softer. "Yeah, I've got one of those too. Come on, I'll show you your room. Hari will be here in the morning. We'll start then."

The next morning, Ikigai munched angrily on her scrambled eggs, still upset with Mickey as they waited. The first floor of the inn was devoted to serving its residents meals. Before them lay a feast of eggs, bacon, tuna sushi rolls, cheddar squares, gouda, oatmeal, sesame seed crackers, rice and corn cereal, smoked salmon, orange, apple, and grapefruit juice, not to mention the available slices of mango, cantaloupe...

("Got it," I said. "Lots of food. What are they waiting for?")

The point was, Ikigai saw many a foreigner walking about, stuffing their faces, demanding service of the Innkeeper, who humbly smiled and bowed his head at every request. This annoyed Ikigai and made her ashamed she had spoken to so many Innkeepers in the same manner the night before as she searched for Mickey. She would have to amend this in the future. But for now, she needed to focus on her mission.

"What's taking so long?" she asked Mickey.

On cue, Hari silently appeared and sat at their table.

"You got him?" Mickey asked.

Hari nodded, carefully laid a satchel on their table, reached gently into it, and pulled out a bird no bigger than one of his hands. But this was not just any bird.

"This little guy will help you communicate with our homeland," said Mickey.

"What is it?" Ikigai asked, entranced. The bird looked almost like an eagle, but with a glowing golden body and fiery red wings. She had never seen anything like it.

"A baby Garuda," Hari said. "When fully grown he will join the stable of Vishnu himself, to serve the God of Protectors as a loyal mount in the fight against Chaos and Injustice."

"That's... intense," said Ikigai.

"He's still a baby," Mickey said. "Not strong enough to work for Vishnu, yet. But he's fast. He can go anywhere in the world at a speed second to none."

"This makes him the perfect messenger," said Hari.

"Wow," said Ikigai. Hari smiled and lovingly petted the Garuda, who cooed softly. "Few things to be aware of though," Mickey warned. "He'll freeze sometimes."

"He'll freeze?"

"He'll freeze. Completely motionless. Won't do a thing. Not even blink."

"Why?"

"No one knows. It'll happen randomly. Also, every now and again, you try to get him to send a message and he just won't do it. Especially in remote areas."

"Not particularly reliable," said Ikigai. The baby Garuda mewed and lowered his head. Hari clutched the Garuda to his chest. "You hurt his feelings."

Mickey was annoyed. "We work with what we got, Ikigai. Tarkshya will help us a lot."

"Tarkshya?"

"That's his name," confirmed Hari.

"Okay," Ikigai went on. "Tarkshya. Can I call you Tark for short?" The Garuda picked up his head and chirped. "I didn't mean to insult you," Ikigai continued. "I'm new here and I'm still learning. Can you send a message to a fellow warrior in my homeland? She is known as the Amazon. Trust me, you can't miss her. Can you tell her I've arrived safely?"

Tark the baby Garuda cawed. Then he vanished in a flash of light.

As Ikigai's brain tried to process what had just occurred, another flash of light blinded her and Tark re-appeared. Her senses couldn't keep up with the wonders of this magic. Tark chirped repeatedly. "That's how he tells you he has a return message," Mickey told her.

Ikigai was astonished. "What's the message, Tark?"

Tark's eyes grew wide and turned neon blue, which, with his body of gold and wings of fire, made for a beautiful sight. He spoke with words that sounded human, but not quite, as if they'd come from the flip side of the universe. Regardless, Ikigai understood the message. And it set her teeth on edge.

A little after Mom first arrived in the Philippines, I was in homeroom one day, re-organizing my binder to keep my mind focused on something that didn't remind me how abandoned I felt. Our teacher, Ms. Broner the stoner droned on. Her voice fell neatly into the din of twenty-three sixth graders chatting away about important topics ranging from the latest album dropped by the latest pop star that we didn't realize was just the latest one-hit wonder, to arguments over the best strategies for winning the latest M-rated video game that we probably shouldn't have been playing anyway. Sixth grade was a funny place, full of kids who were either eleven going on sixteen, or eleven going on six.

I was going on six. I wanted my Mom. Bad. I placed another paper reinforcer on a page whose hole was torn and falling out of my binder.

"Guys, listen up," Ms. Broner said.

I ignored her. I couldn't have a page fall out.

"We have a new student joining us." I still ignored her. I especially couldn't lose this page. It had the practice test she'd given us in preparation for our math exam the next day, and everyone with a pulse knew her practice tests looked exactly like her real tests.

"This is Lily," Ms. Broner announced. I really needed to memorize this practice test. We were working with these funny things called monomials and…

I poked my head above the crowd of kids, which was easy, I was the tallest in class, and looked to the front of the room. It was her. All paper thin and pale eyed and staring at the floor.

"Would anyone like to be Lily's help-mate for at least a week? She could use…"

I was already halfway across the room. "I will!" I shouted. The class laughed. I didn't care. Lily looked up at the sound of my voice and gave a little gasp of surprise. We locked eyes and smiled. Ms. Broner noticed. "Do you two know…?"

I wasn't paying attention to Ms. Broner. "Come on," I said to Lily, grabbed her little bird bone hand, and led her to my group of tables.

Maybe things weren't going to be so bad after all.

"Maybe things aren't going to be so easy after all," Nate said to Geri as they stared at a list of numbers on a computer screen in Nate's lab. "I think Evan knows we found something."

"Good thing he gave us the number to his new phone," Geri replied, looking at the rows of digits on the screen. "It's got a lot of activity. You think it's with them?"

"Don't know if it's *them*, them," Nate said. "But there's a lot of back and forth with this one." Nate pointed to a 12-digit number that appeared repetitively. "That's international." He pointed to the first two digits. "Six three, country code for the Philippines."

"How do you know? You google that shit?"

"I googled that shit."

"Rest of these digits mean anything else? An area code telling us where that phone is?"

"They're texting, so it's probably a cell phone. Could be any-where in the country."

"I haven't heard from Ikigai."

Geri's phone buzzed. She checked it. "Speak of the she-devil."

"That her?" Nate asked. Geri nodded, read the message, then emailed Ikigai back: *Glad you're safe. FYI - we're looking at the pen reg-ister on Evan's new phone. He's been texting the Philippines. A lot.*

"I'm glad you are safe. But be aware," Tark the baby Garuda had said, in that otherworldly voice. "We have been watching Tagagawas. He has his own manner of communication and he is sending messages to The Land of 7,000 Islands."

"Son of a dog," Ikigai said to her new companions. "Lord only knows what he's telling them. We need to find these children. Now!"

Mickey and Hari exchanged a glance. "Well," Mickey said to Ikigai, "what have you got?"

The three warriors finished their meal quickly, then went to Mickey's quarters to avoid the prying eyes of the other guests in the dining area. There were many foreigners at the inn, and it was widely known their purposes for visiting this land were not always honorable. From the satchel in which Ikigai carried her belong-ings, she produced the evidence indicative of Tagagawas' crimes. She lay this evidence before her compatriots. It comprised three watercolor drawings and several letters.

The first drawing was of two boys, aged twelve or so, standing under a waterfall, waist deep in a natural pool, the sweetness of their faces reflecting the sense the surrounding water gave, a sense that all was well in the world.

The second drawing was of an older boy, perhaps fifteen. He stood on a dusty road, looking off into the distance, vast blue sky above, wide green plain around. The sun was at his back, drawn almost as bright as the budding manhood alight in the look of his eyes – eyes that stared into the infinite spread of all that surrounded his frame.

The third drawing was the one Ikigai and the Amazon first encountered in their homeland: the one that alerted them to Tagagawas' transgressions in The Land of 7,000 Islands. It was of a girl, no older than ten, kneeling in an alley, surrounded by stone, tin, and cardboard, her dark eyes silently screaming. When Ikigai and the Amazon saw this picture, they knew it would haunt them the rest of their days. Ikigai heard the Emperor's Ghost whine at the base of her skull as she looked at it once more. This girl was the key to everything. Ikigai needed to find her.

The evidence also consisted of several letters Tagagawas had written. Letters that detailed how he had stolen the Innocence of these children. The problem was, as Mickey pointed out: "Can we prove these letters were written to these children?"

"Not yet," Ikigai replied. "That's why we need to find these children and speak to them."

"Got it," Mickey said, looking over the letters. "But nothing in here specifies the identity or location of whoever he's talking to. He mentions visiting their barangay. But *barangay* is like our word for village, or neighborhood. There are thousands of those on each island."

Mickey turned to the pictures. "Now these, let's see." He held the picture of the fifteen-year-old. "We see the boy, we see some sky. That could be anywhere." He picked up the picture of the girl. "This could narrow things down a bit." Ikigai's ears perked up. "But not much," Mickey said. "She's in an alley. I'm guessing this barangay is a slum in one of the more populated city-islands. That knocks it down to about ten islands. Narrowing her location down, to what, ten thousand barangays? Doesn't help much." Then Mickey held up the last drawing, the two boys under the waterfall.

Hari narrowed his eyes.

It was a slight movement, almost imperceptible, but when Hari did this, Mickey froze and focused his full attention on his friend. Ikigai chose to respect the sudden tense silence, not sure what it meant. Mickey held up the picture for his friend. Hari stared at it intensely while holding Tark, gently stroking the baby Garuda's head. Then Hari pointed to the upper right-hand corner of the drawing, where only a few leafy branches of a tree outside the drawing's frame could be seen. "Tagagawas is a good artist," Hari said. "Those look like the leaves of a *kaningag*."

"What's kaningag?" Ikigai asked.

"A cinnamon tree," said Hari. "Found on one island only: The Island of Traders."

"Yes!" Mickey exclaimed. "That would make sense, that's a city-island."

"But with cities surrounded by wilderness," Hari continued. "And The Island of Traders has only one waterfall."

Ikigai gathered the evidence, placed it into her satchel, and jumped to her feet. "Then let's get there. Now!"

Mickey and Hari traded a look. "Yeah, a little rude," Mickey muttered. "We'll get her up to speed."

"Please and thank you?" Ikigai tried. "Come on. Let's go."

Tark mewed and shook his head.

CHAPTER 5

When Evan Campbell returned to his place of employment, his days were spent mostly alone, in a bureaucratic rubber room, avoided by his colleagues, so as not to infect them with the airborne virus of his guilt. The state had dropped its charges, and the internal investigation by Portland Public Schools, his colleagues knew, would result in nothing, followed by paperwork, followed by more nothing, then by his return to the classroom. But his colleagues always thought Mr. Campbell was a little strange, you know, that way. I've since talked to several of them. Not one was surprised at the time this whole affair came to light.

I asked these colleagues, why didn't you say something? And the general response I received from these men and women, most retired at this point, was: Say what? We had no proof. What could we say or do based on a jittery feeling in the pits of our guts when we saw him place his hands on the shoulders of a child in the hall. I place my hands on the shoulders of children all the time, should I be suspected a pedophile as well?

But you had a feeling, I would say calmly, though I was railing inside. You had a sense of things. You could have watched, followed, looked, prodded, poked your head inside his door during his after-school classes, you know, just to make sure everything was okay.

And the usual response was a slow nod, and a sad smile, and a sorry honey, I couldn't go doing that just because I had a bad feeling. And this is when I would have to smile back, say I understood, and walk away having received my answer. These people were not indifferent. They were good men and women. They were just afraid, afraid of looking foolish, of endangering their own careers, of getting involved in a cloudy mess.

So, Evan Campbell would have sat in his rubber room during the day, then went home to his small, asphyxiated world of stark black and white. And there, he would have ruminated, seeing probabilities open before him like the black branches of a tree, growing, stretching and coalescing into a mass of nausea. How much was left unencrypted? Would they find the Facebook chats? Had they already? If they had, will they, would they, could they, follow through and develop a case? If they could…

Evan would have picked up his cell phone and reviewed a set of text messages, tapped the call icon and listened to the staggered rhythm of an international dial tone.

A voice would have answered on the other end. "It's me," he would have said. "No, no. Don't hang up. Just listen. I can't explain this over text. Some people may come to you. Do you understand? They will ask you about me. Do *not* talk to them."

Evan would have waited while the voice let loose a barrage of questions. "Listen," he would have responded slowly, enunciating his words to make sure they were understood. "They are why I had to leave when I did. They are dangerous. They will tell you lies. They will kill you."

★★★

Ikigai put her head between her legs and fought not to vomit. The last thing she needed was to appear weak before her fellow warriors. Hari looked at her with concern. Mickey laughed. The Great Crane of the East they rode upon was smaller than the Cranes of the West she was used to, and was thus more susceptible to the wind currents meandering between the thick clouds above and the islands below. With each gust, the Crane found its path altered, and had to change elevation drastically to stay on course.

The three warriors sat together, Mickey between Hari and Ikigai. Ikigai peered in her satchel and checked on Tark, who she was charged with carrying. Tark slept peacefully like the baby he was. Ikigai broke the silence. "You two don't like being apart for long."

Mickey and Hari bumped fists. "Bromance," Mickey said. "No shame in that."

Hari smiled and shook his head. "Can't have too many friends out here," Mickey said. "But me and this guy? We're family. Brothers. You know?"

Ikigai winced and Mickey, a perceptive observer of body language, noticed this. Ikigai, just as perceptive, noticed that he noticed this, so she turned away. She didn't want to deal with the question she knew was coming next, and observant Mickey saw that she did not want to deal with it but asked anyway. "And you? You got any family?"

The Crane jolted, dropping elevation. Ikigai controlled her breathing. "Yes," she said, annoyed at everything about this situation. "I have a daughter."

(And here, my ears perked up.)

"Aw," Mickey said. "How old?"

"Eleven," Ikigai relaxed a little. "You have...?"

"Nah. Never found the right woman, to, you know..."

"Impregnate," Hari added, and the two men laughed like twelve-year-old boys.

"Husband? Parents?" Mickey asked Ikigai.

"Ex-husband. And both parents have been gone a while now."

"I'm sorry," Mickey said.

"Not your fault."

"What about siblings? Sisters?" He watched Ikigai carefully. "Brothers?"

Ikigai turned away to look at the cluster of islands below.

I zoned out at this point.

"Do you want me to keep going?" Mom asked gently. I snapped back to attention. Something roiled inside me, filling my brain with a mist that seemed to waft in from the sky over The Land of 7,000 Islands.

I blinked, trying to force the mist away. "I'm not tired yet," I told her. "Keep going."

"Sorry," Mickey said. "Didn't mean to pry."

"Yes, you did," said Ikigai. The Crane jolted again. Ikigai clenched her fist and looked out over the ocean to her left, which was east. She noticed a large irregular-shaped island with a cone-shaped mountain, whose frosted crest poked gently above the clouds.

"That is some mountain," Ikigai observed, awestruck.

Hari smiled.

"Is that the Island of Traders?" she asked.

"No," Mickey said. "That's the Island of the Beautiful Lady. We still have a little further south to go."

Ikigai stared at the mountain, wordless. Mickey laughed. "Welcome to The Land of 7,000 Islands."

★★★

Back home, Geri was trying not to be annoyed with the rain as she parked her car a safe distance east of Evan Campbell's home. It was still the middle of the day. He would notice her if she parked too close. The rain was fogging her view, but if she turned her windshield wipers on, it would alert bystanders someone was sitting there. So, she let her wiper swipe once and clear her view, then she looked: nothing. A minute passed, one swipe again, clear, look: nothing. Another minute, swipe, clear, look: Evan exited the house.

"Subject leaving," Geri hissed into her radio.

Nate's voice answered, "I'll take him. You stay long, he's seen you a lot more than he's seen me."

"Copy," Geri said. She scrawled in her notepad: *13:22 – J leaves*. She watched Evan get into his Camry and back out of the driveway. Nate, in his Chevy Impala, casually pulled away from the curb and followed the Camry after it passed him, heading west. Geri waited about ten seconds, started her engine then followed Nate, keeping a safe distance between them.

They followed Evan to a strip mall less than a mile away, where he parked on the north side of the lot, stepped out of the Camry and walked into a bank. Nate's voice came in over Geri's radio, "I'm getting on foot."

Geri kept her distance on the south side of the lot, in a spot where she had a perfect view of the bank entrance. She watched Nate walk into the bank a moment after Evan. She jotted in her notepad the time of this observation. She waited. The job was mostly waiting. Writing and waiting. Even when there were exciting things going on, like now. After approximately thirteen minutes, Geri watched Evan leave the bank, get back into the Camry and drive away. A moment later, Nate left the bank, got into his Impala, followed Evan and came on over Geri's radio. "Let's stay on him a bit longer. Dude just pulled out a lot of cash."

"What's a lot?" Geri said, turning her engine back on.

"We can come back with a subpoena to get the exact amount, but from what I could see of the teller handing it over: ten k, easy."

★★★

In my school's cafeteria, I could tell from the way Lily kept rubbing her nose and tilting her head that she was doing her best to ignore the compost smell of wasted food. After she got off the lunch line, her partitioned plastic tray filled with mac and cheese, she crossed the warehouse-sized floor with all its shouting middle schoolers and sat at the end of a table, alone.

I watched her from the line while I got my lunch. I watched her sway her thin little body, neck to waist, dancing to some song in her head. I filled my tray with mac and cheese, ignored the vegetables, grabbed two cartons of chocolate milk, and made a beeline for my new friend.

Those pale blue eyes widened when I sat across from her. "Oh, there was chocolate milk," she said in that broken glass voice and reached for a carton. "Thank you."

I knocked her hand away.

"Both mine," I mumbled from a mouth stuffed with processed food.

Lily drew her hand back as if it were burnt and made a funny motion with her lips, sucking them both into her mouth, like a reverse pout. She fluttered her eyelashes, picked up her fork and played with her food. "Sorry," she whispered.

Burning shame welled up again. Being a jerk just seemed to be my default mode. "No, no. Here." I put a carton on her tray. She gingerly reached for it. "Here," I said, placing the second carton on her tray, "Take both." She opened a carton.

"Where was your last school?" I asked.

Lily swayed her body and sipped the chocolate milk. "School of what?"

"The last school you were at? Before here?"

Lily guzzled the milk, wiped her mouth with her sleeve and stared at her tray. "School of what?" she muttered again. "Can't learn there. How would..." She trailed off, then made eye contact.

"I miss kindergarten. Remember kindergarten?"

I met her gaze and blinked. "No."

She blinked back. "You don't remember kindergarten?"

I shook my head.

"You don't remember naptimes?"

I shrugged. "Who remembers naps?"

"I do," she said, and stretched her arms across the table, grabbed my elbows, and put her head down. "Naptimes are the best times."

"You can't take a nap now."

She smiled, nodded silently and closed her eyes, still gripping my elbows. I couldn't help but laugh.

★★★

Ikigai and her companions survived the turbulent ride and arrived at the Southern shore of The Island of Traders. When they landed, Ikigai instantly understood how the island got its name. Merchant vessels sailed to and from its harbor. The warriors walked inland, through the coastal region markets where all manners of people peddled their wares — rice, fish, jewelry, even a few baby Garudas.

Something in one market stall caught Ikigai's eye and she approached it. In the stall stood a pretty young woman with coal-black eyes, dressed in clothes that were modest and loose fitting, her hair covered with a purple scarf. The woman smiled at Ikigai and Ikigai smiled back, pointing to what had caught her eye — a hanging string of pearls. "Two minutes on this island," Mickey muttered, "and of course, that's what you immediately go for."

"Shut up," said Ikigai. "They're pretty." She asked the woman, "How much?" The woman spoke only a few words of Ikigai's language, but she spoke enough to be able to trade. "Five hundred pesos." Ikigai turned to Mickey and Hari and they knew the answer to the question in her eyes.

"About ten bucks," Mickey told her.

"No, it's not!" Ikigai responded, shocked.

"Your money stretches a lot further here."

"A lot further," Ikigai smiled. "I could get so many."

"I am so happy to see your feminine side. But maybe we should stay focused on the mission at hand?"

"I am focused on the mission," Ikigai snapped, turned away from the woman with the coal-black eyes, and took off like a rocket, leaving her compatriots behind. "Let's go, let's get to the waterfall!" she shouted.

"You're, uh," Mickey called out after her. "You're going the wrong way."

It was a full day's travel by foot, heading north, into the heart of the Island of Traders. They walked on a singular dusty and disjointed road, at times lined with nothing but redwood and mangrove trees, at others bursting with human activity. When these outbreaks of humanity occurred, what struck Ikigai most were the colors. The redwoods and mangroves would take to the background, while the foreground would be populated with shops and residences, their exterior walls painted in bright greens, yellows and reds. The shops and homes were built low to the ground, so the sky opened above. The tropical heat gave the sky a more intense shade of blue: a blue that not only comprised blue, but also the gray of pearls and the purple of dye in scarves, as if the heat evaporated pieces of the wares on the Island of Traders and carried them into the air.

For the most part, the citizens who shared the road ignored Ikigai and her companions. They had their own things to do. They carried their wares by foot and by bicycle. They surged and receded like waves, or breath, flowing in and out of shops, residences, and the alleys between. Ikigai wondered how such small buildings and alleys could accommodate so many. At one point, they encountered a man, stick thin and skin brown like leather from honest work in the sun, pulling a yellow carriage with his bicycle. He pedaled to the three warriors and gestured, asking if they wanted to use his services. Mickey and Hari deferred to Ikigai, who politely declined. She was strong and she could walk forever. She had no desire to travel to her destination upon the legs of another.

Later, a small boy and girl with dry mouths and dusty faces walked toward the three, hands outstretched. This broke Ikigai's heart and she reached for her satchel. Mickey quickly advised, "Don't do it." Ikigai looked at him questioningly. Mickey explained, "You give these two money, we'll get mobbed by twenty kids hiding in the alleys over there." Ikigai closed her satchel. "Hang on to that tight," Mickey told her. "Make sure Tark's okay in there." Tark woke at the sound of his name and gently mewed.

The boy and girl headed straight for Ikigai. When she moved, they shifted accordingly and continued to walk directly at her. A collision became unavoidable, and as it happened, Ikigai felt their small hands tugging gently on her satchel, searching for an opening. She gripped it tighter, the children let go, and they continued down the road. Ikigai turned and watched the children walk in the opposite direction, kicking up dust with their bare feet and holding on to each other for support. They were weak from hunger. Tark mewed softly again.

As the sun set, the purple dye in the sky brightened and took its short-lived moment of prominence. Mickey suggested they find an inn for the night. They veered off the main road and entered a town. Hari suggested, "Ask Tark where the nearest inn is."

"He does that too?" Ikigai asked.

"Tark does everything," Mickey assured her with a grin.

"We just have to keep feeding him. He runs out of energy when he's awake. Tomorrow, he'll direct us to the waterfall."

Ikigai gently pulled Tark from her satchel. He cawed at being startled awake, then perched on Ikigai's shoulder and nuzzled into her neck.

The inn Tark directed them to was surprisingly comfortable and inexpensive. The next morning, after eating a quick and simple breakfast, and ensuring Tark had eaten as well, the three warriors and the baby Garuda set out on the road and continued pushing north. After an hour of walking, through an area outside of human activity, Tark, perched on Ikigai's shoulder, said in that otherworldly voice, "In two hundred meters, turn right." So they did, walking through thick bushes surrounded by the calls of parrots and trillers. When the birds ceased and there was an instant of quietude, they all heard it: the sound of rushing water.

They moved toward the sound, down a short hill damp with wet grass and moss-lined tree roots. And there it was. The warriors looked up to see a rocky ledge, several stories high, from which water cascaded into a large natural pool below. The crashing water created a dense mist of droplets. The waterfall was beautiful and it was popular. Though still early, several people had already arrived to swim. Laughing children stood at the pool's damp edge and back-flipped into the water. The mother in Ikigai prayed they wouldn't hurt themselves.

"This be it," Mickey said. He put down his bag and sat by the pool. "What now?"

"Let's be thinking," Ikigai said and rolled her eyes. She reached into her satchel and pulled out an evidentiary drawing: the one with the two boys under the waterfall. She looked around then pointed to a cinnamon tree at the side of the pool. "Hari, that's the kaningag."

"Excellent find, my man, if I may say so again," Mickey told him.

Hari chuckled.

Ikigai said, "This place is not easy to get to. Can Tark tell us where the nearest towns are?"

"Tark's got a map of the whole world in his head," Mickey replied.

"Tark?" Ikigai said to the Garuda. "I don't need the whole world. I just need a map of the immediate area."

Tark glided off Ikigai's shoulder to the ground, and with his beak, drew a detailed map in the damp soil. Ikigai knelt and pointed to the symbols Tark had made. "Here's the main road we came on. There's one town nearby if we keep moving north. Here's the only other road that leads out of this place, going east."

"Want to split up? Check both directions?" Mickey asked.

"Maybe," Ikigai answered. Then she bolted up a short hill to the road heading east away from the waterfall. Tark dutifully fluttered behind her. When Mickey and Hari caught up to her, she was standing in the middle of the Eastern road, surrounded by wide empty plains. She faced the rising sun and held up another drawing: the one with the man-boy, sun at his back, looking off to the distance. "Do you see it?" Ikigai asked as they approached. They looked at the drawing, then at their surroundings. "You see it, right?" Ikigai said again and giggled.

("You giggled?" I asked.)

Mickey also lifted an eyebrow and said, "Did you just giggle?" Ikigai ignored him. "Come on, guys. Don't you see it?" Hari looked at the drawing. Then he and Ikigai shared a smile.

"Mickey, look at the sun in the background of the drawing," Ikigai said. "If this boy was on the Northern road and had the sun at his back, there would be trees or shops or houses in the picture." Ikigai spread her arms wide in a feeble attempt to match the expanse of blue sky and green plain before them. "Look around. This drawing was made here," she said. "These kids probably live in a town off this road. We should stay together. We should keep moving east."

Mickey smiled, impressed. "It's your world lady. We're just living in it."

"Shut up," Ikigai said, and punched him on the shoulder.

★★★

The warriors walked until they reached a city on the Eastern road. It couldn't be missed. It was huge and its appearance was sudden, as if a behemoth of buildings and people had materialized into existence with a wink. Bicycles, carts, carriages, and the denizens that rode them, flowed onto the road like a flash flood.

"There's gonna be thousands of barangays here," Mickey sighed. "Where do we start?"

"At the one closest to the road," said Ikigai. "Tagagawas wouldn't have taken the children to the waterfall if it was too far."

They walked further, past tall buildings – some still under construction – and dodged men and women in fine clothes who strode with an air of importance in and out of these buildings. Then they came upon a bright yellow sign over a narrow side road that read: *Barangay Tormenta*. Hari pointed at it and translated, "Village of the Storm."

They turned onto the side road and entered the Village of the Storm. The world changed. The bustling grew silent, leaving only dusty streets of stone. On the main roads, the warriors were ignored, but once they entered the barangay, they were the center of attention. The Villagers halted conversations as they sat outside their homes and shops and glared at the warriors. Women and men, gaunt with the fierce look of hurt and hunger, walked in and out of the alleys between the shops. Ikigai wondered again how such small alleys could hold so many. A small girl changed an infant's diaper on the stone street. The infant boy barely had the energy to coo, his ribs showing, his face thin at a time of life when it should be fat and full. Ikigai thought of the breakfast feast in which she and the other foreign travelers had partaken on her first morning in this land. Her face flushed with discord, with heartbreak, and with shame.

An old woman walked by the warriors, staring, and Ikigai swore the woman had murder in her eyes.

Then Ikigai heard that familiar high-pitched whine at the base of her skull. It was so loud it made her tremble. Tark, perched on her shoulder, ruffled his feathers and vigorously flapped his wings. "You hear it too, huh?" Ikigai whispered to the baby Garuda. Tark nuzzled into her neck. Mickey noticed this interaction but chose not to press with any questions.

Hari approached a man sitting in front of a shop. The man, wearing a thin shirt with missing buttons and dusty shorts with bare feet, stood up straight to meet Hari eye to eye. Hari asked, *"Punong Barangay?"* The man squinted, spat on the ground, and pointed to the top of a small building a few meters down the stone street.

Hari rejoined his compatriots and told them, "The Village Captain's office is over there." They walked to the building under the gaze of the Villagers who seethed quietly, and went up a staircase built on the exterior of the building. They reached the top after three flights, walked on to a small balcony, and squeezed past a short, round woman who wore brass hoop earrings that jingled as she moved. The woman stood on the balcony, looking over the village, and ignored the warriors as they passed her to open a door to the office on the top floor. The woman and Ikigai locked eyes briefly, and the pitch of the whine at the base of Ikigai's skull increased. Ikigai tried to steal another glance at the woman's face, but the woman turned her back to the warriors.

The warriors entered the office and took a moment to let their eyes adjust. The office was dimly lit with floors and walls painted pastel blue and yellow.

"Yes?" A voice commanded from the front of the room. The warriors faced its source: a tall, stout man, standing behind a plastic desk. They instantly knew he was the Village Captain.

"What do you want?" the Captain demanded.

★★★

Back home, Geri and Nate continued reviewing the data from their pen register. Geri pointed to the digits on the screen representing the durations of Evan's recent international calls and said, "These are getting longer. This one's over four minutes."

"He's graduated from texting," Nate agreed. "Those are actual phone conversations."

"Unbelievable."

"Witness tampering?"

"If we can prove it." Geri pointed to another series of digits. "What are these?"

"I was getting to that. Those are texts."

"That's a lot of texts with the same number. Only five digits long?"

"He only receives texts from that number. Never sends any back."

"Is that one of those automated notification thingashits?" Geri asked.

Nate nodded grimly. "Delta Airlines."

"Would I be right if I guessed Delta flies direct to Manila?"

"Only a little. They stop in Tokyo enroute."

Geri rubbed her temples. "Fuck."

"Playing devil's advocate," Nate said. "We can't tell from this where he's planning to go. Dude could be taking a trip to San Diego or some shit. Trying to get out of the rain."

"With ten thousand dollars in cash?"

"We don't know he's gonna travel with that. And if he is, I don't know, maybe he's just planning to move to San Diego, get a new job, start over."

"In San Diego, ten thousand dollars goes as far as my dick," Geri said.

"You have a dick now?"

"No. That's the point. Now, in the Philippines? Last I emailed Ikigai, she explained how everything's less expensive over there. With ten thousand dollars, he could live like a pig in shit for a year or two."

"Or he could pay his victims off. Shut them up," Nate grimly suggested.

"Or both." Geri let out a deep breath, trying to keep her blood pressure down. "How's your wife?"

"She thinks I'm having an affair. With you."

"I wish," Geri responded and they laughed. "You know that's about to get worse, right?"

"Oh, I know."

"We gotta pull surveillance on Evan twenty-four-seven now."

"The affair would have been easier."

"We could..."

"Don't start."

★★★

"You speak the language of my homeland?" Ikigai asked the Village Captain.

He sneered at her with disdain. "I speak enough," he told her.

Ikigai said, "I am seeking..." Hari stopped her with an outstretched hand. "Let Mickey," Hari muttered.

Ikigai looked at Hari, confused. Hari whispered, "In this man's eyes, you and I, we're the same as him."

"Then shouldn't we be talking to him instead of Mickey?" Ikigai whispered back.

Hari simply smiled. A slow, sad smile. A smile Ikigai knew well, for she herself had often smiled this way. It was the smile of compromise. The acceptance of how things were. The relinquishment of how they should be.

Mickey threw back his shoulders, puffed out his chest, and winked at his friends. "One order of white privilege, coming right up." Hari shook his head, both humored and embarrassed. Mickey approached the Captain in the most arrogant fashion he could muster. What amazed Ikigai was that it worked. The Captain's sneer of disdain changed to a downward gaze of deference. Mickey showed the Captain his badge of Authority.

"My companions and I, we seek information."

"How may I help you?"

"We are looking for these children," Mickey said and gestured to Ikigai, who pulled the evidentiary drawings from her satchel and handed them over. As he took them, Mickey said under his breath, "I get everything?"

"We need the children's testimony," Ikigai prompted.

"We need the children's testimony," Mickey said haughtily to the Captain.

"What will you do with this testimony?" the Captain asked.

"Redress the wrongs of Tagagawas who stole their Innocence," Ikigai told Mickey.

"Redress the wrongs of Tagagawas who stole their Innocence," Mickey said, and handed the Captain the drawings. The Captain looked through them and shook his head. "I do not recognize these children," he handed the drawings back. "They are not in this barangay."

Ikigai took the drawings from Mickey and would have felt a sinking sense of disappointment, but she didn't get the chance. For the Emperor's Ghost appeared. Tark cawed, startled. Apparently, he could see the Ghost too. Ikigai heard something jingle.

This time, the Emperor appeared as a grown man instead of a little boy. When he appeared in this fashion, he sought forgiveness – and knowing this forgiveness had to be earned, assuming it could ever be granted, he'd provide some sort of guidance. So, Ikigai watched the Ghost carefully as he stood silently beside the Captain. She heard another jingle. Tark cawed. The Emperor raised a hand and pointed to something behind Ikigai. Ikigai turned and saw where the jingling came from: the brass hoop earrings of the woman they'd passed on the balcony, staring through a window from outside. Ikigai and the woman locked eyes again. This time, Ikigai did not miss it. The woman's face was rounder, fleshier, older, with bags of work and stress and too many sleepless nights under her eyes. But those eyes, they were the same; her mouth, the same; her ears, her cheeks, her nose.

The woman looked like an adult version of the girl from the drawing: the girl kneeling in the alley, the girl with the screaming eyes.

Ikigai's face lit up with recognition, and the woman, alarmed by this recognition, ran off the balcony and down the staircase.

Ikigai sprinted out of the office and chased after her.

"I don't like this Emperor's Ghost," I interrupted.

"Why not?" my mother asked patiently.

The mist had wafted into my brain again. "Just pedal. Just go," I mumbled.

My mother narrowed her eyes. "What was that, baby?"

"Nothing," I answered and yawned. "Tired."

Mom watched me closely. "Ok," she said, and kissed me on the forehead. "We'll continue tomorrow."

★★★

When Lily rang the doorbell of my Dad's house, I shot down the steps from the second floor. My new friend had accepted the invitation I'd extended the day before to join me for dinner at my home. I opened the front door to her shy smile, grabbed her hand, and pulled her into the living room from the porch.

"Dad!" I yelled, "Lily's here!" Dad poked his head out of the kitchen. "Hey, Lily," he called and smiled gently. "Come on in, guys. Food's good to go."

Lily didn't say anything, she just looked at the floor and muttered to herself. To be honest, I wasn't paying attention to what she was saying. I was dragging her to the kitchen, but she resisted. Then she firmly planted her feet and I found I couldn't move her.

She pulled her hand away from me and hyperventilated. "Is your, um, your mom here?" she asked.

"My mom's still in the Philippines," I told her, confused.

Dad stepped out of the kitchen and Lily flinched. "I um…" she muttered. "Sorry? I have… Sorry."

Then she turned and rushed out of the door.

★★★

Ikigai was a fast sprinter. Tark, perched on her shoulder, dug his little talons deeper into her flesh to hold on. Ikigai ignored the pain and focused on her target.

The woman with the jingling earrings had already hit the ground and was moving toward the alleys. Ikigai chased after her, down the steps to the ground, across the stone pavement, and into a narrow alley between two shops.

When Ikigai ran into the alley, the world changed again. She slowed down to let her brain wrap itself around the new information presented before her. She now understood how these alleys could accommodate so many people. The main road did not show one to the village. The sign that read Barangay Tormenta, leading to a dusty street with shops and a Captain's office, did not show one to the village.

No, the village was in the alleys.

And the alleys were a tight maze of hidden homes: homes of aluminum, cardboard, tin, rubber, chain-link fence, canvas tarp, concrete chunks, and broken planks of wood. The homes bled into each other. They were built on top of each other, around each other, next to each other. You couldn't tell where a family's living room ended and their neighbor's bathroom began. This was a place built diligently and chaotically from the world's leftovers and refuse. But there was life here, so much life: cooking, arguing, laundry, children and dogs playing, people showering under pipes. This was the real Village of the Storm, hidden behind the primary colors of its pleasantly painted exterior shops.

Ikigai's deceleration caused her to lose the woman. She couldn't run as fast here without crashing into someone. The Villagers in the maze of alleys glared at her, some angry, most confused. Foreigners never came to this place. Ikigai closed her eyes and listened, past Tark ruffling his feathers, past barking dogs and squealing children and the clanging of pots and pans and singing and... There! That jingling. She chased after the sound, dodged villagers, jumped over cats, bonfires, and sprinted through a running shower, disturbing the three men sharing it, who covered themselves with their hands in shock.

("Seriously?" I asked.

"Seriously. That really happened.")

Ikigai ran around, over, and through people's homes as they shouted in the Language of Traders what she guessed were the harshest of obscenities. She felt terrible for violating their privacy. It was a wrong she would later have to amend. Right now, she needed to catch that woman.

A glint caught Ikigai's eye and a jingle caught her ear. Ikigai glimpsed the woman before she vanished behind a sheet of tin that passed for a door. Ikigai approached the door, cautious. Someone shouted behind her, "You cannot do this!" It was the Village Captain. Mickey and Hari were with him. They had finally caught up.

Mickey grabbed her arm. "We need to get out of here."

Ikigai pulled away. "Absolutely not."

Mickey set his jaw. "What would you do if you had an intruder in your home?"

"I hear what you're saying but..."

"I know what I'd do." Mickey gazed at the crowd of Villagers who had come out of their homes and surrounded the warriors. "We're intruders. This is their home."

"I don't need your lectures right now. That woman looks just like the girl." Ikigai took Tark off her shoulder and placed him in her satchel, then pulled out the drawing of the kneeling girl.

The Village Captain, red-faced, demanded, "What is it you want here?"

Ikigai held up the drawing. "The alley in this picture," she said, and pointed to the small space between the tin door of the jingling woman's home and the cardboard of her neighbor's residence. "This is the alley," she continued. "This is where this picture was drawn." Ikigai stepped up to the Captain, looked him dead in the eye, and growled, "This girl lives here. You lied."

★★★

When Lily rushed out of my house, I ran after her before I had a chance to think. By the time I got to the sidewalk, she was already down the block, turning the corner. Dad called out, "Junior!" and jogged up to me. "Maybe let her go," he said and scooped me up in a hug before I could keep running.

"Let me go," I whined. "Why is she…? I don't understand."

Dad put me back down. "Sweety, I get the distinct impression she wasn't comfortable with me being the only adult in the house."

"Why?"

"I wouldn't know, but she looked scared. Let's just respect that."

My head was in a mist. Something was there, on the far periphery of my thoughts, something I could almost see. But the lining of the thought, the memory, the feeling, the whatever, was tainted. I couldn't get at it, intermingled as it was with Lily and with what had just happened, intermingled as it was with my loyalty to my father. Why would she be afraid of him? He was not a perfect man. I knew that, even then. But he had a good heart. There was no reason to fear a man like him.

I stuttered nonsensical vowels under my breath, trying to get at words I knew the sound of but couldn't speak. "Eh," I muttered. "Oh… Eh… Oh…" I looked at my Dad, forlorn, wanting him to know those words, not knowing if he could.

"You okay, baby?" he said gently. "It's alright, you'll see her tomorrow." I gave him a blank stare and he asked, "You said she transferred to your school, right?" I nodded. "Do you know why?" he asked. I shook my head. "Let's get inside," he said. "Let's get some grub in you."

***

Ikigai and the Village Captain stared each other down. Ikigai refused to blink. The gathered crowd was subdued, more curious than angry.

The tin sheet door parted and the woman with the jingling earrings stepped out and said, "*Unsa imong gusto?*"

Ikigai turned away from the Captain and approached the woman. From her satchel, she produced a drawing of Tagagawas' face and held it up.

The woman, distressed, shouted, "*Mamumuno!*" and retreated to her door.

"Wait!" Ikigai shouted back and followed her.

The Captain reached out to grab Ikigai but Mickey stepped in front of him. "Don't touch her. Let's please stay calm," Mickey said. "We only want to talk."

"You were not sent here to talk," the Captain said, sliding his index finger across his throat. "You were sent here to silence."

"Nuh-uh," Ikigai said. "No! Mickey and I are warriors from the same land as Tagagawas. We know he hurt people in your village. We want to hold Tagagawas responsible for what he did."

The woman shouted at the Captain, "*Kanang duha murag kami!*"

"What did she say?" Ikigai asked Hari, who shrugged and said, "I don't speak the Language of Traders."

"But you asked that guy for the Captain," Ikigai said, confused.

"I asked in my language, The Language of the Capital. We'll understand a few words of each other's tongue, but they're very different."

Ikigai sighed, annoyed she had to ask the Captain, "What did she say?"

The Captain pointed at Hari. "That you and him do not look like you are from Tagagawas' land. You look like us."

"Tell her I am. I am from the same land as Tagagawas."

"Might want to throw a please in there," Mickey muttered under his breath.

"Please!" Ikigai added, controlling her temper. "And thank you."

The Captain spoke to the woman. The woman responded. The Captain reported, "She does not believe you. She says Tagagawas told them you would come with lies and you would kill them."

"Tagagawas said...? Did you speak to him?" Ikigai asked the woman. "When? Ask her when!"

The Captain did so and the woman retreated to her tin sheet door again. "She does not want to speak with you," the Captain informed them.

"Please," pleaded Ikigai. "Tell her we do not want to hurt anyone. We're here to help."

"No one wants your help," the Captain said, and the crowd murmured and Ikigai's heart sank. Then a boy appeared from behind the screen door and glared at Ikigai. "*Datu!*" the woman cried. "*Sulod!*" The boy continued to stare, and Ikigai recognized him as well.

He was one of the boys in the drawing of the waterfall.

Ikigai dug out the drawing and held it up. "Is this you?" she asked the boy. Then to the woman, "Is this him? Is this your son?" Ikigai held up the picture of the girl with the screaming eyes. "Who is this? Is this your daughter?"

The woman shouted and shoved the boy back into their home and they both disappeared behind the tin sheet. "What did she say?" Ikigai asked the Captain.

"That is her daughter," the Captain said. "And her daughter is at peace."

Panic stirred in Ikigai's chest. "What, what do you mean, she's at peace?"

The Captain lowered his head.

"The girl's gone, Ikigai," Mickey told her. "We need to go. We've made things bad enough."

"How?" Ikigai asked the Captain. "How did the girl…?"

The Captain sighed and shook his head impatiently. "The last time I saw her was right before Tagagawas stole her Innocence. She probably took her own life. I have told you enough. Please leave now."

Ikigai and her companions left the Village of the Storm and walked solemnly back west toward the waterfall. As the sun set, Mickey suggested they hurry to the inn where they'd stayed the night before. Ikigai nodded and unconsciously touched her hip where she normally carried her Weapon, her fingers reminding her that it was gone, an artifact of her very identity, left behind. Then she touched her Authority, which thus far had proved useless on this journey.

But her Purpose was still with her, carried on the inside of her shirt, close to her heart. And it burned. It burned so much it hurt, and Ikigai had to say, "give me a minute." She sat by the side of the road, clutched her Purpose, and wept.

Mickey and Hari squatted beside her, concern on their faces. Tark flew out of her satchel, landed in her lap and chirped. She stroked the Garuda's beak. "I'm okay," Ikigai said, embarrassed that she'd shown weakness. "Just," she stammered, "the girl…" Mickey and Hari nodded and silently helped her to her feet. Tark perched on her shoulder.

And the warriors walked down the dusty road toward the setting sun.

"You were right," I said to my mother, and wiped away a tear. "This isn't easy to hear."

Mom watched me silently. Then she said, "Do you want me to continue?" I shuddered. For a moment, I felt as if something was about to lift from my vision, but it didn't. I looked at Mom, confused, and she looked back, carefully, almost clinically.

"Tomorrow?" I said.

She smiled gently. "Tomorrow."

★★★

Detective Geri Bradford was sticking to her word. She'd promised Ikigai she had her back. She refused to let her down. It was not yet four in the morning. Her and Nate were parked outside Evan's house. Their fellow officers had been helping them watch Evan in round-the-clock eight-hour shifts. Since it was Geri and Nate's case, they drew the toughest shift, midnight to eight a.m.

Geri yawned, picked up her car radio and suggested, "Sing me a song, Nate. Keep me awake."

"Maaaaan," Nate's voice came in. "I look like that piano playing motherfucker from that movie? Ain't here for your entertainment, sing me a song, shit."

Geri cracked up. Nate was funny when he was cranky. That wife of his didn't know how lucky she was. "Okay," Geri said, and crooned a 50s tune off-key.

"Oh, no," Nate exclaimed. "Put that away. Put it back in the fridge. Nah, just throw it out. Shit's long past its expiration date."

The two laughed. Then the lights in Evan's house turned on.

"Got movement," Geri said, and fumbled looking for her notepad.

"Could just be up to take a piss," Nate suggested.

"We'll see," said Geri. The lights went off again. Geri and Nate waited. A minute passed. They were about to relax. Then a taxi drove past Geri and pulled into Evan's driveway. Evan's door opened, and he stepped outside. He carried two pieces of luggage, which he threw into the trunk of the taxi before he got into the back seat. The taxi's brake lights went off. Then it backed out of the driveway and left.

"Follow that cab, motherfucker," Nate said, doing his best Cagney impression. "And step on it, see!"

Geri turned her engine on. "You take lead again."

They didn't stay on the backroads long, quickly finding themselves heading north on I-5, which was empty at that time of the morning. The taxi had all three lanes to itself, so Geri and Nate had to keep a long way back so they wouldn't get made. As they approached the Downtown area, the taxi took the exit to head east on I-84.

"Unless he's taking a trip to Mount Hood," Nate observed, "he's going to PDX."

The sky was clear though still dark and Geri could make out the snow-capped mountain in the distant east. "No one takes a taxi to Mount Hood," she said.

Approximately ten minutes later, the taxi jumped on I-205 North, then followed the exit signs to the Portland International Airport. Geri and Nate kept their distance as the taxi pulled into the airport departures area, which, unlike the highway, was surprisingly crowded. The crowd was good though, it gave Geri and Nate something to hide in. They left their vehicles in law enforcement parking spots, entered the airport on foot, and quickly reestablished eyes on Evan, who waited to check his luggage at the Delta Airlines counter.

They watched Evan talk to the attendant behind the counter, who looked as if she desperately needed a shot of espresso. He took his boarding pass and headed for the passenger screening area. Once he was safely out of sight, Nate nodded toward the counter and said, "Let's do our friendly officer thing."

They approached the counter, to the consternation of the people waiting in line who felt they were being skipped. The man next in line opened his mouth, so Nate showed the man his badge. "I don't care," the man responded. "I have a plane to catch."

Nate smiled politely. "We'll be quick, sir. Promise."

"I have rights," the man said. "You can wait like everyone else."

Geri and Nate ignored him and leaned over the counter and introduced themselves in hushed tones to the attendant, showing her their badges as well. The attendant looked as if she was barely registering what was going on, which might have been a good thing because she didn't need to give them any information without a subpoena. But she did, when Geri smiled sweetly and explained, "You'd be really helping us out a lot. Can you tell us what flight the passenger you just dealt with is taking?"

★★★

Ikigai breathed in the tropical air from a window in the small room of the inn, south of the waterfall, in which the warriors stayed. The air, laden with the evaporated effects of so much heartache, did not help. She thought of the stick thin man who hustled his legs for money with his carriage; the little girl and boy who tried to pickpocket her; the self-important men and women in fine clothes as they strode out of their buildings and walked by a young girl changing the diaper of a starving baby on the street. She thought of the woman who jingled and the fear in her eyes, and of her daughter who had to commit the unspeakable to find some semblance of peace. She was starting to understand why Tagagawas came to this place. It filled her with a rage she needed to suffocate, lest it grow and consume her sanity. So, she shut the window and picked up Tark, stroking his head gently. Tark cawed.

"Tark, please send this message to The Amazon. Tell her I've found two of the children, the girl and one of the boys. I've also found their mother. But the mother refuses to speak with me." Ikigai paused and collected her thoughts. "Also, please tell her that the girl is gone. That she is no more."

Tark nodded sadly, understanding the pain in Ikigai's message, and disappeared in a flash of light. A few moments later, he returned, chirping repeatedly. "Go ahead," Ikigai said. "What's the message?"

Tark's eyes glowed neon blue and he spoke in that otherworldly voice. "Ikigai, we are watching Tagagawas right now. He is on his way to The Land of 7,000 Islands. He will leave in two hours. We need to come up with a way to stop him."

Ikigai grabbed Tark and bolted out of her room, into the hall, and banged on the door of the room next to hers where Mickey and Hari were staying.

Mickey opened the door. "What the what?" he said. "Need our beauty rest, what's…?"

"Tagagawas. He's on his way here."

Mickey stayed calm. "Probably heading over to make sure these people keep not talking to us."

"And-slash-or, to stay here and hurt more children," Ikigai said.

"Can you arrest him?" Hari said, sitting up from his bed. "Can the warriors in your homeland put him in jail? Stop him from coming here?"

"If we get the testimony of these children, yes, they could. That would give them enough probable cause to arrest him. But we need to talk to them."

"They don't want to talk to us," Mickey reminded her.

"There are two other boys!" Ikigai exploded. "Maybe they'll talk to us, we have to try again!"

"Okay," Mickey said, trying to stay calm. "First thing in the morning…"

"No, now! We're going back to the village right now."

"It's the middle of the night."

"Tagagawas will be riding on the Great Crane of the West in two hours. If we can get the testimony of just one child, we can stop him."

"I understand all that, Ikigai," Mickey exploded back, the gravel in his voice returning. "But you are not going about this the right way."

"What other way should I go about it?"

"You need to consider the people whose lives you are affecting."

"All I'm doing is considering their lives."

"No, you're not. I've seen this before."

"And what, specifically, have you seen before?"

"A hot-headed, arrogant, temperamental warrior, who thinks she's running around saving the world, when all she's really doing is working out her own inner demons."

Ikigai stepped back and blinked. "Wow," she said, deeply offended. "And you can magically discern all this about me because of what you've seen in some other warrior before?"

"Yeah, I can," Mickey confirmed. "Still know that guy too. See him every day."

"Every day, huh?"

"Every day I look in the mirror, Ikigai."

The humility in Mickey's words gave Ikigai pause. She took a breath. "Fine. What do you suggest, then?"

"Honestly? I don't know. But I think if we're going to resolve this, we need to rely heavily on that man," Mickey said and pointed to Hari, who stood silently.

Hari approached them. He smiled at Tark, who had perched on Ikigai's shoulder. He faced Ikigai and said, "We need to get you a..." but he couldn't think of the word in Ikigai's language. He snapped his fingers and put his hand over his eye.

Mickey laughed, "Eyepatch."

"That's it," Hari replied. "With Tark on her shoulder she looks like..." Hari and Mickey guffawed like children. Both closed one eye each and said at the same time, "Arrrr." Ikigai tried not to, but she couldn't help but smile.

When they caught their breath, Hari looked at Ikigai and said, "You are right. We need to go back to the village and try to get a child's testimony. We cannot let Tagagawas return here." Then he looked at Mickey. "You are also right. We need to enter that village with caution and with respect. We need to speak with the Villagers and win their trust. We cannot go in there screaming and shouting."

The three warriors shared a glance. Tark flapped his wings to stretch them out.

"Okay?" Mickey asked Ikigai.

"Okay," she agreed. "And thanks, by the way. For having my back before. When we were in the alleys."

"Look lady," Mickey said. "Even if we don't agree with you, we'll always have your back."

"I know," Ikigai said. "I guess I'm just not used to that."

Hari smiled. "We should go. There is much work to be done."

CHAPTER 6

"I love the smell of this airport," Deputy District Attorney, now cross-designated Assistant US Attorney, Robert Martel said. "Still smells like maple syrup. When I was on the job, surveilling fellows who were flying, I swear, most pleasant work in the world."

"You a funny ass cowboy," Nate said. Geri cracked up. The three of them sat together in the Portland International Airport, across from the boarding gate where Evan waited. They kept their eyes on him.

"Thanks for coming," Geri said. "You could have done this over the phone."

"Naw," Martel shrugged. "We pull this off? It's best I'm right here. 'Sides, I miss this shit." They chuckled again. "So, Ikigai wants us to arrest this clown," Martel said.

"The girl's dead," Geri told him somberly. "If at least one of the boys talks to Ikigai, testifies Evan sent those messages to them... It'll be your call, but that might give us the PC."

"It might," Martel confirmed. "She doesn't have to write up an affidavit now. I can approve a PC arrest. But she's gotta get any victim testimony documented and sent so I can look it over."

"Copy that." Geri pulled out her smartphone. "I'll email her your guidance."

"We're a little close. What if this asshole notices us?" Martel asked.

"Fuck him," Nate exclaimed. "What's he gonna do if he does? Freak out and not get on the plane? That's what we want anyway."

"Good point," said Martel.

Geri's phone buzzed. She read its screen. "It's Ikigai," she said. "They just got back to the barangay."

"She needs to move fast," Martel reminded her. "That plane's leaving in an hour."

Ikigai and her companions, sweat drenched, rushed through the maze of alleys in the Village of the Storm. They'd jogged from their inn, south of the waterfall. When they arrived, they caused quite a stir. Though well into the dark of night, the village was still lively, and the Villagers were not happy to see the warriors again. Many shouted at them in the Language of Traders. Mickey glanced around nervously. "We're gonna get shanked."

The warriors stopped at the tin screen door of the jingling woman's home. Ikigai knocked. No response. No light inside. No one there. A crowd gathered. Ikigai and Mickey grew anxious, but Hari said calmly, "Someone here has to understand the Language of the Capital." And he spoke to the Villagers.

The Villagers muttered amongst themselves. Hari told Mickey and Ikigai, "I explained in my tongue that we are only here to help, that we are trying to stop Tagagawas from returning here. Hopefully someone understood."

One man, the man of whom Hari had asked directions to the Village Captain's office earlier, came forward. The man was now bare-chested to acquire some relief from the humidity of the night. He spoke to Hari in the Language of the Capital. "He understood," Hari said. "He is asking how we will stop Tagagawas. He said these foreigners come here and do as they please with no consequences."

"Please tell him *I* am the consequence," Ikigai said. "If I can hear the story of at least one child whose Innocence was stolen, we can imprison Tagagawas in my homeland."

Hari translated Ikigai's words into the Language of the Capital. The man responded and Hari interpreted, "He says you are asking these children to stand before you, a stranger and a foreigner, and tell you their deepest secrets."

"I am," Ikigai admitted as Hari interpreted. "I am asking for their Testimony of Deepest Secrets. I know there is no reason to trust me. You don't know me. But I promise you, I will handle this Testimony with the utmost care. I will use it only for the cause of Justice. I will use it only to stop Tagagawas from stealing the Innocence of anyone else."

The bare-chested man spoke to the Villagers. It seemed he was re-interpreting Ikigai's words in the Language of Traders. The Villagers murmured, and the bare-chested man stood silent, appraising the warriors. Then he beckoned with his hand and walked deeper into the maze of alleys.

"Follow him," Hari instructed.

★★★

"Anything?" Martel asked. Geri shook her head. She, Nate and Martel watched the passengers at Evan's gate form into a line. Evan joined the line, but instead of facing the aircraft entry door, he faced the gate across, where they sat.

"He's made us," Martel observed.

"Look at him," Nate added. "He's smiling. Keep smiling, Evan." They watched Evan calmly turn and face the aircraft entry door.

"He knows if we were gonna do something we'd have done it by now," Nate said. The gate broadcast announced, "Delta Flight 637 to Tokyo, now boarding first class."

"Still got time," Geri gritted her teeth. "He's flying coach."

The warriors followed the bare-chested man, until they came to an open area less constricted by the tangle of homes. The area was just big enough to fit a basketball half-court, its arcs and lines chalk-drawn on the concrete. A crooked portable basketball hoop stood at the top of the makeshift court. A gaggle of children played by the hoop as adults watched from homes surrounding the court's perimeter, sharing food and conversation. "Back home, there's this city I like to visit," Mickey said. "A city of legend. They call it The City That Never Sleeps." Mickey shook his head. "It's got nothing on this place."

There were three boys passing and shooting a ball through the hoop. The bare-chested man approached these boys. A woman ran over to the man. It was the woman with the jingling earrings. The jingling woman and the bare-chested man shouted at each other and the woman grabbed one of the boys, who Ikigai recognized as her son from earlier.

Then Ikigai stepped closer and recognized the second boy in the group. He was the other child in the picture of the waterfall.

The third boy shouted at everyone, in a voice that was strong and wild with newfound manhood, and the whole area quieted down. This boy strode toward Ikigai. He was bigger than the other two boys, with a rough look in his eyes and long black hair dyed with streaks of red. He looked like a fighting rooster. As he approached, Ikigai realized he was the man-boy drawn with the sun at his back on the dusty Eastern road.

He looked a little older than he did in the drawing, his jaw heavier, his chest broader. And he understood the Language of the Capital. He met Ikigai eye to eye and the two spoke through Hari as interpreter. "He does not want you to stop Tagagawas," Hari explained.

"And why is that?" Ikigai asked.

"He wants Tagagawas to return. So he can… do very bad things to him. Then kill him."

The rooster stared at Ikigai. Ikigai stared right back. But she found herself at a loss for words. Perhaps this fighting rooster was right. Perhaps letting Tagagawas return would be the best course of action. She understood now what the Great Crane of the West had said. These people had no need for her help. If Tagagawas returned, they could handle the matter themselves. The fighting rooster spoke, the pitch of his voice becoming feverish as he addressed not only Ikigai but the crowd. "He is cursing about all the foreigners who have come to this land over the centuries and stolen from its people," Hari reported.

Ikigai broke eye contact with the angry, charismatic rooster. For once in her life, she needed to speak from her heart and from her gut, with no filter, and she didn't know what to say. She glanced upwards and searched her heart. She searched her gut. She cleared her mind and prayed. Then she knew. To her delight, she found herself speaking with a calm strength she had heard in only one other person: her daughter.

(I smiled at this part.)

"If you kill Tagagawas," Ikigai said. "Your story will never be told."

Hari interpreted and the fighting rooster became the silent one. Ikigai had hit a nerve. She pressed further. "Your story needs to be told. This should not be handled in silence. People need to learn what happened here. They need to learn what's been stolen from you. They need to be angry and they need to stop others from doing the same. If you let Tagagawas come here, if you kill him, and bury him, you bury your story with him. Please, do not bury this."

The fighting rooster absorbed these words then stepped up to Ikigai, nose to nose. Mickey put his arm out and warned, "Violation of personal space alert." Tark, perched on Ikigai's shoulder, spread his wings to look bigger and cawed at the rooster.

"Leave him," Ikigai said and maintained eye contact with the fighting rooster.

The rooster spoke and Hari explained, "He asks, who are you to tell him what or what not to bury."

"Explain to this young man," Ikigai started, "that if he does not take a step back he's going to find out exactly who I am. Please and thank you." Hari interpreted.

The rooster stepped back, smiled mischief and spoke, pointing to the court. "He says you are strong," Hari said. "He respects that. He is willing to make a deal. If we beat him and his friends, then he will talk. He will give you his Testimony of Deepest Secrets."

"Done," Ikigai agreed without hesitation. "Three on three?" she asked as the fighting rooster jogged over to the court and huddled with the other two boys.

"Yes," Hari said.

"Seriously? This is what's happening?" Mickey asked.

"Yes, Mickey." Ikigai put Tark in her satchel. "This is what's happening."

"We need to beat them and beat them quick," said Mickey. "We got maybe a half hour before that Crane takes off with Tagagawas."

"I played ball in high school," Ikigai said with confidence.

"What, thirty years ago?"

"It was… twenty years ago."

"We're not even playing basketball." Mickey pointed to the three boys chalking a rectangle with six interior squares on the ground.

Hari smirked at Ikigai. "You play *patintero*?"

Ikigai froze. "What's patintero?"

Geri, Nate, and Martel were ready to give up. "Flight 637 to Tokyo," the broadcast announced, "boarding all passengers." They watched Evan hand his boarding pass to the gate agent and approach the aircraft entry door. Before he stepped through, he turned, faced the gate where they sat, smiled, and gave them a thumbs up. Geri and Martel grimaced. Nate gave a thumbs up back. "You gonna get yours," Nate grumbled.

Geri's phone buzzed. She fumbled for it and tapped open her email. "What'd she say?" Nate asked.

"It's not her," Geri said. "It's that ALAT she's with, Mickey Sheptinsky."

"What'd he say?" Martel asked.

"He said," Geri read the email. "Ha, ha, ha. Priceless."

They looked at the email: a picture of Ikigai on the ground surrounded by the laughing denizens of the barangay.

Geri scowled. "Come on! What the shit are you guys doing over there?"

Ikigai's back hit the ground, knocking the wind out of her. Patintero was a simple enough game, its objective straightforward. One team lined its members on the parallel lines inside the rectangle, and physically blocked members of the opposing team from running from one end of the rectangle to the other. If the opposing team bypassed them and successfully made a round trip, they scored, then the teams switched places.

However, the way these boys played was comedic in its brutality. The Villagers, at least, found it funny. Ikigai had passed the first boy, the son of the jingling woman, but then faced the fighting rooster, who she thought she had passed, until he grabbed her shoulders from behind and threw her to the ground. The Villagers laughed, which was one thing. What made her blood boil, was Mickey and Hari laughing too.

She seethed and picked herself up. The time limit to score elapsed and the boys stepped off the inside lines, taking their places outside. "Switch up," Mickey said. "Now let's give them a taste of their own..."

"Absolutely not!" Ikigai thundered. "You're grown men, you'll hurt them!"

"They're the ones playing rough," Mickey said.

"Block them," Ikigai said. "But do not lay a hand on them."

"Whatever," Mickey shrugged. "Pacifist."

Ikigai rolled her eyes.

The boys were too fast. They faked left and ran right. Faked right and ran left. At one point, the fighting rooster jumped clean into the air at an angle and spun around Ikigai. It was a thing of beauty. It was also the winning point for his team. He laughed and the Villagers cheered and Ikigai felt her frustration mount as the game closed. Her team never even scored.

Ikigai picked up her satchel from the ground. Tark fluttered out and perched on her shoulder. The boys, smiling, walked over and shook hands with the warriors. The son of the jingling woman, whose face was round like his mother's, grinned and spoke. "He's speaking the Language of Traders, but I think he's asking our names," Hari said. The warriors told him their names. The boy pointed to himself and said, "*Datu.*" Then he pointed to the jingling woman who stood in the crowd, watching, concerned.

"*Akong inahan, Malaya.*"

"I believe he is Datu," Hari explained, "and that is his mother, Malaya."

"Hi Datu," Ikigai said. She shook the boy's hand and waved at his mother in the crowd.

The second boy approached, the one who appeared with Datu in the drawing of the waterfall. A thin woman stepped from the crowd and stood silently behind him. The boy looked like the woman, their faces long and narrow, their eyes set with the memories of a whole island. "*Kidlat,*" the boy said with confidence, then pointed to the woman and said, "*Akong inahan, Tala.*" Hari and Mickey smiled. Ikigai was polite but sullen and distracted. She was still thinking about how to convince these boys to speak to her. She'd come this far. She'd found these children. She refused to fail because of a stupid game.

The fighting rooster approached. His eyes were still angry, but he too was smiling. "*Bayani*," he said, and shook their hands. Then he spoke in the Language of the Capital to Hari who interpreted. "He says to leave Datu and Kidlat alone. They are young and they have been through enough. He will give you his Testimony of Deepest Secrets."

Bayani beckoned the warriors to follow him. "But we lost," Ikigai said.

"Gift horse," said Mickey. "Not to be looked in the mouth."

"Tark," Ikigai said, "I need you to update the Amazon."

Tark disappeared in a flash of light. They followed Bayani into the maze of alleys, the laughter and cheers of the Villagers echoing about.

Geri, Nate and Martel watched the last of the passengers on Delta Flight 637 board. Geri's phone buzzed. Nate and Martel, on either side of her, peered over her shoulders as she checked her email. Geri's hands shook. "She found them. Oh my god, she found all the boys. She's with one of them now." Geri faced Martel. "The boy's talking."

Martel shook his head. "That plane's taking off any minute." Geri looked at her email and whispered, "Come on, Ikigai."

Nate stood and walked toward the gate for Flight 637.

A thin stream of moonlight snuck through an opening of the dilapidated canvas tarp that passed for a roof. The moonlight fell on the sleeping face of a little girl no older than six, curled up on a dingy mattress and covered with a torn sheet. The moonlight fell on the rugged face of Bayani, highlighting the wisps of facial hair he was starting to grow. There was nothing else in the home, save a few items of clothing tossed about. Tark quietly hopped on the dirt floor around the sleeping girl, and it occurred to Ikigai that the

Garuda was defending the girl from the incursion of bad dreams. Bayani's home was crowded with Ikigai and Hari inside. Mickey waited outside. He would not have fit. Ikigai, Hari, and Bayani sat cross-legged on the dirt floor, facing each other. Hari interpreted.

"What is your full name?" Ikigai asked in a hushed tone, so as not to wake the girl.

"Bayani Matapang." Hari narrowed his eyes when Bayani said this.

"Where are your parents?"

Bayani shrugged. "What do you need to know?"

Ikigai held up the drawing of Bayani on the Eastern road. "That is me," Bayani confirmed. "Tagagawas drew that picture the day he first went to the waterfall with us."

"Can you tell me what that day was like?"

"He had been visiting our village for a while. No one trusted him at first and thought of him as strange. But he learned a little of the Language of Traders and he bought us food. He bought everyone food. After a while, everyone loved him and looked forward to when he came.

"He would play patintero with us, with me, Datu, and Kidlat. I never liked the way he played. He would step off the lines and grab us into his arms. One morning he came to the village to play but saw us three as we were leaving. He asked where we were going and we told him the waterfall. He asked if he could come, and we said sure.

"We went to the waterfall. We had figured we were not going to eat much that day, but on the way, he stopped and bought us sweet rice, which we thought was kind. He drew pictures of us, that is one you have, I think there are more. It was quiet at the waterfall that morning. We had arrived early so no one else was there. He asked me to follow him into the woods behind the waterfall. He said he had something for me.

"Behind the waterfall, he asked for my Innocence. He offered me money. I took his money and I gave him my Innocence, not thinking much of it at first. I was hungry and I had not figured out how I was going to get food for my baby sister that day. Besides, I am a man now, what need have I for things like Innocence?

"But I did not feel like this forever. Now I wonder if a man's Innocence is just as important as a child's. But I can do nothing about it now. What has happened has happened. I only wish…"

A long silence. Then Ikigai pressed gently. "You only wish…?"

"I should have protected Datu and Kidlat. They are younger and I should have protected their Innocence. We returned to the waterfall some days later with Tagagawas, and he asked them for their Innocence as well. They ran to me first and I told them. I told them to go ahead and take his money and take his food. I will never forgive myself."

From her satchel Ikigai took the evidentiary letters in her possession and showed them to Bayani, who peered at them, confused. "Those are letters he sent us. Why would he have those?"

"Sometimes people like Tagagawas make copies of things they write, as keepsakes. Do you have the original letters he sent?"

Bayani gently reached under the mattress his sister slept on, pulled out an envelope and handed it to Ikigai. Ikigai's heart beat faster as she opened the envelope. The letter Bayani gave her matched one of the letters she had. It was solid evidence of Tagagawas' crimes.

"Those other letters were not written to me, that is the only one I have," Bayani said. "I keep it to remind me of my failure to protect the others."

Ikigai winced at these words and the Purpose she kept near her heart burned. She fought to keep her voice even. "The rest of these letters, do you know who they were written to?"

"Datu and Kidlat, and Lualhati." When Bayani said this last word, his voice cracked.

"Lualhati?"

"Malaya's daughter. Datu's little sister. I do not want to talk about her anymore."

"Okay," Ikigai said, and took a deep breath. "Bayani, can I keep this original letter?"

Bayani hesitated but conceded. "Take it."

"Thank you. And thank you for speaking to me," Ikigai smiled, "even though we lost."

"I liked how you played. You wanted to win but you played fair. Even when we did not. It made me think you were a warrior who could be trusted."

A fire burned in Ikigai's eyes. "I will not let you down. I need to go write everything. Everything you told me. I need to document it. I will use this document to stop Tagagawas from coming here again. I will get you Justice."

Bayani shrugged and pointed his chin at the sleeping girl. "Justice will not feed her."

Ikigai had no answer to this. She could only awkwardly thank Bayani again as she and Hari left his home.

Ikigai nodded at Mickey as they stepped out into the night, but Mickey was not paying attention to her.

He was watching Hari, who had paused outside Bayani's door, staring at the ground, his jaw set, a sneer of rage on his face, hands balled into fists and trembling. Mickey approached his friend. Tark fluttered out of Bayani's home and toward Hari, who uncurled his fist and held out his hand for Tark to land on. Hari's face relaxed as he petted the baby Garuda and let out a long sigh.

"I hope you grow very big and very strong," Hari whispered to Tark. "Vishnu needs all the help he can get."

★★★

Geri read the email on her smartphone and tried not to shout, "Come on Ikigai, get the report to us."

"What's her status?" Martel asked.

"She did it," Geri answered. "The boy gave his testimony. He even confirmed that was his Facebook account Evan sent some of those chats to."

Nate jogged up to Geri and Martel. "They need to check the landing gear," Nate told them. "Plane should be delayed for another half hour."

"This is federal now," Martel said. "I ain't doing nothing without something in writing. Tell her to bang out that report and email it to us."

"I am, I am," Geri said, frantically tapping at her smartphone.

Ikigai, Mickey and Hari stepped out of the maze of alleys onto the village's main road. It was late and the Village Captain would not be around. They walked over to the building his office was in, up the three flights of stairs, through the balcony, and discovered that, luckily, he left his office door unlocked. They entered. Ikigai sat at his desk, turned on his lamp, and pulled pen and paper from her satchel. She could now partake in the Sacred Art of Documentation.

Documentation was sacred because it was more than truth or testimony. Documentation was Existence itself. If something was not written, it did not happen. And if something did not happen, the writing of it could breathe it into Existence. This was powerful magic, and it was the Authority of Ikigai that curtailed its abuse, for this Authority was only granted to Ikigai after she took a vow: to never, ever, lie.

Ikigai sat at the Captain's desk, put pen to paper, and wrote the truth of what she had heard and seen from Bayani's Testimony of Deepest Secrets. She wrote furiously, as Mickey and Hari watched. She had very little time. It was only a matter of moments before the Great Crane of the West flew from the shore of Ikigai's homeland, carrying Tagagawas.

When she finished, she let out a breath, rolled the paper on which she had written, placed it between Tark's beak, and requested, "Please, Tark. Take this to the Amazon. Quickly."

Tark did not move.

"Tark, please. Now!" Ikigai urged. Tark did not blink.

"Yeah," Mickey observed. "He's frozen."

★★★

Back home, I had my own testimony to chase down. In the school yard during recess, Lily and I stood alone, looking out into a world dissected by the quadrilateral patterns of chain link fence. The shouts of middle schoolers bounced off the bubble we'd thrown around each other.

"Why'd you run away from my house like that?" I asked.

She did that reverse pout thing with her lips and muttered, "Babies are made from light."

"Lily, why'd you run away?"

"If no light, no baby, right?"

I gave in. If she wanted to play word games, so be it. "Sure. Light, baby. Dark, no baby." I said impatiently. But then I mulled it over and wasn't comfortable with that statement.

Lily saw my discomfort and smiled, correcting me. "Light, baby. *Heavy*, no baby."

"Heavy, no baby," I repeated.

"Right?" she asked, a tremor in her voice.

"Right," I said, not even sure what we were talking about.

"It's... really heavy, Junior," she explained, and slunk down the chain link fence to sit on the pavement.

I sat next to her not comprehending the conversation I was having, but somehow knowing what to say.

"I'll help you hold it."

Lily nodded and wrapped her arm in mine and put her head on my shoulder.

This time she kept it there.

The warriors ran through the maze of alleys once more, asking anyone they encountered, "Do you have a Garuda?" Most Villagers ignored them. Some just laughed.

Then they ran into the bare-chested man. "Long time, no see," he told Hari. Hari asked if he had a Garuda, and he said, "I'll go look." Hari thanked him as he ran off.

"I have to write this all over again," Ikigai said, frustrated. "It's stuck in Tark's beak." She sat on the ground and wrote, trying not to scream in anger. "I can't get this done in time."

"Stay positive," Mickey said. "What can we do?"

"Nothing! I'm the one who needs to document the testimony."

The bare-chested man returned and spoke. Hari interpreted. "He can't find a Garuda." Ikigai smacked her hand against the ground and fought back tears.

Then Tark cawed. The paper fell to the ground as he opened his beak.

"Tark, please!" Ikigai shouted, picking up the paper and shoving it back in his beak. "Take this to the Amazon, now!"

Tark disappeared in a flash of light.

"Read," Geri said and handed her smartphone to Martel, who scrolled through the email.

"Faster," Nate urged.

"Shush, guys, I'm getting through it," Martel told them. "Oh, yeah," he said a moment later. "We're good. We got probable cause. Let's..."

Geri and Nate were already running to the gate. They flashed their badges for the agent behind the counter, who, not sure what they wanted, informed them, "Cabin door's already closed, they're about to take off."

"Open it," Geri demanded. "We need to arrest a passenger."

The agent grabbed the receiver of the wall phone behind the counter. "Um," the agent said. "There's some officers here."

Before the agent finished his sentence, Geri and Nate ran through the aircraft entry doorway and sprinted down the jet bridge. They reached the plane's cabin door and banged their fists on it. A few seconds later, the cabin door opened and a stewardess with a confused smile greeted them. They flashed their badges and stepped on the plane.

"Shit, which seat is he in," Geri asked.

"We'll find him. You take left," Nate said. Geri walked down the left aisle and Nate walked down the right, checking the face of each passenger.

Geri reached a passenger who was hunched in his seat, hiding his face. "Sir," she started. "Sit up real quick and look at me, please." The passenger did so. It was the man who'd complained when they skipped him at the luggage check-in line.

"I have rights," he said again, and the little voice in Geri's gut that she had learned to trust after so many years told her that this man was likely traveling to Manila himself with dishonorable intentions. But she could do nothing about him now. She had to stay focused. She moved further down the aisle.

"Mr. Campbell," she heard Nate say from her right.

"Up," Geri said to the passengers in the three seats separating her aisle from Nate's. The passengers quickly got out of her way. She crossed the seats to the right aisle and joined Nate, who stood over a very angry looking Evan Campbell.

"Evan," Geri said, "let's please not make this into any more of a scene."

She traded a glance with Nate, then reached her left hand behind her, under her shirt, felt for the leather case held in place by her belt, and pulled out her handcuffs.

At that moment, the familiar clink of unfurling steel was the best sound she'd ever heard.

Along with the bare-chested man, several Villagers now surrounded Ikigai and her companions, including Bayani, as well as Malaya and Tala, the mothers of Datu and Kidlat. Ikigai bit her fist and hoped.

In a blinding flash of light, Tark re-appeared, and chirped.

"What's the message, Tark?" Ikigai asked.

Tark's eyes turned neon blue and he spoke. "Ikigai," he began. But then the blue of Tark's eyes faded and he fluttered to the ground and pecked at a spot of dirt.

"Tark!" Ikigai said. "What are you doing? What's the message?"

Tark looked up at Ikigai, holding a worm in his beak.

"Really? Right now? What's the message?"

"Let him eat," Mickey suggested. "He's hungry, that might be why he froze before."

"I'm hungry too, I'm still doing my job."

Tark mewed. "Okay," Ikigai said. "I'm sorry. I'm sorry. Finish your worm."

Tark swallowed the worm then cawed and flapped his wings happily. His eyes turned blue again and he spoke in that otherworldly voice. "Ikigai, you did it. We were able to arrest Tagagawas. He's not going anywhere."

"Yes!" Ikigai and Mickey shouted and raised their arms in victory and fell into a hug. Hari smiled and interpreted the message in the Language of the Capital. The bare-chested man re-interpreted the message in the Language of Traders for the rest of the Villagers. Malaya nodded grimly. Tala wiped a tear from her eye and hid her face.

"Now get off me," Ikigai told Mickey and shoved him away. She stood before the Villagers. "I know it hasn't been easy to revisit this. But thank you for letting us into your village." Her words were interpreted through Hari, then through the bare-chested man.

Malaya spoke sharply and the Villagers laughed.

Ikigai looked about, confused.

The bare-chested man spoke, then Hari said, "She says they did not let you in. You are just very stubborn."

Ikigai smiled. "Well, thank you for not kicking us out."

"Or shanking us," Mickey added under his breath.

Ikigai looked directly at Bayani. "And thank you for trusting me."

Bayani nodded, then left the crowd to head deeper into the maze of alleys. Before he vanished, he turned briefly to wave goodbye. Ikigai smiled. For in that moment, when he waved, he looked like a little boy again.

Later, back at the inn, Ikigai curled into bed and breathed. Muscles, tendons, and joints ached. She wished she could take a hot bath, but the inn didn't have such amenities. She fell into a deep sleep, and the next morning, she asked Tark to send a message to the person who, for her, was the most important person in the world.

"Oh!" I broke in. "That was the night you called me and said you were coming home!"

"Exactly."

"And I said, wow, that was way faster than I thought it would be, and you said…" I imitated my mother's husky voice, "That's how Momma rolls baby, I get things done."

Mom smiled. "Yes, I did say that. Do you remember what else happened?"

"I said can my friend come over when you get home. And you

said yeah, of course. Then you asked what her name was. And I said her name was…"

"But I never heard her name," Mom cut me off.

"Right. 'Cuz the call dropped. Then you texted me, you said reception sucked, but you'd be home soon." I caught my breath. "But then you didn't come home," I said, reliving the disappointment.

"No," Mom said softly. "I didn't."

★★★

"My mom is coming home!" I told Lily.

"Oh, yay!" she said. She knew how much I missed my mother. But she wasn't letting me off the hook. "Let's go again," she said and giggled.

We were racing our bikes down the street she lived on. Lily, who on a soccer field was as coordinated as a newborn foal, was amazing on a bicycle. She beat me three times in a row.

After the third trouncing, she rode up to me, past the piles of red and orange leaves, and told me, "You have to take the training wheels off."

"Well, I can't right now," I said.

"Hold on." She rode over to her house. It was a small one level bungalow. It couldn't have had more than one bedroom, though I honestly wouldn't know because Lily never let me in. She dropped her bike on the unkempt front lawn and ran inside. Two minutes later, she ran back out and jogged up to me in that clumsy, gangly way, holding a screwdriver.

"Let's just race, running," I said.

"On foot?"

"On foot."

"Hmm," Lily pretended to think about it. "I like this better?"

She laughed and hummed to herself and walked over to the left side of my bike as I straddled it. She kneeled on the ground and unscrewed the left training wheel.

"Lily, I'm not…" The left training wheel hit the pavement with a clang. She walked over to the other side and unscrewed the right training wheel. "I'm gonna fall," I told her.

Lily smirked and said, "Yeah, you will." The right wheel fell. "Come on." She stood behind me and held my shoulders. "Just pedal. Just go."

And that was the first time I became aware of the mist.

It wasn't a mist out there in the world around us. It was a feeling. Or more like a feeling carrying several feelings that I couldn't quite get at. Like knowing two notes to a song, but for the life of you not remembering the rest of the melody. And you hum those two notes to yourself over and over again, hoping they trigger your brain to hum the rest of the tune, but it doesn't happen. And you're sad because you can't remember the melody.

So, you hum those two notes over and over again, no longer in the hope of recalling the rest of the melody, but for the attempt to draw out the feeling of it, as if you can recreate the complete experience of the song from the repetition of those two notes. But you can't. And you know you can't. Yet, you try anyway, since those two notes are all you have.

"Just pedal. Just go. Just pedal. Just go. Just pedal. Just go. Just pedal…"

Lily's hand on my shoulder made me catch myself repeating those words. I blushed, embarrassed, not certain what came over me.

Lily stared at me with wide-eyed concern. Concern and comprehension. As if she knew something I didn't because she'd been somewhere I hadn't. Add this to the fact that she could beat me at a bike race easily and I wasn't happy. This was not how our friendship was supposed to go. I was the strong one.

"I gotta get back home," I announced and grabbed my training wheels.

"Oh," Lily said, disappointed. I walked away, holding my training wheels with one hand, and guiding my bike by its handlebars with the other. I didn't really need to head home. It turned out me and Lily lived only a few blocks from each other, and the sun had at least another hour before it set. Lily knew this. She looked hurt. "See you at school," she called.

I felt bad. I turned back and forced a smile. "Hey, when my mom gets home, come over to her house? You can have dinner with us this time?"

Lily brightened and ran toward me and almost tripped over her own feet. She gave me a quick hug and touched that feather light head of hers to my shoulder. Then she ran back home.

★★★

If Geri had believed things would turn out so different from the movie she'd directed in her mind, she wouldn't have been so arrogant. That movie went like this:

Evan Campbell would enter the conference room in the US Attorney's Office. He would look intensely forlorn. He would take his seat next to his defense attorney, Zach Weddle, at the long conference table and stare at the grain of its red oak.

Across a margin of window light that sliced the table between them, Geri, Nate and Robert Martel would sit, straight-shouldered and noble, and engage Evan in a reverse proffer detailing the incriminating evidence in their possession: the pictures of the children; the online chats between him and individuals he had sexually solicited; and the documented testimony of the sixteen-year old boy, Bayani Matapang, who FBI Special Agent Ikigai Johnson had tracked down and interviewed in a difficult to access slum on the main island of Cebu in the Philippines. Bayani's testimony identified the other children in the photos as Datu Padilla, Kidlat Aquino, and Lualhati Padilla, who was now deceased. More importantly, Bayani identified these children as the individuals with whom Evan had exchanged the sexually solicitous chat messages, and showed Ikigai his Facebook page, so that Ikigai could copy some of those chats directly from Bayani's account. Bayani's testimony detailed how Evan had sexually abused him over a period of about three weeks when Bayani was fifteen. On each occasion Evan had given Bayani money, usually one thousand pesos, the equivalent of about twenty us dollars, which Bayani took because that money could feed him and his baby sister for months.

In Geri's movie, Evan would crumple; Martel would toss a stack of paperwork across the table, and Geri would say, "Might want to take the plea this time, smart guy." Martel, of course, would keep it professional, but even his voice would take on the steel timbre of victory, and he'd say, "Let's keep it simple. Plead guilty to one count of Travel with Intent to Engage in Illicit Sexual Conduct. Plead guilty to one count of Engaging in Illicit Sexual Conduct in a Foreign Place. Do ten years for each count. Twenty years."

And Geri would smile and Evan would shake and say, "Okay."

But that's not how it happened.

★★★

"Why didn't you come home?" I asked my mother, full of sadness from the memory. Mom took a breath and continued her tale.

Ikigai finished packing her belongings. The warriors had returned to the Island of the Capital. Ikigai prepared to leave the inn she'd first stayed at when she'd arrived, the one she had to search for after Mickey and Hari abandoned her to test her resolve. Mickey and Hari, with Tark perched on Hari's shoulder, were there to say farewell. Ikigai stroked Tark's head gently and smiled as he cawed softly. "Send one last message for me, my friend," she said. "Tell the Amazon I am leaving now." Tark disappeared in a flash of light.

"Got something for you," Mickey told her. "When you weren't looking, I bought this." He held up a pearl necklace, the one Ikigai saw in the market stall with the pretty coal-black-eyed woman on the Island of Traders. Ikigai let out a squeal of joy which caught Mickey off guard.

"Just a little going away present," he laughed. "You did amazing. Never met anyone like you."

"Thank you," Ikigai said and blushed as Mickey placed the pearls around her neck.

A mule drawn carriage pulled up to the inn, and Ikigai clutched her satchel. It was time to head for shore and catch the Great Crane of the West on his return flight to her homeland. Mickey and Hari waved goodbye. Mickey said sadly, "Keep in touch, okay?" Ikigai nodded. She was sad as well. She waved back and was about to step into the carriage.

But Tark reappeared in a flash of light, perched on Ikigai's shoulder and chirped frantically.

"What's the message?" Ikigai asked.

Tark answered in that otherworldly voice. "We have a problem. Tagagawas won't give up."

Everyone froze.

Tark continued. "Apologies, Ikigai. But you cannot yet leave The Land of 7,000 Islands."

CHAPTER 7

Geri stands and fidgets at the memory of it all. "We thought we had him. We laid out everything in the reverse proffer. We were over-confident, showed our hand." She paces a bit then sits. "Martel offered what, I thought, was an incredibly fair plea deal. Plead guilty to a count of Intent and a count of Engaging and do ten years for each count. But Evan and Weddle? After Martel offers them this, they just look at us blankly and say, 'Hey, give us the room for a few minutes.'"

The planet Proxima b in the Centaurus constellation. The nucleus of an atom of gold. These are things physicists cannot directly observe. They only know these things exist from the observable reactions of surrounding entities: the gravitational wobble of Proximus Centauri or alpha particles bouncing off gold foil. My mother loved this about physics.

I am not my mother. To me, those are just factoids I googled online. I did inherit her love for stories though, and to keep this one straight I need to observe another unobservable moment: the subsequent conversation between Evan Campbell and Zach Weddle to which no one, save those two men, could have been privy. My best inference is as follows:

After Geri, Nate, and Martel left the two men alone in the conference room, Zach Weddle would have stood, touched the orange jumpsuit covered shoulder of Evan Campbell, walked to the door, pushed it to ensure it was fully closed, and said, "if you want my help, I am the one cat you need to be fully, uncompromisingly, honest with."

(I take artistic license with the word *cat*. Perhaps he said 'guy' or 'dude' or 'fellow.')

Evan would have leaned back in his chair. "I still have you on retainer?"

"I received those funds you wired," Weddle confirmed. "Five thousand above my last invoice."

"That was a contingency. In case what's happening now, happened."

"Then you are either clairvoyant or self-destructive."

"I'm not either. I'm just not stupid."

"Self-destruction can be a form of stupidity."

"I'm not stupid. I know they've been watching me. Especially that day at the bank."

"That day?"

"The day I wired you the money. The Black guy, Schwinn, I saw him watching me. I was going to clear my account and take off. I was going to wire you what I owed and pull the rest of my cash out, about fifteen."

(Though I take license regarding the use of these funds, Geri and Nate did learn this wire occurred once the bank finally responded to their subpoena.)

"Fifteen thousand?" Weddle asked.

"Yes, but I saw him, so I only pulled out ten and did the wire later, online."

"With an extra five thousand. For contingency."

"Exactly."

"Then, yeah, you have me on retainer. Now when you said take off…"

"I was heading over there."

"Speak to me with no assumptions…" Weddle would have instructed.

"I was going to Cebu."

"…because I need to understand everything, without ambiguity."

"I was going to Cebu. I was going to stay there."

"What, forever?"

"Why not?"

"Ten thousand might keep you a year, but…"

"Long enough. 'Til everything's finalized, with my mother's estate."

"It's still in probate?"

Evan would have nodded. "I should be seeing a little over three hundred thousand."

(I learned this pursuant to a public records request of the Multnomah County Circuit Court.)

"That's a fair amount."

"It would have been all I needed. But right now, I tell you this, so you know."

"Know what?"

"That I can afford you."

Weddle would have remained impassive. "The ten, you carried it on the plane?"

"Nine thousand, nine hundred and twenty-five. They took it from me."

"Well, it's less than ten, so they won't get you on flying with undeclared funds."

"I had to pay the taxi. And the luggage."

"They're going to try for civil forfeiture. My side project will be proving your nine-thousand-whatever was not involved in a crime. That is my side project. My priority, our priority, is getting them to drop or reduce these charges. They take anything else from you?"

"No. Like what?"

"Your phone?"

"Destroyed it before I left for the airport."

"Computer?"

"Never bought a replacement."

"Good," Weddle would have said. "Now, this boy, Bayani."

"I never forced him to do anything."

"He said he was fifteen when you had sex."

"Age of consent in the Philippines is twelve."

"Doesn't matter. US federal violations define a child as under eighteen."

"And that's the problem, isn't it?"

"For you, yes."

"No, for everyone."

"How so?"

"I refuse to be crushed and told what to do and what not to do, by hypocrites and their archaic laws they break themselves every day. I have never raped anyone. Everything and anything that I've enjoyed with anyone else has been with full consent, full mutual consent."

"Understood. But objectively, legally, that will not fly with a jury."

"I'm not taking their plea."

"I think we can get a charge dropped. They can't prove your prior formation of intent."

"I'm not going to be shut away from the world for being someone who figured out how to successfully navigate it. It's just perspective. Over here, a dollar is something you toss at a bum. Over there, it feeds a family for a week. Here, something's a crime. Somewhere else, it's celebrated. All I did was go where I needed to go, for myself, for what I need. I'm not taking their plea."

Weddle would have scratched an itch on his eyebrow. "Then I need to pull my guys in."

"I told you, I can afford it."

"My guys will go out and dig up dirt and poke holes and discredit, but we have to direct them. Bayani, he have any problems? Is he a criminal? Is he a junkie? What's his story?"

"Bayani isn't leaving Cebu."

"That's major. How do you know that?"

"None of them are."

"None of them, who? The other children?"

Evan would have chuckled.

"The children they found in your pictures?"

Evan would have nodded.

"Did you have sex with those children too?"

"Everything was consensual."

"That girl looked under twelve."

"Everything was consensual."

"Then it is imperative you explain to me why you are so sure none of these children will leave Cebu. Because, if that is the case, I see a clear and advantageous path moving forward."

And Evan would have smiled.

"He's wearing this lovely, shit-eating grin when his lawyer says we can go back in," Geri continues. "And he rejects the plea deal. Again. We underestimated how smart he was going out to the Philippines to do what he did. His lawyer basically said, 'Screw you, see you in court. Oh, and we're going to motion the court to require the accuser to be present at trial.'"

"The judge supported this?" I ask.

"Of course. It was Evan's sixth amendment right. And the judge said Bayani had to physically be there. No telephone call, no video conference. He had to physically be at trial."

"Gotta follow the rules everywhere," I say, and pull a document out of my leather portfolio. "Even when it's inconvenient."

"That it?" Geri asks. I hand it to her. She runs her fingers over the words. Office of the Civil Registrar General. Certificate of Death. Province: Camiguin. City/Municipality: Mambajao. Name: Ikigai Johnson.

"You must have gone through some shit to get this," Geri's voice cracks.

"Mickey did all the hard work."

Geri hands the death certificate back and sighs. "So how'd your mom explain what happened?"

★★★

In the Capital, at the inn, Ikigai fought to keep her frustration in check. "It appears," she told Mickey and Hari, "I need to take Bayani home with me."

Tark was perched on Hari's shoulder. Mickey stroked the Garuda's beak and told her, "That'll be harder than you think."

"If the Judge in our homeland says Bayani needs to face Tagagawas at trial to accuse him directly, fine, it's a small hindrance. I'll take Bayani with me, he'll stand before—"

"You're doing that thing again."

"What thing, Mickey?"

"That thing where you're thinking of this only from your perspective. That kid lives hand to mouth, day to day. He's gonna up and go to our homeland, for how long? How will he feed himself? How will he feed that baby sister he's taking care of?"

"Everything you're saying is valid…"

"There's a 'but' coming."

"*However*, you're doing that thing you do."

"Yeah, I'm doing the thing where I'm pointing out the thing that you do."

"Oh my God, Mickey! You know what you're doing?"

"What am I doing?"

"You're being negative. You're bringing up all the problems and all the pitfalls based on your past experience, but this is not your past experience. This is here and this is now and I think we can do this. We have to at least ask Bayani to come back with us. We have to try."

Mickey exchanged a sad look with Hari.

"Come on, guys," Ikigai said. "We can't give up. You know I'm right."

There was a long silence, until Tark cawed lowly and fluttered from Hari's shoulder to Ikigai's.

Mickey chuckled, "Tark just cast his vote." Then he looked at Ikigai and she saw a pain in his eyes that she knew all too well. It was the pain of failure.

"Had a hard case, a lot like this one, years ago," Mickey said.

"What happened?" Ikigai asked. Hari looked at the ground.

"I gave up," Mickey admitted. "It got difficult. Similar complications to what you're dealing with now. I didn't push as far as I should have. Like you're pushing. I couldn't get past the obstacles. Told you, got my own ghost, but, you're right, this isn't that case. So, okay." Mickey let out a deep breath. "We got your back."

Ikigai touched Mickey's arm. "Thank you."

"And uh, those pearls," he said. "They were a going away present."

"And?"

"And you're not going away, so…"

"Let's get back to the Island of Traders."

It was still daylight when the warriors returned to the Village of the Storm, having repeated the journey from the Capital: a turbulent Crane flight and the long walk on the Northern and Eastern roads. They were exhausted. Ikigai was hungry and sleep deprived. But she had her companions' support and this gave her strength. They pushed forward.

They avoided the Village Captain's office, certain he would not be pleased to see them again. Now more familiar with the maze of alleys, they found their way to Bayani's home, where his little sister played with a rag doll outside. Hari asked her in the Language of the Capital if her brother was around, but she only knew the Language of Traders and stared, confused. So, Hari said softly, "Bayani?" The girl smiled a sweet smile, then ran off.

Minutes later, the girl returned with Bayani, Datu, and Kidlat in tow. Bayani looked happy to see them. He shook the warriors' hands and petted Tark, as Datu and Kidlat shyly stood by. Ikigai spoke with Bayani as Hari interpreted.

"Tagagawas?" Bayani asked. "He is in jail?"

"He is," Ikigai answered. "But I need your help again, to keep him there."

Bayani sucked his teeth. "What else do you need? I've given you everything."

"You have, and we are forever grateful. Unfortunately, we need more. We need you to travel to my homeland with me. To stand before Tagagawas and accuse him to his face."

"I did want to face Tagagawas," Bayani said, his voice rising. "I wanted to face him here, in our village. I would have accused him here. And he would have wished he'd never come. Why would I travel all the way to your strange land just to keep him from leaving the prison he belongs in?"

"These are the rules of Justice in my homeland," Ikigai explained. "If you come with me—"

"Tell her I'm not going anywhere!" Bayani shouted at Hari. "Tell her if she wants me to face Tagagawas, bring him here!" Hari interpreted and Bayani stormed away. His sister, Datu, and Kidlat followed.

"What's really wrong, Bayani?" Ikigai shouted after him. "Are you afraid?"

"I will not translate that," Hari said.

"Why won't he come?" Ikigai asked.

A voice answered, "Because he can't." The warriors turned to find the Village Captain behind them.

"Why can't he?" Ikigai, irritated, asked the Captain.

"As much as Bayani believes he is a man," the Captain said just as irritated, "he is not. And children of this land are not allowed to leave without their parents."

"Let's go find his parents then."

"No one knows who his father is."

"His mother?"

"Died. Here. Shortly after his sister was born."

The pressure in Ikigai's temples built. "Relatives? Aunts? Uncles? Someone?"

The Captain shook his head. "Bayani and his sister, they are alone."

Hari nodded. "I knew it. *Bayani* means hero in your language," he told Ikigai and Mickey. "*Matapang* means brave."

"That's some name the kid gave himself," Mickey said, comprehending. "Orphans do that sometimes."

"I don't care if he's an orphan," Ikigai cried, furious. "I don't care if he named himself. He's Bayani Matapang. He's real. This happened to him."

"He's very real," Mickey agreed. "But besides that baby sister, he has no family. He can't leave this land. Not until he's an adult."

"He's sixteen, that's not for another two years," Ikigai seethed.

"Maybe he would be willing to travel then," Hari said.

"We would have to let Tagagawas go in the meantime." Ikigai gritted her teeth and fought back tears of rage. "And that's exactly why Tagagawas came here: to steal from a child like Bayani, a child who wouldn't be able to leave this place and accuse him of his crimes."

Later, at the inn that was south of the waterfall on the Island of Traders, Ikigai held her Purpose. She traced the polished outline of it with the tip of her finger and placed it against her nose and cried. Tark perched on a drawer beside her bed and watched, concerned. She was out of ideas. Bayani was an orphan. Datu and Kidlat would not speak. Lualhati was dead…

"Huh," I cried out in surprise, as if the wind had been punched out of me. Mom watched me with that clinical stare. There was the mist again. Then there was a face. And the face was gone from my mind as suddenly as it appeared, but the feeling of the face lingered: a cold nose against my cheek. *Just pedal. Just go.* My heart rate went up. *It takes bravery to follow. It takes courage to listen.* "Keep going," I said.

"Maybe that's enough for tonight."

"No, keep going."

"There's always tomorrow. Let's get some sleep."

★★★

One day, after I got home from school and lay in bed in my room at Dad's house, still angry that Mom wasn't coming home from the Philippines when she said she was, my phone buzzed. I checked it.

what u doin? the text said.

nothing I texted back.

u home?

yea dad still at work

i come over?

no

(Sad emoji)

jk lol come if you want

My doorbell rang. Seriously? She was outside this whole time? I ran downstairs and opened the door. It was rainy and gray.

Fall was transforming to the wet chill of a Portland winter. Her bicycle was keeled over on my porch. She looked like a soaked, lost pet.

"You're crazy," I cried. I pulled Lily inside, helped her out of her waterlogged coat, and dragged her upstairs to my room. She sat on the floor. I went to the bathroom and grabbed the fluffiest clean towel I could find from the hamper behind the bathroom door, then returned to my room to find Lily playing with my things.

"What's this?" she asked, her expression blank.

I shook my head. She was like a baby sometimes. "Just stuff," I said and sat down and put the towel around her. Lily had found my Little Pouch of Randomness: a small green pencil pouch that contained items of miscellany I'd collected over the years. Items whose significance I couldn't necessarily remember but could never bring myself to throw away.

Lily pulled three items out, one by one, and held them up.

One: a broken piece of thick, colored chalk which left its pink dust caked on her fingers.

"I got that in kindergarten," I answered the unspoken question in her wide, unblinking eyes. "I liked it. I took it off the blackboard and kept it."

"I thought your mom was coming home?" she asked and rummaged further through my pouch.

"Me too," I said. "She's still in the Philippines."

Lily held up another item.

Two: a miniature billiard ball. Blue. Striped. With the number ten.

"I found that in the grass one day. I liked the way it felt."

"It's heavy," Lily said, dropped it and pulled out another item. Three. She held it up. "That... is a rock..." I said and giggled. Lily blinked.

"Just a rock. Can't remember where I got it."

Lily nodded. Peered at the rock. Stood. Walked to my window. Opened it.

"It's cold. What are you…?" I said. Lily drew her arm back.

"What are you doing! Stop!" I screamed and rushed to Lily and snatched the rock from her hand before she tossed it out into the rain. I clutched it against my heart and fought back tears. "Why would you do that?" I whispered, incredibly hurt, but uncertain as to why.

Lily watched me silently. I didn't like the way she was looking at me, like she was trying to figure something out.

Then she sat back on the floor and hummed to herself.

★★★

Lualhati was dead. Datu and Kidlat would not speak. Bayani was an orphan.

"What else can I do?" Ikigai said to herself in her room at the inn, south of the waterfall.

The Emperor's Ghost appeared.

This time he appeared in the form of a child, huddled in a corner, weeping. When he appeared in this manner, he sought compassion. But Ikigai was not in a generous mood. Even Tark cawed at the Emperor angrily. "I am not feeling sorry for you right now," Ikigai said to the Ghost. "You made your choices."

The Emperor rarely spoke. But when he did, his voice floated as words in Ikigai's mind. And now, those floating words said, "I too."

"No," Ikigai responded. "No excuses tonight. I don't care how hard she was. She did the best with what she knew. Can you say the same?"

"Trying now," said the Emperor.

"I don't care," Ikigai said. "Do you see them where you are? Do you see their shame?"

"See yours."

"Good. I'm glad. Do you see the one you destroyed? Do you? No, you don't. Because I keep her here, close to my heart, away from you."

There was a knock at her door, and Mickey's voice said from outside, "You okay in there?"

"I'm fine," Ikigai shouted.

"Can we come in?" Mickey asked. "Got a little surprise for ya."

And a surprise it was. For when Ikigai opened her door, it was not only Mickey and Hari standing before her.

Malaya and Datu were with them.

Datu stood straight and strong and showed a resolution beyond his years. Hari said, "I can only understand a little of what they say. But they followed us all the way here. I think Datu wants to provide his Testimony of Deepest Secrets."

"Okay," Ikigai said a few minutes later, "we have a lot to figure out." The warriors had escorted Malaya and Datu to the inn's dining area, where they all sat at a table. Tark flew about the room to stretch his wings.

Ikigai couldn't help but stare at Malaya's face, taking in every detail. It was the closest of flesh and blood that she was going to get to Lualhati, the one who started this adventure.

Communication was difficult. Hari spoke the Language of the Capital. Malaya spoke the Language of Traders. Datu, with a serious face as round and sweet as his mother's, spoke Malaya's language, and understood a bit of Hari's, but not enough.

Through Hari and Datu, Ikigai determined that The Language of Traders was not the only language Malaya and Datu knew, though it was unclear which others they understood. Then something occurred to Ikigai. The Island of Traders was named as such because of a long history of, well, trading. But, trading with whom?

(After a long silence, I realized this was not a rhetorical question. "I don't know," I said, "I guess other countries that were, like, close by?"

"Exactly," Mom said. "And can you think of any other countries that just so happen to be close by?"

"Oh!" I said excitedly. Then Mom knew that I knew where she was going with this.)

Ikigai decided to try something.

"*Nihongo wa hanasemasu ka?*" Ikigai asked. The faces of Malaya and Datu lit up as bright as twin moons.

"*Hai!*" Malaya said.

"Oh my god, how did I not think of this before?" Ikigai said to Mickey and Hari. "They can speak the Language of my Mothers, the Language of the Rising Sun."

Ikigai and Malaya squared off, half smiling, half ready for battle. Now that communication was no longer an issue, there was much that needed to be said.

"You are insane!" Malaya shouted in the Language of the Rising Sun. "Running through our village anytime you please!"

"You ran away from me!" Ikigai replied. "And you were faster than I thought you'd be."

"Ah, and why would I not be fast? You just met me and you are calling me fat? Only my boyfriends get to do that."

And at this, they laughed long and hard like two old friends. The women's shoulders sagged as they changed topics.

"I'll be forever grateful if you allow Datu to provide his Testimony," Ikigai told her. "But you two would also need to travel with me, to my home, to face Tagagawas and accuse him."

Malaya turned to Datu, questions and concerns in her eyes and Datu said, in the Language of the Rising Sun, "I will go. Not only for me. For my sister."

"Will you come, then?" Ikigai asked Malaya. "To my homeland?"

"I do not have the Freedom to come and go from this land as I please," Malaya said.

"How do you not...?"

"Freedom is a fickle thing here. Like everyone, I had it at birth. Like many, I had to leave it behind, years ago, on the island on which I was born. It would have cost money to take it with me, money my family did not have. We would have to go back there to find it. The island's very far. I don't have the money to travel there."

"I will pay for everything," Ikigai assured her. And the two women planned further.

Ikigai turned to Mickey and Hari and explained. "Datu was born here on the Island of Traders, he has his Freedom. But he can't use it to leave this land without Malaya. She has to retrieve her Freedom from her place of birth. We need to go to the island she was born on."

"And which island is that?" Mickey asked.

"The Island of the Keepers of the Key."

"That's not good," Mickey informed her.

Ikigai ignored him and faced Datu. "Before we discuss anything else," she said to the boy in the Language of the Rising Sun. "Are you ready to provide your Testimony?"

Datu nodded firmly.

★★★

"Alright guys," Geri Bradford said to the bodies in the case coordination meeting at the US Attorney's Office. "Here's where we're at." Geri's laptop was connected to a projector so everyone in the conference room could see what she did on a screen above her head. The roll call was as before: PPB Detective Nate Schwinn, DDA and cross-designated AUSA Robert Martel, Chief AUSA Diane Appelo, and Brent Oberley, the FBI supervisor.

Geri pulled up a map of the Philippines on her laptop and projected it for all to see. She pointed to Cebu's main island. "Our gorgeous and insanely tenacious colleague has tracked down the kids in Evan's chats and photos to a slum on this island."

Geri pulled up the picture of the man-boy on the dusty road. "This is Bayani Matapang. He provided Ikigai with his testimony and verified that was him and the other kids Evan was communicating with in those Facebook chats. Ikigai's interview with Bayani gave us the probable cause we needed to arrest Evan federally and put him back in jail. The judge, thankfully, used common sense in determining Evan to be an obvious flight risk. He's being held without bail. But since Evan invoked his right to face his accuser at trial, shit's gotten complicated."

"How so?" Appelo asked. "We'll bring Bayani over here to testify at trial."

"Can't," Geri explained. "He's an orphan. Bayani might not even be his birth name. Mom's dead. Dad's in the wind, could be dead too, we don't know. No guardians. So Bayani doesn't have a birth certificate, or if he does, we have no way of tracking it down in a reasonable amount of time. Can't help him do a late registration for his birth either. As an orphan he has no documentation supporting his identity. Without a birth certificate, he can't get a passport. Even if we did grease some wheels…" Geri turned to Oberley. "Not condoning we partake in any form of foreign corruption Mr. G-Man, just saying, hypothetically…"

"Duly noted," Oberley chuckled.

"Hypothetically, even if we did, you know, convince someone to grant Bayani a passport, he couldn't travel out of the country anyway. Not without a parent or guardian."

"Then at trial," Appelo went on, "we can use Bayani's testimony as supporting evidence, but it can't be the foundation of the charges."

"We can generate a superseding indictment," Martel offered.

"We'll have to get other victims to testify," Appelo said.

"Just so happens," Geri continued, pulling up the picture of the two boys at the waterfall and pointing to the one with the round face. "This sweetheart is Datu Padilla, thirteen years old. He gave Ikigai his testimony. Now Evan never had intercourse with Datu, he only…" Geri sarcastically made quotation marks with her fingers on the word *only*. "Touched Datu's penis and had Datu touch his. But he was a lot more brazen with Bayani because he knew Bayani would never be able to travel to the United States to testify against him."

"Too bad Evan doesn't understand the federal child sex tourism laws," Oberley said. "Those acts with Datu are still violations."

"Yes," Geri agreed. "But Evan does understand the complications facing a group of people in the Philippines living in abject poverty. Datu is willing to come here and testify, but he can't travel without his mother, Malaya, who does not have a passport."

"Then let's help her get a passport," Appelo said.

"That's what Ikigai, the Assistant Legal Attaché, Mickey, and his partner Hari Cruz from the Philippine National Police are working on. But they can't get Malaya's passport unless they get her a birth certificate first."

"She doesn't have a birth certificate either?" Martel asked.

"Never got one. That's the thing. Why would she spend a few thousand pesos traveling to the island she was born on and a few hundred more to submit a late registration and get the certificate, when that's money that could be spent on, I don't know, feeding her family?"

"Evan's a piece of work," Martel said. "He targeted these victims with precision."

"This shit is par for the course," Nate broke in, quiet until this point. "Dudes like Evan, they know where to go. They discuss it with each other in their online chat rooms. Which areas of which countries can I go to abuse kids who will never be able to follow me home? Philippines. Cambodia. Vietnam. They know these people are living hand to mouth and won't have the resources to press charges." Everyone took a breath.

"I'll let HQ know our budget's increasing a bit, so Ikigai can pay for expenses related to getting Malaya her passport," Oberley said. "Ikigai told me, last time she emailed, she was heading out to, I can't remember the name of the place."

"Claveria," Geri reminded him. "That's the town Malaya was born. They can do a late registration but they have to get the birth certificate there. Here's the problem..." Geri pulled the map back up on the projected screen. "Claveria is not easy to get to. Here's Cebu, where our victims live." Geri pointed to the island. "Here's the island Manila is on. Here's the island Claveria is on. Here's where the city of Legazpi is, right near this volcano, Mount Magayon, better known these days as Mount Mayon. Now, there's no direct route to Claveria from Cebu. Ikigai will need to take Malaya on a plane north from Cebu to Manila. Then a plane back down south to Legazpi where Mount Mayon is. Then a long drive over land, west, to the other side of the island to get here, the Port of Pio Duran. Then keep going west, across the sea, to get to the Port of Claveria."

"Holy shit," Oberley said. "She didn't explain all that."

"Did she explain the problem with Claveria?" Geri asked, cautiously.

"Do I want to know?"

"It's, uh, kinda unofficially controlled by insurgents. From the New People's Army."

"She did *not* tell me that," Oberley replied, keeping himself under control.

"Easier to ask forgiveness than permission?"

"That's not funny, Geri. That's a State Department designated terrorist organization. She gets captured, she gets killed? I can't have that on my conscience." Oberley shook his head. "No, sorry guys. We'll have to find another way. I'm calling Ikigai. I'm telling her to stand down."

★★★

Malaya and Datu took their leave from Ikigai and her companions and returned to the Village of the Storm. Ikigai documented Datu's Testimony of Deepest Secrets. Once complete, she gave the paper to Tark and asked him to take it to the Amazon. Tark did, but when he returned in that flash of light, his eyes glowing blue, Ikigai had a feeling the return message was not a good one. "Go ahead," she said.

"Ikigai," Tark relayed. "Our chiefs say you are not to travel to the Island of the Keepers of the Key. It is too dangerous. That is an order."

Ikigai smashed her fist on the inn's dining room table, startling Mickey and Hari.

"Might be for the best," Mickey had to admit. "That island is home to a group of Angry Insurgents. I don't think it's worth the risk either."

"Tark, delete that message," Ikigai commanded the baby Garuda, then turned to Mickey and Hari. "I'm leaving with Malaya in the morning. Hari, are you willing to go with me?" Hari glanced at Mickey, who sighed and paced the room.

"Here we go," Mickey said. "I never said I wasn't willing to go with you, Ikigai, I just…"

"Hear me out," Ikigai told Mickey calmly. "I think you should stay."

"That's not your call."

"Give me a chance to finish. Hari and I can blend in better over there, we have—"

"You're going to another island where they speak yet another language neither of you know. You'll stand out the moment you open your mouth."

"Fine. And that's why I think you should stay here."

"I'm not following."

"You're right, this might not work. So, let's get a back-up plan going. What if you stay and talk to the Village Captain? See if there's another way we can get Malaya's Freedom in case me and Hari come back empty-handed."

Mickey looked at Hari, who admitted, "I think that's a very good idea."

Mickey stopped pacing. He set his jaw and Ikigai braced herself for another quarrel.

"Okay then," Mickey relented. "Not happy about it. But I do believe in democracy. Two against one wins. I'll stay and try to figure out a back-up."

Ikigai smiled. "Don't pout. You boys won't be separated for long."

"Messing with the maximum bromance, Ikigai," Mickey said and gave Hari a fist bump. "Seriously though, you guys need to be careful out there."

When decisions are made, the world shifts to accommodate and react to them. It shifts in ways Ikigai had stopped trying to understand. The variables involved were simply too numerous. Do you understand what I am saying to you? When you make a decision, make it in the spirit of Righteousness, and press forward. Do not bother trying to understand what the world does in response, for these things are beyond your control.

Ikigai had come to believe this is what warriors referred to as Faith.

Ikigai had Faith and so she slept well the night before her journey to the Island of the Keepers of the Key. If she had attempted to know the forces set in motion by her decision, she would not have slept so well. It was only after her adventure that Ikigai learned that while she, Mickey, and Hari discussed their plans, Malaya and Datu discussed matters with their neighbors, to include Bayani, as well as Kidlat and his mother, Tala.

"You trust the foreigners?" Tala asked.

"I don't trust anyone," Malaya replied honestly. "I just want Tagagawas punished."

"The foreigners could be lying," Tala suggested. "They could be working with Tagagawas. This could all be a trick to get you out of the village. To take you to a far-away place like the Island of the Keepers of the Key. Anything can be done there. What if you don't return?"

Malaya pondered this. Bayani quietly slipped away.

Bayani walked through the maze of alleys and found his way to the home of his friend, the bare-chested man. "What's up?" the man asked.

"I'm tired of these foreigners sticking their noses in our business," Bayani said. "Let's send a message to the Brothers."

On the other side of the world, yet another force was set in motion. Unbeknown to Ikigai at the time, Tagagawas also schemed. Tagagawas' Defender, the man who would plead Tagagawas' case in a Court of Judgment, visited Tagagawas in prison. They were joined by a man and a woman, an interesting pair. This man and this woman were, like Ikigai and her companions, expert practitioners in the art of investigation. Unlike Ikigai, this man and this woman conducted their duties for the benefit of those who had been accused. Their kind were known as Shadow Warriors.

The male Shadow Warrior spoke. "We have received your payment. We are at your service."

Tagagawas and the Defender traded a look. "I think the first step," said Tagagawas, "is to find out everything you can about this warrior. The one they call Ikigai. Everyone, after all, has secrets."

Ikigai and Hari arrived at the Village of the Storm before sunrise as a night rain subsided. They approached Malaya's home, and heard muffled voices talking excitedly behind the tin sheet that made for her door.

Ikigai tapped lightly. Malaya pushed aside the sheet of metal, stepped out, and cautiously put it back in place.

"Everything okay?" Ikigai asked in the Language of the Rising Sun.

"Yes," Malaya said. "Just making sure Datu has everything he needs until I return."

"Sounded like more than just Datu in there," remarked Ikigai. Malaya smiled and lowered her head humbly and ignored the question, of which Ikigai took note, for Malaya never struck her as a woman who humbled herself before anyone.

They traveled by foot toward the Southern shore of the Island of Traders. At one point, Malaya, carrying her belongings in a satchel, fell behind. Hari offered to carry the satchel for her, so they would not lose further ground. Malaya clutched her satchel tightly and refused. Hari and Ikigai spoke in the Language of Ikigai's Homeland.

"What, does she think we're going to run off with her stuff?" Ikigai asked.

"She does not fully trust us," Hari said.

"We're doing this to help her and her family," Ikigai insisted.

"Why wouldn't she trust us?"

"She does not need our help," Hari told her patiently and made eye contact with Ikigai. "Her life was fine before we entered it. Bad things happen. You continue to live. Or you don't. She is living. So why would she need to trust us?"

Ikigai watched Malaya trailing behind them. "I hope she doesn't sprint off again."

"You can speak with her in the Language of the Rising Sun," Hari said. "You want her trust? Gain it. Speak with her."

They finally reached the Southern shore of the Island of Traders, and Tark, who had slept thus far, awoke and cawed. Ikigai opened her satchel to let him fly about. They passed the market stalls and Ikigai saw the pearl-selling woman with the coal-black eyes, who was now wearing a blue scarf. The woman recognized Ikigai, smiled and waved. Ikigai touched the pearls around her neck and waved back. They continued to the area where the Great Cranes of the East took off in flight.

Ikigai and Hari spoke with a Great Crane of the East, and Ikigai found this Crane to be just as infuriating as his Western brother.

"What do you mean?" Ikigai said to the Crane. "How do none of your brethren fly to the Island of the Keepers of the Key?"

"Do you see my neck?" the Crane answered. "Do you see how long it is? How beautiful? How incandescently pleasant to behold? I would prefer it stay in this condition."

"Incandescently pleasant?" Ikigai muttered to Hari. "This one's probably a wannabe novelist." She turned back to the Crane. "So, I guess a few Angry Insurgents up and run around an Island and you just refuse to go there?"

"I will take you north, to the Capital," the Crane told her. "From there, one of my brethren can take you back south to the Island of the Beautiful Lady. From there, well, that's up to you."

"That's insane! You'll fly over the Island of the Beautiful Lady on the way to the Capital. Can you at least take us directly to the Island of the Beautiful Lady?"

"I will take you to the Capital."

And so, a flight to the Capital it was, a night's stay there, then another Crane ride south to the Island of the Beautiful Lady. Ikigai sat between Malaya and Hari on the back of the Crane, and Malaya, perhaps thinking that if her escorts truly meant to harm her in some way they would have done so by now, warmed up to Ikigai.

"Your rudeness has no limit," Malaya told Ikigai in the Language of the Rising Sun.

"Is it not rude to start a conversation telling someone how rude they are?" Ikigai shot back.

"You are not married, are you?"

"From what I gather, neither are you."

"I only care for my children. Men are silly things that come and go."

"Your son will be a man one day."

"And he will be a silly thing."

"Then don't raise him to be one."

"You have a son?"

"A daughter. If I am not careful she too will be a silly thing."

("Hey!" I said. Mom smirked and kept going.)

"Children. They are the world, are they not?" Malaya said.

"Just like the song. What of the rest of your family?"

"You met my sister, Tala."

"Ah, I did not realize you were sisters. So Datu and Kidlat…"

"Cousins."

"I see. Your family's names, they are very beautiful. Do they have meaning?"

"Every name has meaning," Malaya said. "Like yours."

"True. It means The Reason for Which You—"

"I know what your name means. You will laugh if I tell you what my name means."

"Now you have to tell me."

"Malaya means Free."

They laughed. "That is ironic," Ikigai said, "given why we are traveling. And what of Datu, and Kidlat, and Tala?"

"Datu means Chief."

"He does look like a little chief: thoughtful and resolved."

"Kidlat means Lightning."

"He was very fast when the boys conquered us at patintero."

"That was a funny sight. And my sister, Tala, her name means Bright Star."

"Wow. And what does..." but Ikigai caught herself and refrained from asking the question.

A pained look crossed Malaya's face. After a moment, she spoke. "My daughter. It does not matter what her name means. She is so much more than her name. She is a world. She is a flame. With me, in my lungs, in my belly, at all times. Always." Malaya wiped away a tear and took a deep breath. "How did you get the name Ikigai?"

"My father named me."

"Is he still with us?"

"My parents have been gone a long time now."

"That is hard."

"It is not hard. It just... is."

"I know."

"Do you?"

Malaya peered at Ikigai. "Yes. And I know it does not matter how old you are when your parents leave. You still feel like an orphan when they do." Ikigai wanted to change the direction of this conversation, but she was gaining Malaya's trust. And trust, like many things, cannot be received unless it is also given.

"Well, I wasn't very old when they left," Ikigai said.

"I am sorry. Did you know them? Before they left?"

"I knew them very well."

"What was your father like? Stubborn and rude like you?"

Ikigai laughed. "No. I get that from my mother. My father was... very kind and..."

Mom stopped and hid her face with her towel. I placed my hand in hers. "Do *you* want to keep going?" I asked.

Mom wiped her face and nodded.

I sat up, attentive. She never talked about my grandfather.

"His name was Peter," Ikigai told Malaya. "He was tall and thin and beautiful. I don't remember him ever raising his voice to me or my brother. But he talked to us all the time. In the mornings, he would sit with us, and ask how we slept, and of what we dreamed. And we would tell him, and he would listen to every word as if any and every syllable we uttered were the finest treasures of gold and jade and ruby spilling from our lips. Then he would go to work, and while he worked he'd melt the gold we gave him, and carve the jade and cut the ruby and come home late while we were in bed and watch us sleep. I was older than my brother, so I figured my father was doing this and I trained myself to wake when he came home. And when I woke, he would hold me and tell me stories until I fell back to sleep, stories of lost and distant lands, adventures in rivers, mountains and caves. Into these stories, he always weaved the dreams we shared. I'd fall asleep to the sound of his voice. I'd tell him that I loved him, and that I loved his stories, and he would tell me they were not his stories. He would tell me that he could only shape the stories I had given him. And that he himself, and everything he was, was my story. For I was his little Ikigai: the very reason for which he woke up in the morning."

After a long silence, Malaya spoke. "That was a good man. What happened to him?"

Ikigai shook her head. Malaya decided it was best not to press further. She grasped Ikigai's hand and the two shared a sad smile. Hari caught Ikigai's eye and nodded, then pointed to a conical mountain jutting from an irregular shaped island.

"I remember this mountain." Ikigai stared in awe as the Crane flew closer.

"She is a volcano," Hari explained.

"She's beautiful."

"That is why we call her the Beautiful Lady."

"What happened to him?" I asked. "What happened to Grandpa?"

Mom watched me carefully. "Let's continue next time."

"No!" I jumped to my feet. "I want to know! There's so much you don't tell me."

"I know baby, I'm trying to tell you now."

"Then just tell me."

"You have to listen, Junior. Do you want me to keep going?"

It was late and I was tired, but I didn't want to stop. "Yeah, keep going."

"Please."

"Sorry. Please."

They landed on the Eastern shore of the Island of the Beautiful Lady. They needed to get to the Western shore. The Crane of course, was a finicky beast, and refused to travel further. So Ikigai, Hari, and Malaya were forced to walk over land, west, to the opposite side of the island.

The Beautiful Lady, a near perfect pyramidal cone, rose with majesty by the Eastern shore. Her sides were not straight, sloping inward gently, curving toward the ground. But this imperfection, if it could be called that, only added to her attraction. Her mouth, though gray with age, was still sensuous, frost-tipped with snow, even in the heat of this tropical land, and it peaked above the passing clouds that lingered lovingly at her sloping neck. From this mouth Ikigai could see the paths of many scars, carved by the lava of past eruptions. Ikigai was glad they had to move west, away from the Lady. For it seemed, like most women of beauty, she had a tempestuous side as well.

They pushed forward on a main road that would take them to the Port of the Western shore. Ikigai opened her satchel and Tark fluttered happily about. No matter how the road meandered through mangroves and palm trees, the Beautiful Lady loomed behind, clouds hovering around her.

"It looks as if the clouds are stealing kisses from her mouth," Ikigai said to Hari.

Hari smiled. "That is because they are."

Ikigai thought Hari was just being poetic. But Hari saw her reaction and decided to explain he was not being metaphorical. "She was a princess, long ago," he began. Ikigai listened as the three walked and Tark landed on her shoulder. "Princess Magayon, the Beautiful Lady. Her lover, Panganoron, saved her life when she almost drowned one day, and so her father loved Panganoron as well and gave Panganoron his blessing for marriage to his daughter. But the angry warrior Pagtuga also wanted to marry Magayon, and kidnapped her father to try and force her to leave Panganoron for him. But Panganoron was brave and righteous. He gathered his warriors, and went to battle with Pagtuga, right here." Hari waved his arm. "Panganoron succeeded in killing Pagtuga in battle, but then Panganoron was killed himself by one of Pagtuga's warriors. Magayon held the love of her life as he died in her arms. Then she took her own life and lay beside him."

"Think I've heard a story like that somewhere before," Ikigai smirked.

"It is not a story," Hari said patiently. "Magayon, she is very real. She is right there. Her spirit grew into that volcano where she was buried, and Panganoron's spirit is in the clouds that kiss her mouth."

"What is he saying?" Malaya asked Ikigai in the Language of the Rising Sun.

"He is explaining what happened to the spirits of Magayon and Panganoron," Ikigai responded. "Huh," Malaya grunted. "No one ever asks what happened to the spirit of Pagtuga."

Meanwhile, a few hours after Ikigai, Hari and Malaya first set out from the Village of the Storm, Mickey stood in the Captain's office deploying his usual charm. It was to no avail.

"Soooo," Mickey said, "there's really no other way?"

"No," the Captain answered stubbornly. "Malaya has to retrieve her Freedom from her island of birth."

"Well," Mickey said, finally giving up. "It is what it is." Dejected, Mickey turned to leave, but the Captain's gaze softened, and he said, "If a back-up plan is what you want, you should speak with Tala and Kidlat."

"I'm pretty sure Tala wants nothing to do with us."

"I suggest you try again. It would be much easier to retrieve Tala's Freedom than Malaya's. She is younger than Malaya and I believe she was born in a city that is on this island."

Mickey brightened and winked at the Captain. "You the man," he said, and rushed out of the office.

"How will you communicate with her?" the Captain called out after him.

Mickey re-entered. "Oh, yeah, yeah. You mind coming with?"

As Ikigai, Hari and Malaya moved west, the Beautiful Lady shrunk in the distance but continued watching them from afar. They finally reached the Port of the Western shore.

A small crowd of people waited on the white sands of the Western shore, their feet wet from the coming and going of the tide. Ikigai looked out across the sea and saw the shore of the Island of the Keepers of the Key, a little over three kilometers away. Malaya approached the small crowd and, remembering a bit of the Language of the Beautiful Lady, asked them something. A man responded. Then, Malaya said to Ikigai, "The ferry will be here any moment."

At that, there was a rush of water and a huge object emerged from the sea. At first it looked like a boulder. Then it looked like two boulders. Water cascaded down the surface of the first boulder, revealing eyes and a mouth attached to the second boulder by a neck. The second boulder sprouted flippers that wad-dled onto the small beach.

The Giant Turtle was not as large as a Great Crane, but she was still colossal — big enough to carry the group of people waiting to climb onto her shell. Turtles are cute, but at that size they look rather fearsome, and this creature gave Ikigai pause. Tark mewed and fluttered off Ikigai's shoulder and down to her satchel. Ikigai took the Garuda in her hand and perched him back on her shoulder. "Show this turtle no fear," she said to Tark. "From what I understand, you will be much larger one day."

The Turtle spoke in the Language of the Beautiful Lady, with a small, whispery voice that did not match the enormity of her presence.

"A hundred pesos each," Malaya interpreted for Ikigai. "You have enough for us all?"

"I have more than enough," Ikigai said.

"Good, you'll need it."

"What do you mean?"

But Malaya had already bullied her way to the front of the line. Ikigai and Hari jogged to catch up.

Ladders helped the passengers climb onto the Turtle's shell, where they dropped coins for payment into a collection bowl. The Turtle spoke and Malaya interpreted for Ikigai. "She said we are slow." Malaya broke into a deep, gut-busting cackle. "It's funny, because, she's a turtle, and she's calling us…" Ikigai laughed as well, not so much at the Turtle's joke, but at Malaya's reaction. Hari watched them and smiled.

The passengers found seating in the damp carriage fixed to the olive specked shell of the Giant Turtle.

The creature waddled clumsily into the sea. In the water, the awkward turtle was a different beast. She submerged her head and limbs, kept her shell above water, and kicked her flippers gracefully, propelling herself forward with elegant speed.

It was day still. The ocean's cobalt blue, rushing by as they rode the Giant Turtle, tinted the complexion of everything. Ikigai watched the Beautiful Lady shrink into a small hazy pyramid in the distance. But halfway to their destination, the Turtle came to a stop, floated in the open water, raised her head, and spoke in that disarmingly soft voice. Malaya cackled again. "She says she has a cramp in one of her flippers." Ikigai told Hari what happened. He shook his head. The other passengers grumbled and stood and dropped more coins in the collection bowl. Malaya winked at Ikigai and said, "The hidden fees will surprise you."

Ikigai faced Hari. "Apparently this Turtle is corrupt."

Hari shrugged. "Just pay her."

Ikigai gritted her teeth. "I don't participate in bribery. It's a rule of my homeland."

Ikigai repeated for Malaya what she had just said to Hari. Malaya walked toward the Turtle's head, exchanged a few words with the beast, then returned to Ikigai and Hari. "She says her cramp is getting worse. If she sinks, everyone will have to swim. Or drown."

The passengers glared at Ikigai and her compatriots. Many ranted furiously. "They're mad at you," Malaya said.

"I got that," Ikigai responded. "I'm not paying any bribes."

Amongst shouts of anger and panic, the Giant Turtle began to sink slowly into the cobalt sea.

★★★

If you sink into a world, who's truly to blame? If I sunk into Lily-world, into the mire of her word games, what fault was that of hers? The quicksand is what it is. You are the one acting upon it, pushing into it, forcing it to adapt to your weight and envelop you.

"How come you won't talk about your last school?" I had asked Lily one chilly but dry day. It was the weekend. Her mother, who I never saw, kindly left an old, torn up sofa out on the front lawn of their bungalow home. It was comfortable. We sat on it and watched the cars in the road pass under the almost bare trees.

"How come you won't talk about kindergarten?" she shot back, surprisingly short-tempered.

"Kindergarten?" I was confused.

"Where'd you go?"

"Where'd I go where?"

"To kindergarten."

"I dunno."

"What was your teacher's name?"

"I don't... Who cares?"

"You don't remember."

"Guess not."

"But you remember the pink chalk you took? Off the blackboard?"

Wow. She got me there. "Whatever," I said.

"I remember my kindergarten? My teacher's name was Ms. Belle, like the movie."

"Good for you."

"Very good for me. Perfectly normal to remember kindergarten?"

"You're doing it again."

"What?"

"Saying questions that aren't questions."

"That's how I talk?" she said and laughed. I laughed too. Even when I was annoyed with her she cracked me up. Then she froze and said, "There's a cloud."

She touched my arm and nodded toward the road. A car lingered on the street in front of us. "There's a cloud," she repeated. "You don't see it?" It was an old-school car, a Lincoln or a Buick, I can't remember exactly, black or maybe gray. I grabbed Lily's hand.

The driver-side window rolled down. I couldn't see the driver's face because it was covered with a big camera that flashed a bright light twice. Then the car sped away.

"Weird," I remarked. The car turned the corner and disappeared. Lily trembled.

"What was that?" I asked.

Lily muttered, "They called my mom. They told her he was gone."

"He's gone?" I repeated. I didn't know who *he* was, but I somehow knew it was important to confirm this.

She nodded and sucked in her lips. "That cloud shouldn't be there like that."

"Who's *he* Lily?" I whispered.

"Heavy. No baby."

CHAPTER 8

Before we return to Ikigai's predicament with the Great Turtle, let us revisit those other forces set in motion before she'd set off on her journey to the Island of the Keepers of the Key…

Bayani was wet and he was angry at being wet. The Brothers should have arrived by now and a downpour had begun, soaking the dirt of the village alley in which he stood. He needed to run home as soon as possible and ensure the dilapidated tarp that made for the roof of his home blocked at least most of the rain. His chief concern was that he and his baby sister could find themselves with a dry place to sleep as the night wore on.

The rain's pace hardened; striking its rhythm across the tin, canvas, plastic and wood of the homes in the maze of alleys that were the Village of the Storm. Bayani lost his patience and started the return route home with his baby sister at the forefront of his mind. Then a figure stepped out from the maze before him.

"Where are the others?" Bayani asked the man blocking his path.

"They are here. They are listening."

"You are late."

"We needed to make sure it was safe."

"Here? In the Village of the Storm? How could it not be?"

"Foreigners have already intruded, no?"

"That is why I called you."

"And we are here."

"The foreign warriors, they are traveling to the Island of the Keepers of the Key."

"But we are the Keepers of the Key. And only we are to step foot on our Island."

"Well, they're leaving in a few hours. They'll be stepping foot on it soon."

"Only because you and your friends spoke with them."

"They told us they sought Justice."

"Then why call us? Go, deal with your foreign friends and their Justice."

Bayani looked at his wet feet and shook his head with a snarl. "Their Justice is empty and it is weak. It is a lie that covers the true plans all foreigners have when they come to this place. They come to hurt us. They come to help us. But the hurt and the help is all the same."

The man stared hard at Bayani, appraising, evaluating and categorizing the boy's merits and deficiencies. He laid the weight of Bayani's heart on the plate of a balance scale, whose other side held a whole history of anger and subversion.

"You are young," the man finally said. "It is good you see this now. It is good you came to us." The man paused and squinted in thought. "Hm," he mused. "Kidnapping a foreigner, a warrior no less, will bring attention to the cause."

Now, back to Ikigai and the Great Turtle...

"Damn it!" Ikigai shouted, not caring what her daughter would think of her cursing, if she ever got to tell this story.

Everyone's feet became wet with the seawater that crept upwards while the Giant Turtle started to sink. Tark, luckily, could flutter above their heads. "You quit it right now!" Ikigai screamed as she ran up the slippery shell toward the Turtle's head. "I am not paying you another peso! I am an honest warrior from another land and I am going to complete my mission here." And with that, Ikigai displayed the badge of her Authority to the Turtle who turned her great, leathery head to listen to the curious, shouting, little warrior.

Malaya stepped behind Ikigai. "She has no idea what you're screaming about."

Ikigai stamped her feet on the shell of the Giant Turtle and repeated her tirade for Malaya in the Language of the Rising Sun. Malaya interpreted for the Turtle.

"Ah," the Turtle chuckled. "Tell the little foreigner her Authority means nothing here."

Malaya did so. Ikigai gritted her teeth and re-interpreted for Hari. Hari faced Malaya. "Then tell this Turtle mine does," he said and displayed his Authority as well.

"I see," the Turtle conceded. "That is different." The Great Turtle rose. The passengers' grumbling died down, replaced by their quiet scrutiny of Ikigai and her companions.

"Thank you," Ikigai told Hari.

"I don't know if I should be thanked," he replied doubtfully. "Displaying our Authority here was not a good idea."

The Turtle swam on. The blue of the sea gained a tint of green and crashed on a beach with sands layered in white, creamy brown, and a pale shade of red. They'd arrived at the shore of the Island of the Keepers of the Key.

"Wow," Ikigai said, agape. "It's paradise."

The passengers watched her intently.

Hari looked about nervously.

Shortly after their discussion, Mickey and the Village Captain found Tala at her home in the maze of alleys, washing clothes. She scraped the laundry up and down, across the ridges of a wooden washboard in a small basin of soapy water. She was lost in the rhythm of raking wood and wet clothes slapping against the basin's tin. Mickey approached her with caution as one might approach a sparrow, and she noticed this, and he noticed that she noticed this, but she said nothing to acknowledge his presence. Mickey, with the Captain interpreting, initiated the conversation. "I'm guessing you have no desire to speak with me."

"No need to guess," Tala replied.

"I'm really sorry for what happened to you."

"It did not happen to me. It happened to my son."

"I don't have children. But if I did, I imagine whatever happened to them would feel like it happened to me too."

Tala seized up, and threw the laundry forcefully down, splashing soapy water everywhere. Her eyes flared with rage but just for a moment. The fire quickly subsided, replaced by an accepting sadness.

"Why are you here? To sell your Justice? Let us move on."

"I'm not selling anything, Tala. I'm trying to do the right thing."

"My sister has gone with your friends to retrieve her Freedom to travel with you and her son. Do you need more little boys to revisit the horrors of the days their Innocence was stolen?"

"I need to make sure Tagagawas stays in jail, so he can't do this again."

"Again, your friends are retrieving Malaya's Freedom."

"What if they fail?"

Tala said nothing. Mickey continued, "It's an arduous journey. What if something goes wrong? Or they just can't find it? We'll have nothing, and Tagagawas will go free."

"I'm sure they'll be fine. Your girlfriend, it seems she doesn't like to fail."

"She's not my girlfriend. But why'd you say that? You think she likes me? Don't answer. It's beside the point. You're right, she doesn't like to fail. That's why she asked me to pursue a back-up plan."

Tala looked at her laundry. Her long face and sad eyes should have aged her beyond her years, but somehow, she still maintained a semblance of youth. "What do you want?" she finally said.

"I would like, with your permission, to acquire the Testimony of your son, Kidlat."

"I have no Freedom to travel with Kidlat either," she told him warily.

"I would also like, with your permission, to escort you back to your place of birth and retrieve your Freedom. Where were you born?"

"I was born after Malaya, after our parents left the Island of the Keepers of the Key and came here to the Island of Traders. I was born on this Island, in the City of Holy Swords."

"That's a half day's journey away," the Captain explained.

"A half day's… That's nothing," Mickey responded. "It's still daylight, we could head out now. We could have your Freedom today. Are you willing to let Kidlat provide his testimony?"

"We will retrieve my Freedom first. Then I will let you speak with Kidlat."

"I have to justify to the Chiefs in my homeland why I'm spending money helping you get your Freedom. If I don't have Kidlat's testimony, I can't help you."

"Your rules, not mine," she said. "We retrieve my Freedom first or you don't speak with Kidlat."

Mickey thought about this. "You know what? Deal."

"The day is half over. If I go with you, we'll have to return at night. I am not traveling anywhere with you at night."

"If we can get your Freedom today, let's not delay. Do you have family still in the City of Holy Swords? Family you can stay with for the night?"

"Aunts and uncles I have not seen in a long time."

"Good, you stay the night with them, I'll stay at an inn. We'll head back here tomorrow morning."

"Then I will also lose a day's wages," Tala told him, pointing to the clothes in her basin. "I do this laundry for the people of our

Village. This is how I make my living. This is how Kidlat and I do not starve."

Mickey ruminated again. "I'll give you money for your lost wages. Anything else?"

"That should be fine." Tala raked the laundry. "We'll leave when I finish this."

Ikigai didn't want to leave the beach of the Island of the Keepers of the Key. She didn't want to stop sifting the multi-colored sand through her fingers, but the sun would soon set, and they needed to take advantage of the daylight left to search for Malaya's Freedom. Ikigai breathed in salty, humid air. Small, paved roads led up a hill into a beachfront town whose architecture varied from the influences of different conquerors over the ages. The beach was mostly empty. A few fishermen in small rowboats mulled about in the sea not far from shore. The Giant Turtle waded into the open water and Ikigai, Hari and Malaya could see her speaking with one of the fishermen. That fisherman quickly rowed to shore, left his boat on the beach, and jogged toward town. Hari narrowed his eyes and asked Ikigai, "Can Malaya tell what the Turtle just said to that fisherman?"

Ikigai interpreted for Malaya, who responded, "Do I look like a dog? How would I hear that from here?"

Ikigai was too enraptured with the beauty of the place to be as concerned as Hari. She watched Tark hop in the multi-colored sands, from white to brown to red, pecking and searching for tasty beetles and pill bugs to munch on. Ikigai watched the fishermen and the few people who moved about coming to or from the town on the hill. The people were sparsely dressed. It was obvious they didn't have much. Or did they? They had this beach, they had this sea, and they had a town, small and rundown as it was, that overlooked it all. Meanwhile, back in Ikigai's homeland, people worked and strived in small, cramped spaces and longed for a day when they could spend time right here, in a place like this, where Ikigai was sifting sand through her fingers. So, no, she didn't want to leave. But she had a job to do.

"Do you remember," Ikigai asked Malaya, "where you were born?"

"It would be terrible if I didn't, huh?" Malaya replied. "Come all this way, survive a sinking Turtle, and, oops, Malaya forgot how to get to her birthplace."

Ikigai read Malaya's features, not sure if she was joking or not. Malaya rolled her eyes. "Come on," she instructed. "This way."

Malaya led them up a road to the town on the hill. Tark flew above, enjoying the open air. The town was old but looked less rundown as they walked through; its age giving it a sense not of decrepitude, but of history. It was not crowded, only a few denizens walked about. The denizens nodded politely, but Ikigai could tell they were watching her closely.

Malaya appeared not to care who watched them and led them to a little house, painted bright green, off a side road. Frog grass and pasture weed grew wild around the home on a small parcel of land. Malaya knocked on the door. A man answered. They exchanged words. Then Malaya beckoned Ikigai and Hari to follow her inside.

It was dim inside the house, little natural light entered from the windows. The house was small and bare, furnished only with one bed and one drawer. The floor was covered with dusty tiles. Four small children, two boys and two girls, ran about, playing a game that had no rhyme or reason to anyone but themselves. A tired-looking woman sat on the bed nursing an infant. The man's eyes were hard and untrusting. He and Malaya exchanged more words.

Tark fluttered into Ikigai's hands and she placed him in her satchel. She touched Malaya's shoulder and asked, "Do you know these people?"

Malaya replied, "No, but they remember my family. From the days when my family lived in this house, before they left this place." Malaya led Hari and Ikigai back outside and behind the house into what would have been a backyard if it were landscaped, but it wasn't. The growth of bushes, grass and weeds tangled into a small, dense, personal forest for the family that now lived there. The setting sun bathed the yard in red and orange and it was wild, but it was beautiful. Ikigai had to ask as she thought of Malaya's current living conditions in the slum of the Village of the Storm, "Why did your family leave this place?"

Malaya sucked her teeth and ignored the question. "Dig," she instructed. "Right here."

"With what?" Ikigai inquired.

Malaya ignored this question too. Focusing on a specific spot on the land, she began pulling up grass and weeds. Ikigai and Hari chipped in, and the four children ran outside and around Malaya, Hari, and Ikigai, laughing and trying to catch each other. As the children played, Ikigai, Hari and Malaya wore the plant growth down to the soil, then scooped out dirt with their hands. The soil was soft and warm and felt almost like the sand Ikigai didn't want to stop sifting through her fingers.

They dug and dug and then a bright light silently erupted from the earth and momentarily blinded them. Malaya laughed, and her laugh had a weightless quality that blended into the giggles of the children playing around. The children stopped and wide-eyed, approached the three adults digging in their backyard.

Malaya reached into the dug hole and pulled out her Freedom.

She held it carefully in the palm of her hand and the children crowded over her shoulder to get a better look. It had a pale blue tint and if you stared at it too long, you would simply see spots before your eyes before you could make out any definite shape to

it. Ikigai and Hari laughed as well, from joy at the success of their
mission, and from wonder at the beauty of what they had helped
their new friend retrieve. A tear rolled down Malaya's cheek and
she looked at Ikigai and they shared a smile. Malaya placed her
Freedom in her satchel and stood.

Malaya led them back into the house where, once their eyes
adjusted to the dim light, they saw the woman still nursing her
infant. The children's shouts and giggles danced in from outside.
Malaya and the woman exchanged words, which Ikigai imagined
were expressions of thanks.

Hari stiffened and touched Ikigai's shoulder. "Where did the
man of the house go?" he asked. Ikigai saw no one else in the home,
and found herself nervous as well, for the whine at the base of her
skull had returned. Malaya and the woman continued to talk.

But in the corner opposite the nursing woman, the Emperor's
Ghost appeared, in the form of a man, silently pointing at the
door.

Ikigai grabbed Malaya by her arm. "We need to go," she urged,
and pulled Malaya out of the house with Hari directly behind.

"Rude as always," Malaya complained, then drew up short as
they saw, coming up the road toward them, the man of the house.
He was not alone. Behind him were ten more men: scarves covering their faces, weapons openly displayed: knives, axes, bows
and arrows.

"This is why my family left this place," Malaya explained,
annoyed. "Too many people killing and dying for what they say
they love."

"The Brothers of the Keepers of the Key," Hari said. "The
Turtle told them we were here. Ikigai, throw your Authority
away." Hari took his badge and waved his arm behind his back to
toss it without the Brothers noticing.

Ikigai hesitated as she held her Authority. She had been

trained never to part with it. "Do it!" Hari hissed through clenched teeth.

So she did. Ikigai threw her Authority into the bushes nearby. Then she opened her satchel and whispered as the Brothers of the Keepers of the Key approached, "Tark, you awake?" The Garuda mewed softly. "We need you to carry a message," Ikigai continued. "And when you return, land in the bushes over there. Do not let these guys see you."

It was still pre-dawn, but SSA Brent Oberley's cell phone only rang once before he answered Geri's call. Oberley dispensed with any greetings. "You hear from Ikigai?" he asked.

"Good news or bad?" Geri responded.

"Bad."

"Let's start with good: Ikigai got Malaya's birth certificate in Claveria."

"I ordered her not to go there."

"Okay, bad. She's still in Claveria. She shot me an email a few minutes ago saying she's run into a contingent of New People's Army fighters."

Geri could tell from the silence that Oberley probably went sick in his stomach and was forcing himself to remember the ABC's of crisis management. Always. Be. Calm. "You mind heading into my office?" he finally said. "I'll get FBI personnel in the Philippines on the line. If Ikigai's communicating with you, we need you there."

"Oh, I'm already Dick Tracy."

"What's that?"

"I'm on my way."

The Brothers of the Keepers of the Key approached. The man who lived in Malaya's old family home, the one who brought the

Brothers, ran past Ikigai, Hari, and Malaya, and into the house. A moment later he stepped outside, wife and children trailing behind, and they ran up the road away from this scene as quickly as possible.

Before the Brothers were within earshot, Malaya told Ikigai, "You two say nothing." Hari looked at Ikigai questioningly, wondering what Malaya said, and Ikigai put her finger to her lips. Hari nodded.

The Brother who appeared to be the leader of the group stepped forward, a grimy white bandanna with red spots covering his face. He looked over the three. Malaya, thoroughly unfazed, also stepped forward and exchanged words with this leader in the Language of the Keepers of the Key. They appeared to be heated words. Then the leader slowly removed his bandanna, revealing the angriest face Ikigai had ever seen on another human being, and bore his eyes into Malaya's. Malaya looked down and spoke in a softer tone. The leader continued to press, as if he were asking more questions, questions that Malaya seemed increasingly flustered with. One of the Brothers went into the nearby bushes and began looking around. Damn it, Ikigai thought, they probably saw us toss our Authority and they're looking for it. To make matters worse, from the corner of her eye, Ikigai saw a light flash briefly in the bushes. Tark had followed Ikigai's instructions to hide. Ikigai's heart raced as she searched the faces of the Brothers, looking for a sign that any of them had noticed the flash signaling Tark's return. A second Brother joined the first and searched in the bushes. Oh no, Ikigai thought, if they find Tark, they'll know we sent a message.

The Brothers poking around the bushes were in the area where Ikigai and Hari threw their Authority. The leader continued asking Malaya questions, then pointed at Malaya's satchel. The bright blue light erupted as Malaya showed him her Freedom. They're going to take her Freedom away from her, Ikigai thought, we did all this for nothing. The Brothers convened around their leader and muttered amongst themselves.

Then the Brothers faced the three and stepped aside.

Malaya walked through them confidently and beckoned toward Ikigai and Hari who quickly followed her lead. "Just keep walking," Malaya whispered to Ikigai as they headed away from the Brothers. Hari did not need Ikigai to translate, the situation spoke for itself.

Ikigai let out a low whistle, hoping Tark would hear and follow them unseen.

***

In Portland, the colors were fading. Winter stripped the red, gold and orange of the leaves to just brown, then washed them away with sheets of rain. Unpredictable in its capacity for humor or hubris, the season sometimes toyed with Lily and I, playfully tickling our faces, but mostly it launched offensive attacks: gales of stabbing wind that forced shivers from our bodies in the cold wet that darted everywhere. One day, we huddled together, the polyester of our hooded raincoats squeaking as we protected each other as best we could from the elements creeping their way into our bubble.

We were waiting outside school to be picked up by our respective parents so we wouldn't have to walk home in the cold. My Dad's car arrived first. I looked at Lily, concerned. "It's okay," she said. "My mom's coming."

I hugged her, then jumped into the warm back seat of Dad's car. But as Dad drove away, I saw Lily in the rear-view mirror, walking down the road in the same direction we were driving. "Her mom's not coming," I said. "Dad, we have to drive her home."

"Given what happened last time she saw me, I don't think she'd get in the car."

"Let me out then," I said, panicking at the memory of the strange vehicle from a few days ago.

"Junior, no."

"Let me out!" I screamed so hard it hurt my throat.

"No! Not appropriate. That is not—"

"Fuck you!" I screamed, remembering the flash of the camera, Lily muttering about the babies of the heavy and the light, the stone she almost threw away. *Heavy, no baby. Just pedal. Just go.* "Let me out!"

"You stop it!" Dad screamed back and pulled the car over. "I do not care what shitty behavior your mother has been modeling for you, you do not pull this shit. You do not talk to me like this!"

Even through the panic, something inside me smiled. I had him. I was the one who could make him lose control. And now it was my turn to drop a hydrogen bomb. "If I'm like Mom, it's because I care about other people."

That did it. Dad turned red and shouted even louder. It was an attempt to frighten me into submission with a show of force. He pounded his fist on the steering wheel. He turned and put his finger in my face and screamed about respect. He grounded me for decades. He threatened to keep me from hanging out with Lily. And while he distracted himself with his abject fury, I clicked open my safety belt and unlocked the door, watching Lily get closer to our car from the rear-view mirror.

"You are my responsibility," he shouted. "No one else's child is my responsibility."

I glared at him, silent. He knew what he said the moment it came out of his mouth, a perfect expression of the difference between those like him, and those like his ex-wife, those like his daughter. Greg Warner, my father, he was a good man. But he was not a warrior.

I opened the door and ran out of the car toward my friend.

He did not try to stop me.

★★★

It wouldn't be until much later that Malaya would tell Ikigai exactly what was said between her and the leader of the Brothers. Ikigai would be glad she hadn't understood the exchange that occurred between them. The exchange had actually gone something like this:

"Why are you idiots bothering us?" Malaya began. The leader, taken aback by her forwardness, found his confidence greatly decreased as he realized he didn't appear as menacing as he believed. "We... we have been informed there are foreigners about the Island."

"Take that silly rag off your face, so I can talk to you like a human being."

The leader obliged and his face looked as if it was twisted into a permanent snarl. He was an unfortunately ugly man. "Oh, no wonder," Malaya muttered as she looked down to avoid eye contact. "Put it back on, please."

A Brother in the group stopped himself from snickering and meandered into the nearby bushes, attempting to look as if he were busy searching for other foreigners, so he wouldn't burst out laughing and further embarrass his leader.

"I will not put it back on," the leader pronounced in the scariest voice he could muster. "Do you know anything of these foreigners?"

"What would I know of foreigners?" Malaya said. "Do I look like a foreigner? Do I sound like a foreigner?"

"You speak our language, but I have never seen you. I know everyone on the Island of the Keepers of the Key."

"That's because my family left the Island before your father saw your mother and got really excited about, you know, holding her hand."

Another member of the group put his head down, withheld a guffaw, and walked into the bushes to join his friend in trying to appear busy.

"Why did your family leave the Island?" the leader asked.

"Because of extortionists like you, making them pay your revolutionary taxes."

"We are not just extortionists!"

"True that! I remember you're also kidnappers."

"Well... if we make things so bad here, then why have you returned?"

"To retrieve my Freedom. I need to travel."

"Where?"

"Really none of your business."

"Let me see it."

Malaya opened her satchel and the light emitted briefly blinded everyone. The Brothers muttered amongst themselves, and one said to the leader, "If her Freedom was here then she is from this Island. She's telling the truth."

"Then who are these two?" the leader demanded of Malaya, nodding toward Ikigai and Hari. "Where are they from?"

"Do they look like foreigners to you? They are my husband and his sister. I couldn't travel out here alone."

"Why do they not speak?"

"My husband is mute and my sister-in-law is slightly insane. Actually, she's very insane. I can't even begin to tell you. She's also very jealous of me. You know, competitive, always for the attention of her big brother. It's a little weird. A few nights ago, when we were..."

"Just... shut up! Please, shut up," the leader said, and convened with his Brothers. "I don't know, man," one of the Brothers said. "We're looking for foreign warriors. They don't look too foreign."

208 A CRIME IN THE LAND OF 7,000 ISLANDS

"And they don't look like warriors," another giggled. The leader nodded. "Let them through. There's only one way off the Island. If we are mistaken, our Brother at the beach will alert us."

Then the Brothers faced the three and stepped aside.

Malaya walked through them confidently and beckoned toward Ikigai and Hari who quickly followed her lead. "Just keep walking," Malaya whispered to Ikigai as they headed away from the Brothers. Hari did not need Ikigai to translate, the situation spoke for itself.

Ikigai let out a low whistle, hoping Tark would hear and follow them unseen. Then a voice shouted from behind them, "Hoy!"

"Keep walking," Malaya said again. But Ikigai turned to see what was going on and what she saw made her blood course faster. The two Brothers who wandered into the bushes held up objects that glinted in the light of the setting sun. One Brother said, as Malaya would later explain, "The Turtle said they'd have these."

They had found the badges of Authority.

"Okay," Malaya told Ikigai. "We should run now." The leader pointed at them and shouted and the three ran as the Brothers of the Keepers of the Key gave chase.

"Now," Mom interrupted her flow. "Let us take another detour and peer in on the actions of Tagagawas."

"What!" I shouted. "You can't stop now!"

"I'm not stopping. I'm only pausing at a cliffhanger to discuss an important subplot. It's a good way to add tension to a story and keep you on the edge of your seat."

"W-T-F!"

"Oh, please curse again. Let's see if you hear this story from the tomorrow I knock you into."

"I didn't curse." I lowered my voice. "I said W-T-F."

"That counts."

"I won't do it again."

"Good."

Now Tagagawas sat in a cell in his prison half a world away. He was joined again by his Defender and the two Shadow Warriors whose services he contracted. The Shadow Warriors sat beside Tagagawas, pulled forth a packet, and placed this packet on the table they shared.

Tagagawas opened the packet and inspected its contents. "Wow," he exclaimed, surprised. "This is good. This is very good."

"How may we be of further service?" the female Shadow Warrior asked.

"Complete what I could not," Tagagawas replied. "Pay a visit to the Village of the Storm."

"Returning to Ikigai, Hari, and Malaya…" Mom went on.

"Wait," I told her. "Hold on! What was in the packet?"

Mom looked at me sadly. "You know more answers than you give yourself credit for."

The mist came back and now I really didn't like where this story was going.

She was right. I knew exactly what was in that packet. I just couldn't bring myself to say it. If I said it, it would be the first domino tipping, resulting in a cascade of more questions. Questions like, "Mom, how do you know that I know what was in that packet?" I could not bring myself to ask even that. That would have been the brave question to ask because that question would have expressed accountability for my own knowledge. But it's hard for an eleven-year-old to take responsibility for what she knows. It's so much easier to place that responsibility, that awareness, back on the adults charged with your care. So instead,

I asked the weak question, the childish question: the question that returned the onus of all guidance to my mother. "Why don't you just tell me what's going on?"

"I am," she informed me patiently. "I'm telling you everything, just like I promised."

I searched her eyes. I found no trace of dishonesty. No trace of wavering or indecision. "But when all is said and done, baby," she continued, "I'm not going to tell you anything you don't already know."

I shuddered.

Mom's eyes met my own. "I warned you, Ikigai," she said, using my real name again. "I warned you this would be an act of war. Do you want me to continue?"

"Yes," I whispered.

They ran as hard as they could, Ikigai leading by virtue of being the fastest. "Tark!" she screamed. "Come on!" Tark appeared with a caw and a flash of light and flew beside Ikigai, chirping loudly. "You'll have to tell me the return message later!" Ikigai yelled. The sun had almost set and Ikigai realized a few seconds into their sprint that running straight to the beach was not a good idea. She diverted into the forest off the side of the road. Hari and Malaya followed. The best thing they could do now was hide.

Ikigai, Hari, and Malaya plunged into the dense underbrush of the forest, dodging the leaves of the raintrees. They split up, staying within each other's view and found a cluster of eucalyptus to hide among. They burrowed into the vegetation of the forest floor and leaned on the trees while the Brothers crashed about nearby, searching. Tark nuzzled into Ikigai's hands. She gently pinched his beak closed.

The sun set and the sky grew cloudy. This made it hard for Ikigai, Hari, and Malaya to see each other. This was a good thing.

Especially since a Brother was stepping closer, rustling leaves and snapping twigs until he was within striking distance of Ikigai. To strike was something she considered. But even if she won the fight, he'd scream, and his nine Brothers would be upon them. She stayed motionless, and waited, as he stepped around looking, but not seeing. His eyes could not penetrate the dark of the cloudy forest night.

The Brother stalked off, and Ikigai heard his companions join him. The Brothers shouted words Ikigai did not understand. She heard them take off in multiple directions. Some headed back to the road. Ikigai figured they were setting up at different checkpoints where she and her compatriots would have to pass. The best thing to do now was wait.

Hours passed. The sky grew cloudier, covering any light from the stars or the moon and it began to rain. Ikigai's muscles grew tight from lack of motion. She shifted, restless. They did not want to wait too long. The dark of night was their friend.

The warm raindrops bouncing off the thick vegetation were lulling and Ikigai forced herself to not doze off. It did not help that Tark had fallen asleep. She placed him in her satchel. Then, as if to assist her in staying awake, a loud laugh reverberated throughout the woods. She squinted hard to see Hari and Malaya, thinking it was one of them. She could barely make out their outlines against the nearby trees. She waved. They waved back. No, it was not Hari or Malaya laughing. But whoever or whatever the origin of this laughter, it was soon joined by others, until it sounded as if the whole forest was giggling.

The laughter was so loud it occurred to Ikigai she could get away with walking to her friends, for the laughter drowned out the sound of her steps. The three joined each other by the tree Hari leaned against.

"What is that? Is that the Brothers?" Ikigai whispered to Hari.

"*Kuliglig*," Hari said. "The laughing cicadas. They are in the trees."

"They're loud," Ikigai said. "Let's go now. Any Brothers still in the forest won't hear us moving around." She turned to Malaya and told her, "Let's go."

The three headed out of the forest, laughter and rain echoing throughout. They reached the road, where a Brother sat against a tree. They froze. Ikigai's eyes adjusted. She could tell the Brother was motionless, but she couldn't see his eyes in the dark. She decided to take the risk and step forward. Her friends followed and the moment they passed the boundary between forest and road, the laughter stopped, leaving only the gentle patter of night rain. Ikigai shouldn't have wasted time doing what she did next but she couldn't help it. She stepped backwards, away from the road, over the boundary and into the forest again. Her ears were once more deafened by the laughter of the kuliglig. "Wow," she muttered. She stepped forward, back to the road. The laughter ceased. She continued toward the Brother, who did not react. As the three approached him, they could see his eyes. He was asleep. The pattering rain had lulled him into slumber.

They tiptoed past and went down the road, toward the beach, not sure how many more Brothers they would encounter. Surprisingly, none. The Brothers had been posted mostly in or near the forest. Ikigai and her compatriots continued down the road, through the town, past homes shut for the night, and made it back to the beach. The lapping waves and pattering rain made it feel as if the whole world was underwater. The sand slowed their steps.

"We need a boat," Hari suggested. Ikigai nodded. Hari pointed to a lone rowboat beached on the shore, likely the same boat left by the fisherman who spoke with the corrupt Giant Turtle:

a fisherman who, come to think of it, was probably one of the Brothers. It didn't matter now. Ikigai sprinted through the sand toward the rowboat, her companions behind. But when they got to the boat, they froze again. The Brothers were not that stupid. They knew this boat was the only way off the island. They'd posted one of their men inside it: a man who was also sleeping, snoring loudly. And there was no way to take the boat without waking him up.

CHAPTER 9

While my mother was having the adventure of a lifetime, I was staring at a rock.

I sat on the floor of my room in my pajamas: the organic cotton, blue flannel ones that made me feel super cozy. I needed to feel cozy given what I was doing. I'd pulled the Little Pouch of Randomness from my closet and dumped its contents on the floor. Pink dust from the old piece of chalk dispersed in the air. I waved it away. I focused on the rock, its luster and its hues. Its layers comprised shades of brown from yellowish to reddish to almost black, just like, just like... What was it just like?

The floorboards creaked outside and Dad lightly tapped on my door. He slowly pushed it open and poked his head in. I glared at him. Things were still tense.

"You brush your teeth?" he asked, tired.

I ignored the question and asked my own before my brain had time to process what was coming out of my mouth. "Where's the other one?" I demanded, holding up the rock.

Dad didn't react. That made me angry. I could tell it was the non-reaction of someone suppressing his reaction. It always amazed me how adults could do that.

"There were two of these," I said. "I remember now. Where's the other one?"

"Baby," he said gently and stepped inside. "Let's talk about what's coming up for you."

"No!" I screamed at him. "Just tell me what's going on! Where's the other one?"

He walked toward me with caution, hands outstretched, like he was approaching a wild animal. Why was he treating me like this?

"Leave me alone," I told him, the fight leaving me. I jumped into bed, holding the rock. "Leave me alone," I muttered as he stood over me, afraid to touch me.

He sighed and turned my light off. "I'm here if you want to talk," he said, before leaving my room.

I clutched the stone to my heart and cried myself to sleep.

Let's rewind a bit. For when Ikigai, Hari and Malaya were still on the Island of Traders, arguing with the Great Crane of the East who refused to take them directly to the Island of the Keepers of the Key, which we now know was thoroughly understandable, Mickey the Expatriate was having a far easier time.

He escorted Tala to her place of birth, The City of Holy Swords. The journey was simple, especially since they hired a horse-drawn carriage to take them most of the way. Mickey had also convinced the Village Captain to accompany them so he could interpret between Mickey and Tala when necessary.

Tala's Freedom was to be found in the one-room school-house she attended as a child in the City of Holy Swords. Her old wooden school desk was in the same place, never having been moved. It was evening when they arrived, and the schoolhouse looked strange to Tala, dark and empty without the din and roar of groups of children. But she remembered. She remembered how this was the place where, often in boredom, and sometimes in inspiration, she dreamed of leaving the City of Holy Swords on the back of a Great Crane and finding the new and strange places that lay beyond her homeland's shores.

"We had to leave before I got very far in my schooling," Tala said, and the Captain interpreted for Mickey. "There was no work for my parents here. So we moved to the Village of the Storm. They are always building things around that village. Always there are jobs for building: many things to build and fix. They never fix the village, though."

Mickey listened, not sure how to respond to the sadness in Tala's voice or the frustration in the Captain's as he interpreted. Tala knelt by her old school desk and shook it. She removed a hollow wooden leg, which caused a flash of light. She peered down the opening of the leg and laughed, then turned it upside down and caught her Freedom as it tumbled out.

Mickey laughed with her. "Too easy," he said. "Let's get you to your family for the night. We'll head back to the village tomorrow." The Captain interpreted for Tala. She nodded and they left the schoolhouse and stepped out into the open air. The Village Captain clapped Mickey's shoulder. Mickey was surprised by the show of affection. "She has her Freedom now," the Captain said. "This will help her and her family no matter what happens."

"Just doing my job, bro," Mickey told him and held out his fist. The Captain smirked and bumped it with his own.

Mickey and the Captain escorted Tala to the home of her aunt and uncle nearby, then found an inn and retired for the night. The two men took their time waking the following day, enjoying a sumptuous brunch before picking up Tala, which was fine with her, she hadn't seen her relatives in years. They also took their time returning to the Village of the Storm in another horse-drawn carriage. On the ride back, Tala would often peek inside her satchel and gaze at the emitted light, and Mickey would smile at her joy and think to himself that these were the moments which gave meaning to the toils and sufferings of the warrior's path.

The sun was setting when they returned to the Village of the Storm. They went to the Captain's office to sit and talk. "I know this is hard," Mickey said to Tala, the Captain interpreting. "But it would be really helpful if I could document Kidlat's Testimony of Deepest Secrets now."

Tala replied, "You kept your word. I'll return shortly with my son." She left the office. Mickey and the Captain nodded at each other.

Then there was a blinding flash of light. Tark appeared, fluttering and chirping.

"Tark, buddy, everything okay?" Mickey asked.

The baby Garuda spoke in that otherworldly voice. "The Amazon has been courtesy copied on this message from Ikigai."

"Okay, what's up?"

"We have retrieved Malaya's Freedom. But we are now surrounded by the Brothers of the Keepers of the Key."

The Captain shut his eyes and shook his head. Tark perched on Mickey's shoulder. Mickey stroked the Garuda's beak. "Get back to Ikigai and Hari, buddy. They need you." Tark mewed and trembled.

"Future mount of Vishnu," Mickey said sternly, the gravel in his voice returning, "there is no time for fear."

The baby Garuda nuzzled into Mickey's neck, then fluttered into the air and cawed the bravest little caw he could. "That's what I like to hear," Mickey said. "Tell them to head toward the Beautiful Lady if they can escape." Tark vanished in a flash of light. Mickey grabbed his belongings and told the Captain, "If you can explain to Tala why I had to run off, that would be much appreciated."

"She will be beyond concern for her sister," the Captain replied.

"Tell her I'm on it."

"What will you do?"

Mickey set his face and headed for the door. "Call in lots of favors."

On the shore of the Island of the Keepers of the Key, Hari tapped the sleeping Brother's shoulder. The Brother awoke and sat up in the boat, groggy. He wore two bandannas, one covering the lower half of his face, the other covering his head. He was not an adept watchman, but he was still an obstacle. The Brother shook the sleep from his eyes then jumped to his feet, realizing three people were staring at him in the dark. He opened his mouth to shout, but Hari cracked a fist into his jaw. The Brother fell back asleep.

Ikigai jumped into the boat, searched the Brother, and pulled a knife from a sheath on his hip. She held the knife to the Brother's throat. But the rain stopped and the clouds parted for a moment, allowing moonlight to shine on the beach. In that moment, Ikigai saw, even with the bandannas covering his face and head, that this Brother was still more child than man.

Ikigai shook her head and handed the knife to Hari.

"He's going to warn the others," Malaya told her.

"Then he comes with us," Ikigai said. She jumped into the boat and gripped its two oars. "He can't warn anyone from the middle of the sea."

"And when we get to the other side?" Malaya asked.

"He can row himself back here and warn his people if he wants. That will give us a big head start."

Hari nodded, agreeing with this course of action. He pushed the boat, with Ikigai inside, into the sea, then jumped in and beckoned for Malaya to do the same, which she did. Hari reached for the oars. "Let me row," he suggested.

"We need you to sit behind the boy and keep him under control. I'll row."

"The whole way?" Hari asked, positioning the Brother at the front of the boat and sitting behind him.

Malaya sat behind Hari. Ikigai sat at the rear, where the oars were located. "We're wasting time," Ikigai said, and with that she began to row.

The sea appeared black as it reflected the starless night sky, and there was a thickness to the water, created from the depth and temperature of the ocean. This was not the small river Ikigai was used to paddling in her homeland. She had the distinct impression she was rowing through molasses. Her shoulders and lungs began to burn quicker than she'd expected.

"You know which way you're going?" Malaya asked. Ikigai looked around. She needed to keep rowing away from the shore of the Island of the Keepers of the Key. That much she knew. She looked up, finding no constellations to assist. Malaya laughed, "You don't know which way you're going."

Though he did not understand her words, Hari could guess what Malaya had said. "East," he told Ikigai. "Head east."

"How am I supposed to know east once the shore is out of sight?" Ikigai asked, flustered and already sweating. "It's pitch black out here."

"Ask Tark," Hari instructed.

"Yes," Ikigai agreed. Then she asked Malaya, "Can you get Tark out of my satchel?"

Malaya reached behind her, grabbed Ikigai's satchel and gently scooped out the baby Garuda. Tark awoke and mewed.

"Tark," Ikigai said between the heavy breaths of her burning lungs. "Can you point us east, toward the Island of the Beautiful Lady?"

Tark didn't even blink.

"Tark?" Ikigai said again. "East?"

No response.

"He's frozen," Ikigai informed them.

"We're going to die out here," Malaya said.

"Stop it!" Ikigai snapped. "What's our other choice, head back to the Brothers?"

Ikigai continued to row. Her shoulders warmed up with perspiration and their burning did not bother her as much. But she still struggled with the air, thicker and more humid than she was used to. She felt as if she were inhaling the sea itself.

After some time, three things happened that everyone feared would happen, but knew they would have to deal with eventually. First, they could no longer see the shore from which they had departed. Everything appeared as a dark watery sameness in all directions. Second, the sea became choppy with the invisible battle of its deeper currents, pushing and pulling the boat in ways Ikigai could fight only so much with the oars. These two things were challenging enough, making it impossible for the group to tell if they were still heading in the right direction. Then the third thing happened: the young Brother woke up.

The Brother sucked in his breath and looked around frantically. He tried to jump to his feet but Hari grabbed him in a headlock to keep him seated. The Brother was young but he was strong, and his struggle with Hari shook the boat violently. "Stop it, you idiot!" Malaya screamed at him in the Language of the Keepers of the Key. "You'll overturn the boat!"

"Overturn the..." the Brother croaked hoarsely as he began to comprehend exactly where he was. As it hit him, he shouted at the top of his lungs.

"See?" Ikigai told Malaya. "Nobody's hearing him out here."

Malaya and the Brother exchanged words. The Brother shivered. Malaya laughed.

"What are you saying?" Ikigai asked.

"I told him," Malaya explained, "that to say he screams like a little girl would be an insult to little girls. I never hear my daughter scream like that when she is afraid. I told him to calm down and enjoy the ride. Then he asked if we even know where we're going. I told him the truth, we don't. And that is why he is now shaking. Like a baby."

"Well, we're not turning back," Ikigai said, and continued to row. But, as the burn moved from shoulders to triceps to forearms, fingers, and lower back, Ikigai grew concerned. This was a hard and long row. She needed to travel in as straight a line as possible back to the Island of the Beautiful Lady. If she wavered too much, they might not make it.

Ikigai closed her eyes and focused on the humidity coursing through her lungs. She pondered what had brought her here, to this moment: a picture of a girl with screaming eyes. Screaming for what exactly, Ikigai would never know. According to Malaya she never would have screamed from fear. Was she screaming for help, then? Screaming to be seen?

Ikigai's mind shifted to what else had brought her here: tracking down Mickey and Hari in the Capital; chasing Malaya through the Village of the Storm; playing patintero with Bayani and Datu and Kidlat. Ikigai shook her head and opened her eyes. Those thoughts were stupid – stupid and pointless, and of no use to her in this time and place.

Ikigai stopped rowing. Her fingers found her Purpose in the pocket near her heart. She shut her eyes again and was about to pray. But before she began, a wordless sense of a deeper Faith surged through her with the humid air. It was a brief sense, but it was all she needed: a reminder that her actions, even when misguided, were taken in the spirit of Righteousness. And in that moment, Ikigai realized that to pray even, was to think. But there was no need for thought, no need for prayer. She herself was a prayer, a prayer in the screaming eyes of a little girl half a world away. Malaya too was a prayer, chased down like a feverish dream in the alleyways of a slum most will never see. The children of this land, whose Innocence was stolen, Bayani, Datu, Kidlat, even the angry Brother shouting on the boat, they too were prayers. And Hari, steady and sure in the impeccability of his speech and action. They were all prayers. The boat was a prayer. Its oars were a prayer. The wind and the choppy waves were a prayer. The thick air, the black sky, these were all prayers. So, there was no thing to pray to. There just *was*.

Malaya turned her body to look behind Ikigai and laughed again, harder than before. She pointed over Ikigai's shoulder.

"Steer more to your right!" she cried. Hari and the Brother turned their heads as well. Even in the dark, Ikigai could tell Hari was smiling.

"The Beautiful Lady," Hari said. "She is showing us which way to go."

Ikigai turned her head. The Beautiful Lady was erupting. Ikigai could make out the red glow of the lava spilling from her mouth in the distance. All Ikigai had to do was aim for that glow. She grasped the oars. "Keep correcting the course," she said to Malaya.

"A little more to your right," Malaya replied.

★★★

"Mount Mayon didn't erupt while she was there," Geri says, smiling. "But in the context of the story she made up for you, that makes sense. She did have to row toward it."

"She really rowed that whole distance?" I ask.

"Apparently, it was a little rowboat with a shitty motor thrown on the back. Halfway through, the motor gave out. She had to row the rest of the way. Still damned impressive. And she did have to use the volcano as a landmark to head in the right direction."

"How'd she see it?"

"Flashlight?" Geri says, laughing. "And there were lights on the dock at the Port of Pio Duran where she had to land."

"Okay, so, this next part is where things in her story get a little, fantastical."

"More so than the cranes, turtles, and baby Garudas?"

"No, it gets… I don't know. When I was a kid, I just took in everything. But thinking back on it, this part sticks out. It's like she wanted to make sure that out of everything she told me, she needed me to remember this next part."

"What'd she tell you?"

"You first. I think if I learn what happened in reality it'll help me think things through. What were you guys doing this whole time?"

"You guys?"

"You, Nate, Martel, the FBI."

"Losing weight."

"Huh?"

"'Cuz we were shitting tons of bricks."

The command post in the FBI Portland Division's office was a flurry of activity. Agents and analysts were throwing up the timeline of events that led to Ikigai's encounter with the New People's Army on whiteboards and Post-it pads. A screen projected a map of the Philippines for everyone's visual context.

SSA Brent Oberley strode through the chaos. "Geri," he called out, "anything?"

"Negative," Geri replied.

A landline desk phone on speaker emitted a ringback tone then clicked off. "Please keep trying," Oberley urged Nate, who sat by the phone. Nate nodded and dialed a series of digits again.

Another ringback tone. Then: "Mickey Sheptinsky."

"Listen up guys!" Oberley shouted and the room quieted down. "Mickey, where are you?"

"Who is this?"

"Mickey, this is Brent Oberley, supervisor of the Portland..."

"Hey Brent, what's up?"

"Where are you now? Are you with Ikigai?"

"No, sir. Ikigai escorted a victim's mother to—"

"Against my direct order."

"Maybe let me finish?"

"She sent an email about an hour ago. She's apparently encountered a contingent of New People's Army fighters."

"I got that email too."

"Can you get to her?"

"What do you think I'm trying to do right now, Brent? That's a lot of noise in the background, you got a command post going?"

"Affirm."

"You got the prosecutor there?"

Martel spoke up. "Yes, Mickey. Robert Martel here."

"Hi Robert. I had to help Tala, the woman I just escorted from Cebu City, find records from her freaking elementary school a few hours away in Toledo City to verify her identity, so she could get her birth certificate, so she could get her passport, so she can accompany her son to testify. And I can't bitch and moan about that as I would like to because Ikigai, who loves one-upping me on everything, is with a bunch of terrorists. You better take this all the way if we get these victims to the u.s. We're going through a lot of shit over here."

Martel was about to speak, but his cell rang. He stepped away to answer it.

"No response from the lawyer," Mickey said.

"He had to answer a call," Oberley told him. "Can you get to Ikigai?"

"I'm about to catch a flight to Manila, then I'll catch one down to Legazpi. If Ikigai's still in Claveria, I have to drive over land to the Port of Pio Duran, then catch a boat to the Port of Claveria. If I'm lucky and I haul ass I can maybe make it in five hours. Maybe."

"What can *we* do?" Oberley asked.

"I already sent her an email, but if you hear from Ikigai tell her to move toward Legazpi, if she can. I'm calling in some favors with the Philippine National Police there. I'll get them to travel with me toward Claveria. If Ikigai's moving toward us, we'll get to her quicker."

"I imagine the PNP don't want a kidnapped American in their territory."

"If they go with me, it's because they're worried about Hari."

"Either way, please tell the PNP we'd be grateful—"

"Let me off this phone so I can move." There was a click and a dial tone. Mickey was a lot more acerbic in real life.

Oberley sat down and took a breath. Martel walked back over to Geri. "Wife told you get your ass home for dinner?" she asked.

"Worse," Martel said. "Defense attorney."

"What does Weddle want now?"

"To verify the addresses of the victims Ikigai interviewed."

"It's all in the report."

"I told him just that."

"He needs that now for what?"

"Probably gearing up to send his private investigators to interview the victims."

"Shit."

"Yeah."

"They can do anything while they're out there: pay them off, threaten them."

"Yeah."

"That would have been a good thing to give Mickey a heads up about."

Martel shook his head in frustration. "One problem at a time, Geri."

"Okay," I say. "That makes sense."

"What's the issue with the way she told it to you?" Geri asks.

"Well…"

★★★

They finally reached the Port of the Western shore on the Island of the Beautiful Lady. Ikigai's arms and shoulders were stiff as iron, and her legs, cramped in one position in the overcrowded boat for several hours, felt like jelly. When she stepped out of the boat, into the shallow water where sea met land, her legs collapsed. She landed on all fours and crawled through the water toward the dryness of sand and stone.

Malaya rushed over and helped Ikigai to her feet. Ikigai leaned on her to keep moving. Hari kept his arm around the Brother's neck and the knife at the Brother's back.

"Let him go," Ikigai told Hari. Hari did, and the Brother ran back to shore. Ikigai heard a familiar rush of water and turned to see the Giant Turtle emerge from the sea. The Brother ran toward the Turtle and climbed onto her back.

"Seriously?" Ikigai said.

"Should have killed him," Malaya said. "That Turtle will get him back a lot quicker than the rowboat."

"There goes our head start," Ikigai muttered as they watched the Turtle swim away.

They quickly found their way to the main road that would take them back to the Eastern shore. As the blood returned to Ikigai's legs, she let go of Malaya and led them into a slow jog. But after a few minutes, she stopped. The humidity was getting to her. She vomited beside the road. Hari and Malaya traded a look of concern. Hari offered Ikigai water from his canteen which she gratefully sipped. She continued to move forward. Hari and Malaya followed.

They walked east, toward the Beautiful Lady, but the road was hard to see and the glow of the Beautiful Lady's eruption was dying down. She had been quick to anger this night, but quick to calm as well. Tark, snuggled safe in Ikigai's satchel, was still frozen, so he was no help. Ikigai worried that, in the dark, they could find themselves on a side road that would take them away from their destination. Then, two things happened.

First, the sky cleared. A soft glow of moon and starlight bathed the road. Now, they could see enough to safely stay on it. Ikigai looked up at the sky. She flinched. She looked away, then looked up again. She knew what she was seeing but needed a moment to process it.

It was the Milky Way.

Ikigai had never seen it like this. Nothing could compare to this view, here, in this distant land, on this remote island, where one could look at the sky and see it as one's ancestors had. It really looked like someone spilled the milk of stars across the roof of the world. And each star appeared clear and distinct with its own size, its own color, its own luminosity. Ikigai felt awe.

The second thing was the Emperor's Ghost.

Ikigai was so exhausted that when he appeared, she was uncertain as to whether she was really seeing him or not. The paradox of this thought did not escape her. The Emperor, in the form of a man, walked ahead of Ikigai, waving her on. She spoke to him, muttering at first, then louder as the conversation continued. "Go away," she told him. "I don't want your help."

"Have it anyway," the Emperor insisted underneath the whine at the base of her skull.

"You will never make up for what you did. You can do this as much as you like, for as long as you want. You will never undo your acts of destruction."

"I know."

"Then why are you here?" Ikigai's voice cracked as she shouted the question. Hari and Malaya traded another look of concern, but something told them to not interrupt as she shouted into what, to them, appeared to be nothing more than empty night.

"Still love you," the Emperor said.

The wind left Ikigai. She sunk to her knees. Malaya and Hari rushed to help her. She fought them off, still talking to the

Emperor's Ghost. "It was my fault," she sobbed. "I should have protected you. Mom was so hard on you after… Of course you turned out how you did."

"No excuse for me."

"I could have found out what you were doing. I could have stopped you."

"Not your fault."

"I ran my whole life into the ground. I got so caught up in the fight, in being a good warrior, fighting for Justice and Righteousness. I was so arrogant. I thought I was a hero. I thought I was going to change everything and save the world." The tears flowed freely down Ikigai's face. "I couldn't save my own family."

"Look around," the Emperor ordered.

She did: into the clear vastness of forest and sky. Though they'd traveled hours from the Western shore, she could still taste the sea in the air. If she listened hard, she could hear its waves in the distance. She looked up again at the Milky Way and sighed.

"This," the Emperor said, "is the world." The Emperor smiled, and for a moment, he no longer appeared as a ghost. He looked as real as Ikigai and Malaya and Hari. So real in fact, that Malaya and Hari saw him as well, gasping in surprise at the sudden appearance of this man in the night forest. Ikigai kept her eyes on him, not sure if she could trust what was about to happen, but the Emperor continued to smile.

Then he asked Ikigai a question, and before she could think to answer, he vanished.

Ikigai knew that was the last time she would ever see him. But his question lingered, echoing in the wind rustling through forest leaves, carried by the distant crashing of waves against the shore. Ikigai knelt on the road and pondered his question.

"How can you save the world," he had asked, "if you won't let the world save you?"

Ikigai felt a restlessness inside her and realized it just might have been some semblance of Inner Peace. It did not feel the way she always thought it would. It was calm but not so silent. There was a buzz to it, a vibration, a ringing chord that quivered underneath the cadence of the question posed by the Emperor.

Ikigai jumped to her feet.

"Who... What was that?" Malaya asked.

"I'll tell you some other time," Ikigai said. "Let's keep moving, the Brothers..."

Then they heard a rumble. They looked toward the Beautiful Lady but she was not erupting. The ground quaked and they frantically looked about. From their rear, a band of horses rushed toward them. The men upon those horses wore bandannas over their faces.

"It's the Brothers! Let's go!" Ikigai screamed. They ran but found themselves moving toward a similar rumble. They stopped, confused. Were they surrounded? Another band of horses appeared before them, men and women atop the equine beasts with bows and arrows in full view. This group did not look like the Brothers of the Keepers of the Key.

"Run toward them!" Hari shouted. There was no time to ask questions. Ikigai grabbed Malaya's hand as they ran toward the group, the Brothers at their rear, closing in. As the group they ran toward became easier to see, Ikigai screamed in delight as she recognized one of the men on horseback.

"Mickey!" she shouted.

"I am *so* saving the day!" he shouted back. "Move it! Get behind us!"

Mickey had brought a contingent of Hari's fellow Local Warriors. Hari ran to one of these warriors, who grabbed Hari's hand and swung him up onto her horse so he sat behind her.

Malaya did the same with the first warrior she saw. Ikigai ran straight for Mickey. He grabbed her hand and helped her up.

"I kinda meant hide behind us while we face these guys down," Mickey explained.

"I'm not hiding behind anyone," Ikigai responded.

"You're behind me right now."

Ikigai sucked her teeth, tapping the back of his head with her palm. Then she put her arms around his waist, you know, so she wouldn't fall off. "I'm not hiding though."

The two contingents, Local Warriors and Brothers of the Keepers of the Key, faced each other, arrows at the ready.

The rain started again.

"Do you see the problem?" I ask Geri.

"So what?" Geri says. "She got a little philosophical. She was telling a kid a story, explaining it as best she could to an eleven-year-old to get her to understand everything she needed to understand."

I rub my temples, frustrated.

"She was actually pretty accurate in telling you how it went down," Geri says.

"Listen up!" Oberley shouted above the din of the FBI command post. "It's ALAT Sheptinsky." The room quieted down. Oberley put the phone on speaker. "Mickey, we're here."

"Yeah," Mickey's voice came in. "We got her. We got Ikigai."

The room exploded in a roar of claps and cheers. "Quiet down!" Oberley had to shout. "Please!"

"Sounds like a lot of masturbatory self-congratulation going on over there," Mickey said. "Like you're the ones who called in favors with the Philippine National Police, rounded up a bunch of trustworthy and non-corrupt local officers with vans and rifles and stared down a group of armed and very angry New People's Army fighters *West Side Story* style."

Geri snickered and said under her breath to Nate, "Love this guy."

"More than me?" Nate joked.

"Never," Geri said.

"Is she okay?" Oberley asked Mickey.

"A bit dehydrated, but she's fine. Toughest agent I've ever met. Lot tougher than you guys sitting around your command post pretending you're helping resolve the crisis."

"Hey, Mickey," Oberley reminded him, "we're all on the same side here."

"If we were all on the same side you would have sent more agents with Ikigai. She wouldn't have been the only one out here risking her life for your squad's case."

"Shit just got real," Nate whispered to Geri.

"Listen, I can't tell you how much we appreciate..." Brent started.

"I know you appreciate it, Brent, because it'll sound great when you write it all up in that FD-954 for your next promotion. I'm sure you'll make it sound like you're the one who resolved this whole matter from your bullshit command post 6,000 miles away."

"Mickey, that's not fair. I ordered her to not go there."

"Yeah, and she went anyway, because she has balls. Because she knew it was the only way to bring this child predator to justice. And you knew she would. You knew that. That's why you sent her. People like you *use* people like Ikigai. You climb up the ladder off their guts. If she'd failed, you would have put your hands up and said, 'I ordered her not to.' But she succeeded. So, what are you gonna do? Write her up for not following orders? Course not. You're gonna ride on the coattails of her success as far up as you can go."

"Mickey, I can only imagine how stressed you are right now. I think..."

A dial tone. Mickey had hung up. Oberley stared ahead and took a breath. The room was silent. "Awkward," Nate whispered.

Geri whispered back. "We still need to tell them about the private investigators."

"That's the problem," I say.

"What, honey? I still don't get it." Geri responds.

"Mom's accurate in how she lays it all out, right? Mickey and the Philippine National Police showing up. The way she had to row from Claveria to Pio Duran."

"But...?"

"Look, it was months after she returned from the Philippines before she told me this story. Months she spent preparing it. She's got it carefully constructed up to this point, everything's consistent. Then, here, we get these gaping freaking plot holes."

"Like...?"

"The Great Turtle. Mom's the hero of this story. She's sharp. She's trained. She's competent. So how would she have been stupid enough to show the Turtle her badge?"

Geri smiles. "In real life, the Turtle was the ferry that took her to Claveria. She couldn't take the ferry back to Pio Duran to get away from the New People's Army because it wasn't coming back for two days, that's why they had to improvise and rent a fisherman's boat. It wasn't really the ferrymen she showed her badge to. She showed it to a bureaucrat in Claveria's Town Hall who was being a pain in the ass, telling them to come back some other time because the office was about to close, subtly letting them know she'd only stay and take care of them if they slipped her some extra pesos. Ikigai and Hari had to display their badges to get her to stop dicking around. The bureaucrat completed the late registration of Malaya's birth in Claveria, but she alerted the New People's Army there was an American FBI agent in their territory. Sounds like your mom conflated and simplified characters and events to explain them to eleven-year-old you."

"Fine," I say. "Then what about Hari's fellow Local Warriors?"

"That's what happened."

"Yeah, but again, in the story, they come out of nowhere, saving the day on horseback. We don't see or meet any of these guys before this point. Where'd all those horses come from, by the way? If there were so many horses around why didn't Mom and Hari and Malaya ride some instead of walking all that way?"

"In real life they were in cars. You're overthinking this."

"I don't think I've been thinking about it enough. Least not 'til now. Mom could have taken the time to set up the entrance of Hari's fellow warriors a little better."

"Okay, she missed something. It must have been pretty hard putting that story together."

"But why did she miss it? What does her missing these things in the telling of the story say about her state of mind when she was telling it?"

"I don't know, Junior. What?"

"She wasn't focused on the Turtle and the horses and Hari's fellow warriors because she was focused, overwhelmingly, on a different character in this story: the character whose existence required the biggest suspension of disbelief."

Geri narrows her eyes. "The Emperor's Ghost."

"Exactly! And no matter what, she wanted me to remember everything she said about her final meeting with the Ghost. Everything."

"But we know now who the Ghost was," Geri says patiently, "and why she told it to you like that." I clench my teeth.

Geri leans forward in her chair. "Does this have to do with that inaccuracy in the obituary?"

I nod.

Geri lets out a breath. "Oh, sweety…"

Now I'm fighting back tears and Geri smiles sadly. "Keep going," she urges. "What'd she say happened next?"

The Brothers of the Keepers of the Key were not stupid. They were far from their base and they were outnumbered. One by one they turned their horses and slunk off into the darkness.

"Yeah, that's right," Mickey shouted. "Go back home to your mommas." Ikigai dug a finger into his rib. He yelped.

"They're leaving," she said. "Don't provoke them."

"Whatever," Mickey said. "They don't understand what I'm saying anyway."

"I understood you," one of the Brothers called from the dark in Mickey's language. "And I will remember that you insulted my mother."

"No, no," Mickey called back. "I didn't insult your mom dude. I just said, I meant, like you should go back home to your mom."

"Just stop," said Ikigai.

"I was insulting you, really," Mickey continued. "'Cuz you know, you still need your mom? But I wasn't insulting your mom. I'm sure she's awesome!"

"Seriously! What is wrong with your friend?" one of Hari's fellow warriors asked.

"There is a thing most have," Hari replied, "a thing that stands between their inside thoughts and the words they use with others in the world. That man does not have that thing."

(I laughed at this point. "How'd you know Hari and his fellow warrior said that to each other?"

"What do you mean?" Mom asked.

"What language are they talking in: The Language of the Capital probably, right? How'd you know that's what they said to each other?"

"So observant," Mom winked. "Maybe I made that part up.")

The warriors turned their horses and rode toward the sun that was starting to peek through the clouds that were kissing the mouth of the Beautiful Lady. Ikigai wrapped her arms tighter around Mickey's waist as the horse's strides jostled her. It was a struggle to stay awake. She passed in and out of consciousness.

When they reached the Eastern shore, they dismounted and parted ways with Hari's fellow warriors. Mickey had to carry Ikigai in his arms. She fought, of course, but it was no use. "Come on, lady," Mickey insisted. "You've done enough. Let someone else be the hero for once."

She smacked him in the face, lightly, and said, "Fine."

"Thank God you're so small and light and clearly watch what you eat," he said.

"And... moment ruined," said Ikigai.

Mickey, Hari, Malaya and Ikigai approached a Great Crane of the East who waited by the shore. A caw sounded from Ikigai's satchel. "Ah," Ikigai muttered. "Now he wakes up." Tark chirped loudly. "Oh yeah, you still have a message for me."

"Probably the one I sent," Mickey remembered.

"Go ahead, Tark," said Ikigai.

"Ikigai," Tark relayed in that otherworldly voice. "It's Mickey. Head toward the Beautiful Lady, if you can escape."

"Thank you, Captain Obvious," Ikigai teased Mickey.

Mickey chuckled. "Tark, buddy. Send a message to the homeland. Tell them I have Ikigai."

After that, truthfully, everything was a blur. They flew back to the Island of the Capital, then to the Island of Traders, flights through which Ikigai mostly slept. She came to when they landed on the Island of Traders and found an inn closer to the Southern shore from where the Cranes took flight. "We'll stay here for the night," Mickey told her. "You need to rest. We'll take Malaya back to the Village of the Storm tomorrow."

They each got their own room. Ikigai was still out of sorts, so Mickey requested the room next to hers. "Just bang on the wall if you need anything," he said as he helped her to bed, and turned to go. But before he could leave, Ikigai smashed her fist against the wall.

"Okay," Mickey said. "What do you need?"

"Just stay. Please," Ikigai whispered. Mickey sat by her side. He opened his mouth to say something but she cut him off, "Maybe don't talk, though."

Mickey smiled silently. And he held her hand. For a really long time.

"You didn't hold hands Mom! I'm not stupid!" I said.

"What do you mean? We held hands."

"You did more than hold hands."

"What more would there be?"

"You did it!"

"Did what?"

I eyed my mother and she stared back. For the first time in my life she broke first and looked away.

"We held hands," she said again, blushing.

The next morning, as she woke in the inn on the Island of Traders, Ikigai felt much better.

("I'm sure holding hands all night helped," I said. She ignored me.)

After breakfast, she and her compatriots escorted Malaya back to her home in the Village of the Storm.

They arrived at the village late in the day and entered the maze of alleys. When they reached Malaya's home, her son Datu, her sister Tala, and Tala's son Kidlat were there, waiting. Datu rushed into his mother's arms, relieved she was okay. She hugged her son and kissed him and showed him her Freedom. Datu did not look as happy to see it as Malaya expected. Something was wrong. "What is it?" she asked her son.

Datu nodded toward the maze, and from the alleys two figures stepped into view. Tala flinched when they appeared, and Kidlat instinctively put his arm around his mother. The figures, a man and a woman, wore long, dark coats that stood out in the heat and humidity of this place. And they had the look of those who had traded their souls for something. What that something was, Ikigai did not know. Usually it was money. It did not matter. What mattered was that they were there.

"Damn it," said Mickey. Hari's eyes, normally calm, blazed with fury. Even Tark, perched on Ikigai's shoulder, cawed angrily at the figures.

"Who are they?" Malaya asked.

"They're from my homeland," Ikigai told her through clenched teeth. "Here to conduct their own investigation on behalf of Tagagawas. They're his Shadow Warriors."

CHAPTER 10

Mickey the Expatriate stared down the Shadow Warriors. "Well, this ain't good."

"No, it's not," Ikigai agreed as they approached them. "What do you want here?" she asked. Tark cawed again.

The male Shadow Warrior spoke calmly. "The same as you, Ikigai: to learn the facts."

"That's crap!" Ikigai responded sharply. "I know your kind. I know what you do."

"We have the same right to be here as you. We only wish to conduct our own gathering of the testimony of the accusers."

Mickey put his hand on Ikigai's shoulder. "They do have that right. By the rules of our homeland, if we obstruct them we could ruin everything."

Ikigai glared at the Shadow Warriors. "If you do or say anything shady, pun very much intended, to these villagers, I will find out and I will hunt you down."

At this, the female Shadow Warrior laughed, a cold, haughty laugh. "Such bold words," she said, "from one with so many secrets."

That stopped Ikigai in her tracks.

The male smirked and waved his hand. "We will speak with the accusers now."

"Malaya," Ikigai urged, "quickly, gather everyone and come here. Please."

Malaya beckoned for Tala and Datu and Kidlat to join her and they huddled around Ikigai, fear in their eyes.

"We will speak with the accusers now!" the male demanded again.

"You will wait!" Ikigai shouted. Then she turned to Malaya

and her family and spoke in the Language of the Rising Sun. "Malaya, translate if they don't understand everything I'm saying. Listen, do not be afraid of these guys. No matter what they do or say, there is nothing they can do to harm you. Nothing. If they ask you questions, just answer with the truth, nothing more, nothing less. If you don't want to talk to them, you have the right to say that too."

"*Sore de jubun da!*" the woman Shadow Warrior said. Damn it, the woman also spoke the Language of the Rising Sun. "This is getting dangerously close to obstruction of our investigation," the woman said.

"Come on," Mickey told her, putting his hand on Ikigai's shoulder again. "We have to leave."

"Do not be afraid," Ikigai repeated as Malaya, Tala, Datu and Kidlat walked toward the Shadow Warriors. Malaya turned back and looked at Ikigai. "Do not be afraid," Ikigai called out to her once more.

Mickey, Hari, and Ikigai left Malaya and her family. Tark fluttered ahead. "They're not here to investigate anything," Ikigai said. "They'll threaten or try to bribe them."

"Hopefully your pep talk helped," Mickey replied. "We'll just have to come back tomorrow and see what happens."

Ikigai clenched her fists as she and her companions left the Village of the Storm.

★★★

"Eight-O!" I shouted, laughing deliriously. Lily and I had gone over to the soccer field at Columbia Park to practice. I wasn't supposed to have left the house but it was Christmas Break and Dad couldn't take off work the whole week to watch me every day. Lily shook her head and muttered to herself, but she was smiling and I could tell she was having fun too. Even if she was losing.

"Post up, don't let me cut this angle on the net," I advised, dribbling the soccer ball over the damp grass toward her. "Don't cross your legs like that," I said, exasperated as she gave a gangly, half-assed attempt to defend and tripped on her own feet. I slipped past her and the ball found the inside of my foot and rocketed into the goal. "Nine-O!" I cried, dribbling the ball back to the top of the half field.

"What's game?" she asked impatiently.

"Eleven," I told her, checking the gray sky to see if it was going to rain again.

"I think you won," she conceded, shoving her hands in her coat pockets and bringing her shoulders up around her thin little neck. "It's cold."

"Game's eleven."

"I'm not catching up. Ever."

"You can. You have to try. It'll be the great Lily comeback."

"I have zero," she reminded me. I dribbled up to her and when I was close enough she giggled and threw her arms around my shoulders.

"That's a foul!" I laughed. "You can't do that!"

I pushed past her and she jumped on my back, but she was so small I kept dribbling forward. "You can't do that, Lily!"

We were both cracking up as I carried her tiny frame on my back. I lost my balance as I kicked the ball and we crashed on to the damp grass and I shouted as the ball found its way past the goal line. "Ten-O!"

That's when something inside me clicked open.

Lily was laughing, her arms around my shoulders. But I'd curled up into a fetal position on the ground. It took a few seconds for her to realize something was wrong. She sat up on her heels. "Junior?" she asked and stroked my hair and nuzzled her nose into my face like a worried puppy. She shook me gently as I lay on my side rocking.

242   A CRIME IN THE LAND OF 7,000 ISLANDS

"Ten-O, Ten-O..." I couldn't stop saying it. There was a sym-
metry to it: in the ten and the O, in the visualization of the digits -
the one and zero. My memory spanned beyond the digits, beyond
the binary pointers, hazy and pixelated. It was right there. I could
almost see it. If I could just make the image more detailed. If I
could just define the signal. "Ten-O, Ten-O..."

"Junior!" Lily shook me hard. I snapped out of it. I met her
eyes and she cocked her head, peering at me from different angles,
like she was trying to solve a Rubik's cube. I looked at her the same
way. A three-dimensional puzzle we were. I wondered if we'd ever
get all our sides and colors into a uniform shape.

"We'll figure it out," she said, reading my mind and stroking
my hair. "We'll figure it out."

★★★

Ikigai found herself wide awake in the dark of early morning.
When the sun finally rose, she held back the urge to shout at it for
taking so long. She ran, fully packed and dressed, out of her room
at the inn on the Island of Traders that was just a bit south of the
waterfall. Tark slept peacefully in her satchel, and she did her best
not to jostle him too much as she rushed into the hallway. She was
surprised to find Mickey and Hari in the hall already, packed and
dressed, waiting for her. The three exchanged glances. Nothing
needed to be said.

They set out on the route they knew so well, along the
Northern then Eastern roads, past the waterfall.

Walking on the Eastern road, after over an hour of silence,
Mickey turned to Ikigai and asked, "What's a *tenno*?"

(At this point I froze, believing in my own mind that I'd successfully deployed that adult skill of forced non-reaction. In reality,
my body probably exhibited a hundred tells my ultra-perceptive

mother picked up on, but she did not prod. She simply watched me and continued.)

"You say that word a lot," Mickey told her. "You said it in your sleep, when we were on horseback on the Island of the Beautiful Lady. And the other night, when you fell asleep after we, uh, held hands. It sounds like a word from the Language of the Rising Sun."

"It is," Ikigai admitted.

"So what's a *tenno*?"

"A *tenno*," Ikigai said, "is not a what to me."

"Okay, what is the not-what that it is or is not then?"

Silence.

Hari gently touched Mickey's shoulder and shook his head. Mickey put his hands up. "Sorry," he said. "I'll leave it alone. I just want to know you, that's all."

They walked further, quietly. Ikigai considered to what degree she could trust this man whose voice would bubble like mineral water then evaporate into gravel at a moment's notice. To what extent could she trust his soft-spoken friend, whose well-chosen words circumnavigated the whole of 7,000 islands before they reached the ears of their recipients? But had they not been loyal? Had they not been faithful and true? Had they not gone above and beyond anyone else in her life in proving their dependability? Their friendship?

Ikigai took a breath, and slowly spoke. "*Tenno* means Emperor."

Mickey said, "You don't have to explain anything you don't…"

"My father loved my mother dearly," Ikigai continued. "And he loved her language. He loved listening to her speak in her language, even though he didn't understand it. He insisted that she teach their children her language. And he insisted his children have names that came from the words of her language. So, he called me Ikigai because he said I was the very reason for which he got up in the morning. And when my little brother was born, he told us, 'This boy has the look of an emperor,' and he named him Tenno."

"Where's Tenno now?"

"His is the ghost I used to see."

"Used to?"

"I don't think I'm going to see him anymore."

Mickey ventured forth. "How'd he die?"

I'd broken out into a cold sweat. "Ten-O," I muttered, "Tenno."

"What do you remember, baby?" Mom whispered and stroked my hair.

"Uncle Tenno."

"That's right. What else do you remember?"

I shook my head. It was right there, but I still couldn't get it. My mother took my hand. "It's okay," she said. "You're being so brave. I'm going to keep going, okay?"

I nodded and gripped her hand tight.

Ikigai ignored Mickey's question. They walked the rest of the way in silence and when they arrived at the Village of the Storm they proceeded with trepidation, down the dusty main road, through the maze of alleys, and finally, to the home of Malaya. Ikigai tapped the tin sheet door and called to Malaya softly in the Language of the Rising Sun.

"Go away, Ikigai!" Malaya shouted from inside her home. Ikigai clenched her fist. Mickey and Hari looked down. Their worst fears were coming true.

"Malaya," Ikigai responded hoarsely. "Please come outside. Please come and speak with us."

"I will not! I want nothing to do with any of you people from your crazy foreign land! I am done! My family is done! You bring nothing but pain and fear!"

"Malaya, calm down. Please. What did the Shadow Warriors tell you? I told you, they can do you no harm."

"You don't know that. Once we leave our land and go to yours, they can do anything."

"They cannot. I don't know what they told you, but I promise you, they can do nothing to harm you. I won't let them."

"Go away!"

"Please, Malaya…"

Then Malaya burst outside, facing Ikigai and her companions with wild eyes and a knife in her hand. "After everything we've been through together," Ikigai said, keeping her eyes on the knife. "You still don't trust me?"

"Leave my family alone," Malaya said through gritted teeth.

Mickey and Hari each gently took an arm of Ikigai's. "Come on," Mickey said somberly. "They've made their decision." Ikigai did not fight them. There was no fight in her left. They turned away and left the Village of the Storm.

Heading back west, on the road toward the waterfall, Ikigai gently awoke Tark and pulled him out of her satchel. "Please send this message to the Amazon."

Geri clutched her steering wheel with one hand, her smartphone with the other, and pulled over on the shoulder of the freeway. "Run that by me again?" she said into her phone.

Ikigai's voice was choppy over the connection. "I don't know what Campbell's private investigators said, but they scared them. Malaya and her family are done. They refuse to travel back with me."

Geri smashed her steering wheel with the palm of her hand, making her horn blare.

"Feeling the same way, Geri," Martel's voice came in on the

line's conference call. "Are they dead set in their refusal, Ikigai? I mean, after everything, everything you've done."

"Malaya pulled a knife on us," Ikigai explained. "I'd call that dead set."

"Ikigai, this is Brent," Oberley's voice came in on the conference. "Need you to come home now, okay? You did your best. You went above and beyond what anyone else would have done. Those efforts will be recognized. I'm putting you in for an award. But I need you on the next plane back—"

"I have exactly one shit left to give," Ikigai said. "And it is not for any goddamn award."

Geri couldn't help but laugh, even over her heartbreak. "Must be a special shit."

"That's the one I keep for my daughter. I'll be on the next flight home." And with that, Ikigai disconnected herself from the conference call.

"Geri," Martel said over the line, "you on your way to my office?"

"I was."

"No point now."

"'Cuz you're going to drop the charges."

"I'll call Weddle first, try to bluff him into a plea with a lower sentence. I'm thinking one count of Coercion and Enticement. But we all know he won't go for it. Sorry, guys."

"Everyone did their best," Oberley said.

Geri rubbed her eyes and fought back the tears. "I'mma go drink now."

I'm sure Evan Campbell laughed. A hard laugh. Metallic in its reverberation off the plaster, concrete and bulletproof glass of his prison's visiting room. I don't know if Zach Weddle laughed too. It may have been just another job to Weddle, a job well done, a job that guaranteed a good referral and further business.

"I talked to Martel. You've won," I imagine Weddle would have said.

"Are they going to drop the charges?" Evan would have asked.

"Without the victims willing to face you in court and stand by their testimony, Martel's not going to get you on Engaging in Illicit Sexual Conduct. Now he is saying they will use the Facebook chats between you and Bayani, corroborated by Agent Johnson, to buttress a charge for Coercion and Enticement. Martel is, once more, offering a plea deal: for you to plead guilty to one count of Coercion and Enticement and accept a sentence of ten years."

"He was trying for twenty before. What do you think?"

"I don't think anything, I know. He's bluffing."

"You're confident of that?"

"Absolutely. He's using the chats with Bayani because they're the most explicit and because Agent Johnson was able to find evidence of those communications in Bayani's account. But look, there's still an element to that charge of you having to have *known* that Bayani was a minor. There's no point in those chats where you discuss Bayani's age. And they still have the same fundamental problem they had before. Bayani is an orphan, for whom documentation regarding his true name and age do not exist. We know him to be a minor, only because he says he's a minor. He can't show up to court and face you, as is your right, and stand by his testimony. Even if, slim chance in the land of maybe, he did show up in court, he can't actually prove he's under eighteen. This goes to trial, any wet-eared neophyte with ADHD and a public speaking anxiety could convince the jury that reasonable doubt exists."

Evan would have considered this. Then he would have smirked. "Let's meet Martel anyway."

"For what? I call him on his weak bluff, he folds, and you're free in a matter of days."

"But now this is fun for me. Ask him to come and talk to us about the plea deal in person. I want to see his face when I tell him to shove it up his self-righteous cowboy ass."

Weddle would have stood and packed his briefcase. "You're the boss."

★★★

I never liked it when Lily and I fought, but I was stubborn and tended to not let things go. I was walking her home after school. Even though we were arguing, we were linked arm in arm, drawn close together against the winter cold.

"I already told you," she said, shivering. "Couldn't learn in my last school."

"Fine. What about what happened that day with the car outside your house? What was that?"

"I don't know."

"You looked like you knew."

"The heavy couldn't be there, they told me he was gone."

"What does that mean?"

"What about you?" she turned the tables. "Look at what you're carrying."

"Carrying what?"

She lunged and shoved her hand inside my coat. I yelped and blushed, thinking she was grabbing at my not yet formed breast. Then I realized what she was feeling for.

"Stop," I told her.

"You stop." She struggled with me, forcing one hand into the top of my coat, shoving the zipper down with the other. "Take it out," she ordered.

"What is wrong with you?"

"Take it out. I see you holding it in class, all the time. Staring and staring." She shoved me with a surprising strength. "What do you carry?" she screamed. "Take it out!"

Trembling, I reached into my inside pocket and let the tips of my fingers find it. I pulled it out, held it in my palm, gazed at its layers of brown, different shades all in one, just like...

"Where'd you get it?" Lily asked.

"I don't remember."

"That's not just a rock. I know what that is. It's a piece of tiger eye."

Tiger eye. Something inside me clicked open again.

Tiger eye stone. Shiny tiger. I said, "It looks like your eyes. It looks like I said, "It looks like your eyes." Damn it, what was her name? "It looks like your eyes." I giggled and she laughed and she stroked my hair.

She said, "It looks like your eyes too, Ikigai. Little tiger eyes, my little Ikigai."

Damn it, what was her name? She nuzzled her nose to my cheek when I cried my leg hurt when the concrete hit it. "I can't do it!" I said. "I can't do it!" I cried. The pedals were slippery from the rain.

She said, "It's okay, little Ikigai. You can do it. Just pedal, just go. Just pedal, just go."

I couldn't see Lily. I could only see *her*. Her brown curly hair and hazel eyes. She looked just like me, only older, taller. I blinked. Hazel shifted into pale blue and there was Lily again, sighing patiently, grabbing my wrists, burrowing her little head into my chest.

"I'm sorry," she whispered.

"It's, it's..." I stammered.

"What happened? What just happened?"

"The girl with the tiger eyes," I mumbled, looking at my stone. "She had the other one. There were two of these. She had the other one."

"Who is she?"

"I can't remember."

The wind bit through my open coat. I shivered and Lily zipped me up and grabbed my hand and gently led me down the sidewalk.

So why are we strong, Junior?

★★★

Ikigai sat in her room at the inn on the Island of Traders and pulled her Purpose from the pocket near her heart. It burned in her hand. She had never before wanted so badly to throw it away, far away, where its burning and its song could no longer disturb her. Where it could no longer invade her dreams and force her to get up in the morning with all her failure and all her rage, all her heartache. She wanted nothing more than to be rid of this thing: to be rid of it and to forget. To forget what it was like to dream for more. To forget what it was like to dream for a better world.

Ikigai watched Tark, hopping about the floor and stretching his wings. She put her Purpose back in her pocket. Even now, she could not bear to give it up. What, then? If her Purpose was intact, then who was she there truly to save? Malaya and her family wanted nothing to do with her. Tagagawas had won. Ikigai put her head in her hands and convulsed, sobbing and fighting the urge to vomit.

She rummaged through her satchel and pulled out the picture, the one of Lualhati, in the maze of alleys in the Village of the Storm. She'd wanted to save Lualhati, save her from being reduced, cast aside, minimized to being just another victim, just another number. What number could possibly represent this girl? She'd been destroyed by suffering, destroyed by one who reduced her to a trinket, to a toy. And now she was gone — any reference to her was relegated to that of the past tense. What happens now? What happens to the number of a girl…?

"What happens to the number of a girl in the past tense?" Ikigai said out loud and jumped to her feet, electricity shooting down her spine.

"Tark, let's go," she called. The baby Garuda quickly flew and perched on her shoulder as she ran out of her room, into the hall. "Mickey! Hari!" she screamed. Mickey poked his head out of his room. She did not give him time to talk.

"I'm going back!" she shouted. "Come with me or don't!"

"Oh, now this is the good part," Geri says to me with a twinkle in her eye. "The *really* good part." She raps her knuckles against her desk. "I show up at Martel's office the next day and the first thing he says to me is…"

"You sure you want to come?" Martel said to Geri from behind his desk. "Just gonna be more heartache. Me and Weddle, we're gonna go back and forth, both of us knowing we're full of shit. I'm bluffing and he knows I'm bluffing. He just wants to give me hope that maybe I can salvage this. Then Evan's gonna rip that hope away, refuse the plea deal, laugh at us and that'll be that: case closed. Period. No question mark. No exclamation point."

"I just want to look in his eyes," Geri muttered, still hungover from the night before.

"You're not planning anything rash, right?"

Geri stared at the wall.

"You can't bring your gun into the prison," Martel told her.

"I'll be good. I promise."

"I'm only doing this so I can say with good conscience I did everything I could. But don't fool yourself. There will be no divergence, no surprises, from what I just described."

Martel's cell phone rang.

He looked at the incoming number and answered it. "Ikigai?

Yeah, I hear you. Yeah…" His hands trembled. His face turned red. "Copy that."

He hung up. "Let's go," he said to Geri, bolting for the door.

"What was that?" Geri asked, following.

"A divergence," Martel said.

"What happened?"

"Come on, dammit," Martel said. "I'll explain on the way."

"And you know what's funny?" Geri says, still rapping her knuckles on her desk. "He did *not* explain it on the way. He was so jittery it took all his energy to stay focused on driving. And honestly, I was so hungover, I was all, just go with the flow. Then we get to the meeting and Martel goes cold as ice. Starts out by offering the plea deal for a reduced sentence like nothing happened. Perfectly calm."

"That's your offer?" Weddle said.

Once again, Geri Bradford and Robert Martel sat on one side of a table, facing Evan Campbell and Zach Weddle, a stack of papers between them in the prison meeting room.

"That *was* my offer, yes," Martel replied.

And Evan actually did laugh. He laughed and said, "Absolutely not."

Martel kind of crinkled his nose. "I'm confused. Absolutely not, what?"

"I'm refusing your offer," Evan scoffed.

"I think you missed something, son. I said that *was* my offer. Not *is*."

"I teach math, not English," Evan reminded him. "Screw your semantics. Either way I refuse."

"Cool," Martel said dismissively and packed his briefcase. "See y'all in court. We're still pursuing the charges for Engaging in

Illicit Sexual Conduct."

Geri did a double take. She still didn't know what was going on.

"Woah, big guy," Weddle said. "What in the world are you playing at?"

"Not playing at anything, boys. This ain't no game."

Everyone except Martel gave each other confused glances.

"What?" Martel said, with barely controlled anger. "You *really* thought sending your private eyes out there to threaten that family with whatever you threatened them with, would work?"

"We did no such thing," Weddle replied with practiced incredulity.

"Neither here nor there. But it's obvious you're under the impression, a mistaken impression, that the victims are not traveling to the United States. Check your sources. See you in court." He turned to leave.

Geri followed, dumbfounded. Martel turned to Weddle and Evan once more before he left the room. "We're adding a few more charges too. Expect a superseding indictment."

"Are you serious?" Weddle said.

"Serious as an STD," Martel told him. He and Geri left the room.

As they walked down the hall, Geri couldn't help but smirk. "Which STD?"

"What?"

"I'm just saying, they're not all serious."

"STDs are pretty serious."

"Syphilis? Sounds scary, but penicillin will clear that shit right up. You should have stuck to serious as cancer. That shit is serious."

"I was trying to avoid clichés."

Geri cracked up. "Are you going to tell me what's going on?"

"Your mom tell you this part?" Geri asks. "Please tell me she told you this part. It would be so sad if in her whole story she didn't explain the bestest best part of all."

"She did," I say, laughing and fighting back tears at the memory.

Ikigai's feet were blistered. She'd run the whole distance to the Village of the Storm. Now each step made her want to shout in agony. She ignored the pain. Mickey and Hari had kept up with her. They all struggled for breath as they entered the maze of alleys.

"That was my work out for like, the year," Mickey announced.

"The decade," Hari said.

"The century."

"The…" Hari snapped his fingers, not remembering the word. "You know, a thousand years?"

"Millennium," Mickey laughed.

"That," Hari said. "That was our workout for the millennium."

They fist bumped. Ikigai ignored them. They followed her to Malaya's home. The Village Captain appeared, walking his rounds in the maze. "Enough already!" he said. "Leave them alone!"

"You!" Ikigai screamed and lunged for the Captain. "You liar!" Mickey and Hari grabbed Ikigai, holding her back. "Liar!" she screamed again.

"Ikigai, stop!" said Mickey. "Talk to us! What's going on?"

Malaya stepped outside her home, wondering what all the commotion was about. "This woman again!" she shouted, adding to the chaos. "Where's my knife!" she asked in the Language of Traders and ducked back inside.

Hari said, "I think she's getting her knife."

"Getting shanked," said Mickey.

Malaya came back out, knife in hand. Ikigai, still screaming at the Captain, noticed this. She did not care. She turned her rage on Malaya, shouting in the Language of the Rising Sun. "You lied too! And you didn't even do a good job of it! Do you realize that you never, ever, ever, ever, referred to your daughter in the past tense?" Angry spittle flew from Ikigai's lips. "Lualhati. She's not dead, is she?"

Mickey and Hari, not understanding what Ikigai said to Malaya, simply looked at each other. "Yes," Hari said. "Getting shanked."

Malaya screamed back at Ikigai. "Don't you call me a liar! I never said she was dead!"

Ikigai pointed at the Captain. "He said that you said she was at peace!"

"I don't care what he said about what I said or what he said or what whoever said! That idiot is originally from the Capital, he still doesn't fully understand the Language of Traders. He must have misunderstood. That's what her name means, Lualhati: *At peace*."

"Oh my God," the Village Captain said.

For in the commotion, the tin door of Malaya's home was pushed aside, pushed aside by a little hand. And out stepped the little girl attached to that hand.

It was Lualhati.

"Oh, my God," the Captain said again, facing Ikigai. "I did not mean to lie. I thought, I thought she was gone." The Captain faced Malaya and said in the Language of Traders, "I thought she was gone. I haven't seen her since..."

"No one has," Malaya explained. "She's refused to leave the house since then." Then she turned to Ikigai and repeated herself in the Language of the Rising Sun.

Mickey and Hari stared at the little girl in shock.

As for Ikigai, she did not know whether to laugh or cry. So, she did both, and sunk to her knees as Lualhati walked slowly toward her.

Malaya said something to her daughter in the Language of Traders, probably telling her to go back inside. But Lualhati's eyes were just as intense as they were in her picture, and one look into them told Ikigai that the girl was even more headstrong than her mother. Lualhati ignored Malaya.

Ikigai and Lualhati stared at each other for a moment. Then Lualhati gingerly touched the pearls around Ikigai's neck. She smiled and Ikigai smiled with her. The girl gazed at Tark, perched on Ikigai's shoulder, and her face lit up. She petted the Garuda and he jumped off Ikigai and fluttered about the girl's head. She giggled. Tark perched himself back on Ikigai's shoulder.

"Do you speak the Language of the Rising Sun?" Ikigai asked.

"A little," Lualhati replied. "I am still learning. One day I will understand it completely."

"No one ever understands any language completely."

"Why are you here?"

"I am here because of you."

"You retrieved my mother's Freedom."

"Your mother retrieved her own Freedom. I was just there to help."

"Can you help me? Can you help me retrieve my Innocence?"

Ikigai's heart broke and she trembled and she gave the only true answer she could. "No, I cannot."

"Then why are you here?" Lualhati asked again.

Ikigai pulled out her Purpose, her burning Purpose, and showed it to the little girl.

"This is the reason I get up every morning," Ikigai said. "I thought you were gone, destroyed by the loss of your Innocence as that loss has destroyed so many other children. This is why I fight. This is why I do my best: for those children. To keep them from being hurt, the way you and too many others have been hurt."

Ikigai wiped the tears from her face and continued. "There were three things that defined me as a warrior when I took the journey to find you: my Weapon, my Authority, and my Purpose. My Weapon and my Authority are gone. I no longer have them. They were useless and meaningless in this land. My Purpose, that is all I have left. I thought my mission was to come here to find you, to help you, to save you. But I have since learned better. I am not here to give you my help. I am here to beg for yours. I am not here to save you. I am here to beg you to help me save others, to save all the children that Tagagawas will hurt if he is allowed to walk freely in this world. I can do nothing to return your Innocence to you. But you can help me protect the Innocence of so many others who have not yet had it stolen."

Lualhati pondered these words. Then she looked at Ikigai with a seriousness far beyond her years. "You are a strong and brave warrior. I am a little girl. How could I help you?"

"You can face Tagagawas. You can face him and accuse him of what he did to you."

"I am afraid," Lualhati whispered. "I am afraid to see that man again. I have stayed in my home, where it is safe. I do not want to leave again. I am not strong and brave like you."

The tears flowed freely from Ikigai's eyes and she shook her head. "No," Ikigai told her. "You have faced the fire of horror and shame, and you have survived. You are here. By virtue of that alone, you are stronger and braver than I have ever been."

Lualhati glanced at Ikigai's Purpose and a thought crossed Ikigai's mind: to give away the last thing that made her who she was. But Ikigai hesitated. How could she give away her very Purpose? What would she be without it? Lualhati stared into Ikigai's eyes, and must have read the thoughts there, for she said, "Keep your Purpose. I guess I have my own now."

Lualhati turned to Malaya and said something in the Language of Traders. Malaya, flustered, said something back, and they continued this conversation. Lualhati crossed her arms and glared at her mother with that fiery gaze.

"What are they saying?" Ikigai asked the Captain. "And translate accurately, please."

The Captain was about to speak, but Malaya cut him off. "Let's not have any more misunderstandings," Malaya said in the Language of the Rising Sun. "She wants to help you. She wants to provide her Testimony of Deepest Secrets. She wants to travel with you and face Tagagawas."

Ikigai's heart leapt with joy. But she kept herself under control. "You are her mother. She cannot travel without you. Please, will you come?"

"I am afraid of the Shadow Warriors," Malaya said, and looked at her daughter's burning eyes. "But if she can be brave, so can I. We will go with you."

Ikigai bowed. "Thank you," she said. "Thank you so much."

Ikigai turned to Mickey and Hari and smiled. "Do you guys know what everyone's been saying?"

Mickey grinned. "I think we figured it out."

Now, this was the power of Lualhati. With her mother, the Village Captain, Mickey, and Hari as witnesses, she stood without fear and gave Ikigai her Testimony of Deepest Secrets. Her courage placed the rest of her family in a state somewhere between shame and inspiration. Her brother, Datu, who had already provided his testimony, did not need to be convinced to travel with his mother and sister to face Tagagawas. Now her cousin, Kidlat, demanded of his mother, Tala, a good reason as to why they too were not joining this fight. If his little cousin could be so brave, he asked, how could he live with himself if he too did not go?

Everyone, Malaya and Tala and their children, Mickey, Hari, Ikigai and the Captain, took a short walk to the Captain's office so they could talk. Tala stood by her sister and spoke with Ikigai in the Language of the Rising Sun. She had many questions. She was more analytical and much slower to action than Malaya, her foremost question being:

"How will you protect us from the Shadow Warriors?"

"What exactly did they tell you?" Ikigai asked.

"They were not specific in their threats."

"That was smart of them."

"They said if we traveled to your land, we may never see our homes again."

"They will come nowhere near you while you are in my homeland."

"But they can speak with us freely while they are in our homeland? That makes no sense. How can you tell me they would not have more power in their own land?"

"They don't have *any* power," Ikigai tried to explain. "They have the right to seek the truth, just as anyone does. But once you are in my homeland, we will be preparing to stand before a Judge and Jury to accuse Tagagawas. At that point, neither they nor I can go seeking more information."

"Your Justice is strange."

"I will not argue that point with you. It is strange. But if you face Tagagawas and simply speak the truth, and if Tagagawas cannot convince the Jury that there is anything that should make them doubt this truth, then he will be isolated from the world as punishment."

Tala did not look fully convinced.

"We will protect you," Ikigai said. "When we arrive in my homeland, a contingent of warriors will be there to watch over you. They will escort you everywhere. You will stay at a comfortable inn, and these warriors will stay in that inn and they will guard you all day and all night. I give you my word. We will not let any harm come to you or your children."

"Malaya and I have retrieved our Freedom, and for that we thank you. But there is still work that needs to be done to get all permissions in order for us and the children to travel with you. How long will that take?"

Ikigai turned to Mickey, Hari, and the Captain. "She's asking how long it will take before everything is in order for them to travel." At this, the Captain stood, and bowed his head. "I will take care of that," he assured them. He looked at Lualhati, and her brother and her cousin, fighting back the tears in his eyes. Then he looked at Ikigai. "I see now your intentions are pure. I am sorry I did not see this before. We have to be careful here. There has been so much pain."

Ikigai bowed as well. "You were doing the best you could with what you knew, to protect the people of your village. At the end of the day, that is all a warrior can do."

"I will get all the permissions in order," the Captain said. "Just give me three days."

"Yeah," Geri says, with a grin so wide it threatens to split her face. "That's pretty much how it happened." She lets out a long sigh. "Your mom was really something. She did it. She tracked all those kids down and convinced their mothers to bring them to court. I can't even tell you how I felt when Martel finally explained what was going on."

"Are you shitting me!" Geri screamed.

"She got that Village Captain fully on their side," Martel said as they drove back into the city. "He'll use his contacts to help them get their passports."

"And the girl's really alive?" Geri asked. "She's coming? This is really happening?"

"We lost Bayani. But we have Lualhati, Datu and Kidlat. That's three minor victims, coming to testify, and charges against Campbell for each."

Geri screamed with joy.

Martel laughed. "Ikigai's coming back with all of them."

CHAPTER 11

"Can you run that obituary by me again," Geri says.

I read: "Ikigai is survived and greatly missed by her daughter, Ikigai Warner. A celebration of life and cremation will take place at 10:30 am, November 19, 2021, at Ryan Hollywood Chapel, 4644 NE Tillamook St, Portland, Oregon."

"Junior…" she says sadly.

"It's a long shot," I persist. "But it might work."

"Junior," she shakes her head. "What did she tell you about your family?"

Back in my eleven-year-old life the girl with the tiger eyes was gone and I really couldn't blame her – what was there to stay for? The cold dampness of reality was seeping its way into my nerves, rippling past the puppet shows, the cartoons, the video games, the weekly top streamed pop songs.

Reality was the cold and the wet. Reality was the river, every morning with my mother. I hated that river. I hated her. I hated the paddling but it was real and I missed it because it was real. And the real was very, very hard. It was hard and I needed someone to guide me through it. I needed my mother.

The real was hard and with that recognition came the mist: the mist that covered my eyes; the mist that most would term the onset of adolescent depression. But it was more than that because depression is an internal state formed by thoughts formed by chemical imbalances. This mist was more than a thought. This was a mist that was palpable. This was a mist that had a Purpose. But I couldn't discern that Purpose at eleven years old, going on twelve. I could only feel its effect: that seeping sticky sense of loss.

I didn't even know what I'd lost but I searched so desperately for distraction. I really just wanted to watch television. I was still in my father's house and he couldn't control what I did all day, but when he came home he could prevent me from watching television. It hurt because I wanted so badly the cartoon show pop songs and the sitcoms that made me feel like I was older than I was, when I laughed at innuendos I only half understood. I'd cursed at my father. I'd sworn at him in my arrogance. *I know who you are*, I'd thought as I did these disrespectful things. *I know you are a weak little man. You are not like me. You are not like my mother. You are not a warrior. I know who I am*, I'd thought. I am strong, I am noble, I am righteous, and I will fight for what I love. *I will never stop and I will never back down the way you ran away from Mom because she was real and she was difficult and she was hard.*

And now I didn't feel so superior. I didn't feel so arrogant or so sure. I'd screamed at my father and I'd screamed at the world. I told the world, *bring it on.* I told the world, *I am my mother's daughter. I am Ikigai. I am a hero.* And the world responded, *little warrior, little Ikigai, little hero, you are so brave and so bold and so loud. What if we remove your mother? What if we give you a soul mate who you do not understand? What if we place a mist before your eyes, a mist to be waded through each and every day in pain and longing and fear? How brave now little Ikigai?* the world whispered.

I tried to escape in sleep but the world's voice came in through open windows and ripped open my heart. I thought of my Lily, so frail, so afraid. I thought of the girl with the tiger eyes. What was her name? Of course, she was gone. Of course, she left this cold damp real. Who would want to stay here?

One night, from my room in my father's house I could hear the television downstairs. I could hear him laugh at a show. I thought I have to go to him, I *have* to. I crept downstairs. He heard me and turned the volume down. He was still upset with me.

"What's up, Junior?"

"I'm sorry," I choked out words between sobs and ran into his arms. "I'm sorry," I bawled. His arms wrapped around me. His belly softened. His voice rumbled from his chest. "Come on, calm down."

"I'm sorry I screamed at you."

"Which time?" he chuckled.

"All of them. And that day in the car. I'm sorry I cursed at you. I just wanted to stay with my friend."

He sighed. "I'm sorry too. I'm the adult, I shouldn't have lost my temper. I know Lily's very important to you but you're very important to me. That's all I was trying to say."

"You're important to me too."

"I'm glad I am. You're still not watching TV though."

"Who's the girl with the tiger eyes?" I blurted out.

"The girl with the what?"

I stared at him. I knew he understood the question.

"You're the girl with the tiger eyes, sweety," he said slowly.

I didn't let him off the hook. "Who is she Dad?"

"You're the girl with the tiger eyes," he repeated.

Then he picked me up and carried me upstairs and tucked me into bed.

Years later, I sat with my father on the same couch in the same living room and he told me that after he tucked me in that night, he walked back downstairs, grabbed his phone, and sent a text message to my mother. He could not, of course, remember his exact wording, but it was, in substance:

Ikigai, I don't care what the hell you're doing gallivanting about in the Philippines but you need to come home. Wasn't sure before but am now. Junior is starting to remember. Really not fair for me to deal with all this alone. It was your family that caused this.

★★★

The Village Captain asked for three days.

Three days, he said, and he would have all permissions in order for Malaya, Tala, Datu, Kidlat, and Lualhati, to travel with Ikigai to her homeland to face and accuse Tagagawas.

On the first day, Tark carried messages between Ikigai and the Amazon, who scrambled to arrange Ikigai's flight with the Great Crane of the West. The trial against Tagagawas, the Amazon relayed, was in seven days. If Ikigai was returning in three, that gave the Amazon and her team just enough time to prepare the children to face Tagagawas and his Defender.

On the second day, Ikigai spent time with Mickey at the waterfall. They once again watched as children performed backflips into the natural pool at the foot of the fall. Mickey, in a juvenile attempt to impress Ikigai, backflipped into the pool as well. Ikigai shook her head and had to admit that it was remarkable Mickey could be so youthful in body and spirit.

They lounged by the side of the pool and Ikigai asked, "So what happened to your ghost?"

A grave look crossed Mickey's face. "He's close," Mickey told her.

"How close?"

"Tell you some other time?"

"Who's being secretive now?"

"I will tell you. Sometime. Let's just enjoy the day."

"I'll let it go."

"You should come back here."

"Where?"

"Here. When this case is over, you should come back. Hang out with me and Hari. Keep doing this kind of work. You're good at it."

"I have my daughter."

"Bring her."

"Her father would never let me."

"Hey," Mickey forced a smile. "Had to try."

So, they held hands and enjoyed the second day.

On the third day, her last in The Land of 7,000 Islands, Ikigai packed her belongings before the sun rose and set out from the inn with Mickey, Hari, and Tark by her side. They joked and laughed and tried not to miss each other as they walked on the Northern and Eastern roads one last time. Ikigai savored these final moments with the fellow warriors she now called her friends, moments that would always be in her heart. They had shared a great adventure.

When they arrived at the Village of the Storm, they walked straight to the Captain's office and entered, smiling. The Village Captain did not look up from his desk, remaining focused on the papers he was reading. "What is it you want now?" he asked.

Ikigai was confused by the coldness of his demeanor. "You said three days."

"What are you talking about?" the Captain asked with a sneer.

Ikigai's heart pounded. "You said three days. We're here to pick up Malaya and her family. You said you'd have all the permissions in order for us to travel. Today."

"Crap," Mickey muttered under his breath.

"Was there a miscommunication?" Ikigai asked. "You said to give you three days and you would take care of everything. I need to travel with Malaya and her family. Now. We need to get to the Great Crane of the West today. We only have a few days until Tagagawas' trial."

The Captain smiled coldly. "I have no idea what you are talking about."

Ikigai felt sick to her stomach. Her brain reeled, slowly

catching up to what the sinking feeling in her gut already told her. She looked at Mickey, who stared at the floor dejected, and Hari, who stared at the ceiling, seemingly trying to control a temper he never showed.

"Why did you do this?" she asked the Captain, trembling. Then she answered her own question. "The Shadow Warriors. They got to you, didn't they? How much did they pay you?"

The Village Captain betrayed no emotion, remaining silent as he gathered his thoughts. Then he snickered. "The look on your face," he said. "I wish I could have kept this going longer."

Ikigai was tired and confused. "What is going on?"

"I have the permissions, I have the permissions," the Captain said, still snickering. "We just wanted to have some fun before you left."

Mickey and Hari exploded into laughter with the Captain. Adrenaline pumped through Ikigai's veins. "You two were in on this?" Mickey and Hari nodded, unable to catch their breath. Mickey put his arm around Ikigai's shoulders. "Come on," he said. "You gotta admit, that was good. We got you good."

Ikigai shoved Mickey and stormed out of the office. The roars of laughter followed her outside.

Stupid, stupid men. Everything was a joke to them. But once she was out of their sight, she allowed herself a smile. A small one. It was a little funny. Ikigai walked toward the maze of alleys, shaking her head. It was time to pick up Malaya and Tala and the children.

★★★

In his prison, Tagagawas smashed his fist on the table in the cell in which he was allowed to meet with his Defender and the Shadow Warriors.

"You should have made stronger threats!" he screamed at the Shadow Warriors.

"Slow down," the Defender said. "They did what they were supposed to do. Their threats were vague enough that they could be denied. If we'd made them any stronger, we'd be committing another crime you could be charged with."

Tagagawas seethed.

"What else will you have us do?" the female Shadow Warrior asked.

"Absolutely nothing," Tagagawas said, then turned to his Defender. "I don't want to be kept in isolation from the other prisoners any longer. It's lonely."

The Defender was confused. "I requested isolation for your safety."

You see, by stealing the Innocence of children, Tagagawas had committed a crime so despicable that even hardened murderers and thieves hated him for his transgression. For even murderers and thieves love their children.

Tagagawas fixed his gaze on his Defender. "Request that I no longer be isolated from the other prisoners."

★★★

The good thing about not having much, Ikigai noticed, was that there was not much to pack when traveling. Malaya, Tala and the children had fit all the belongings they needed for their journey in two satchels that Datu and Kidlat insisted on carrying for their mothers. Ikigai smiled at the boys, wondering what it would be like to have one of her own, a little brother for her daughter one day, perhaps? Who knew what the future could bring?

Ikigai, Mickey and Hari led Malaya and her family on the long walk to the Southern shore of the Island of Traders. The Amazon had arranged for Ikigai's transport with the Great Crane of the West directly from the Island of Traders, so they would not have to fly first to the Capital. They needed to hurry, but as the day wore on, while the children ran ahead, the steps of the adults grew slow, but not from weariness, they were all used to these journeys by now. For Malaya and Tala, it was the fear of the unknown, they had never left their homeland. For Ikigai and Mickey, it was the fear they would never see each other again. Hari watched his friend with concern, hoping Mickey would not have to suffer too much heartbreak. As for Tark, he refused to leave Ikigai's shoulder, nuzzling into her neck at every opportunity.

"So, you learned the Language of the Rising Sun from your mother," Mickey said to Ikigai to break the bittersweet silence. It was clear he just wanted to talk to her about something, anything, before she left. But he could see from her wince that he'd struck a nerve again.

"Never mind," he said.

"Tell you what," Ikigai told him. "I'll talk about it if you tell me about your ghost."

"Deal."

Ikigai took a breath. "I learned a little from my mother. But I had to study it on my own when I was older to really get it."

"She didn't teach you?"

"She started. But she wasn't around to finish."

Ikigai watched Datu, Kidlat, and Lualhati running ahead, playing in the road. "After my Dad was, uh, killed, by two stupid warriors, who thought he was someone else, she had to be, hospitalized. Me and Tenno, grew up in the system, bounced around foster homes."

There was a long silence. "I'm so sorry," was all Mickey could think to say.

"Everything happens for a reason, I suppose," she said sadly.

"That's why I became a warrior myself. I thought maybe I could, I don't know…"

"Make things better?" Mickey said. "Save the world?"

Ikigai nodded. "Is that why you became a warrior?"

"Me? No. I just wanted to have adventures and look cool doing it."

"Then why do you have a ghost?"

Mickey traded a glance with Hari, then looked up the road as he heard a shout from Kidlat ahead. Lualhati had crouched behind him and Datu had shoved him so that he tripped over Lualhati and fell to the ground. Tala yelled at them, reprimanding. Malaya laughed.

"Remember that case I told you about?" Mickey said, his voice neither gravel nor mineral water, but something in between. "The one I failed at? It was very similar to your case. It involved a boy, who also had his Innocence stolen by someone from our land. This boy was an orphan too, and I couldn't get him to our land to provide his Testimony of Deepest Secrets."

"We couldn't bring Bayani either," Ikigai reminded him. "I'm sure you did your best."

"No, I didn't," Mickey admitted. "Not like you. Like I said, I became a warrior for the wrong reasons. I became one because of my ego. Then when it came to the actual hard, grinding, frustrating work of being a real warrior, I fell short. I should have done what you did. I should have tracked down other children who could have provided their Testimony. It would have been hard, but I should have kept fighting."

"What happened to this boy that you see his ghost?"

Mickey looked uncomfortably at Hari, who stared ahead and said nothing. That's when it hit Ikigai.

"He became a warrior," Mickey said. "He promised to never be corrupt and to do whatever it took to help kids like the one he once was." Hari continued to walk without speaking and Mickey continued, fighting back the tears. "He became a good man when God knows, he would have been perfectly justified in becoming a bad one. Everyone thinks he quietly follows me. They don't get it. I'm the one following him. But when I follow, I don't see him all the time. I see the ghost of the boy he once was. The one I failed to find Justice for."

Ikigai absorbed all this and looked closer at Mickey and Hari. It always seemed they were the same age, like twin brothers almost. But Mickey's story changed her perspective, and she realized how young Hari was, aged by his experience, and how much older Mickey was, kept young only by a stubborn grip on his own boyishness.

Ikigai grabbed Mickey's hand. "You're a good man too," she said, then looked at Hari. "You both are. The best."

Hari pointed to the activity of the Southern shore that came into focus as they drew near. They could see the long neck of the Great Crane of the West rise against the horizon.

"We are here," Hari announced. Then he breathed deeply and smiled. "We are here."

★★★

Tagagawas walked in the prison yard during the hours the inmates were allowed to partake in fresh air and activity. He kept his own company, but ambled about in circles, smiling to himself in an odd manner.

A group of four hardened inmates, all murderers, approached Tagagawas. "You new?" one of them asked.

"I am not," Tagagawas said and giggled nervously.

The inmates traded glances. "If you aren't new," the inmate said, "then you were in isolation before."

"True," Tagagawas agreed.

The inmate sneered. "Why were you in isolation?"

★★★

"I think this is where we leave you," Mickey said. "We've got another night at the inn, south of the waterfall. We'll head back to the Capital tomorrow." He and Ikigai exchanged a long hug. "Keep in touch?" he said.

"Of course," she nodded. Then she let him go, though she really didn't want to.

"Hari," she said and hugged him as well. "Look out for this guy."

"I will try," Hari replied with a smile.

Ikigai took Tark off her shoulder and cradled him in her hands. He mewed. She stroked the feathers of his crown. "You are going to be the bestest mount for Vishnu," she whispered, and nuzzled his beak with her nose. "You are so brave. I am forever in your debt." Tark cawed gently. "Just stop freezing so much," she suggested. Tark hid his face under a wing.

"Don't make him feel bad," Mickey chided and took Tark from her.

"It was constructive criticism," said Ikigai.

"Stop, he's just a baby," Mickey passed the Garuda to Hari.

"Okay, sorry," Ikigai responded. She faced Mickey and fought back the hot surge of missing someone before they're even gone. "See you around?" she asked.

"See you around," Mickey smiled. They turned slowly and walked in opposite directions. Hari, Mickey and Tark headed up the Northern Road. Ikigai led Malaya and her family toward the Southern shore where the Great Crane of the West awaited.

Ikigai and Malaya and her family walked through the bustling market on the Southern shore. Ikigai noticed the pretty young woman with the coal-black eyes that sold pearls. That day she was wearing a bright red scarf and she recognized Ikigai and waved slowly. Ikigai waved back, touched her fingers to the pearls around her neck, and smiled at the woman. The woman did not smile back. She kept waving at Ikigai, her face expressionless. Ikigai found this strange, but touching her pearls made her think of Mickey, and this distracted her. She turned and faced the direction in which Mickey and Hari had left, hoping she could catch another glimpse, but they were long gone. Ikigai sighed. Datu, Kidlat, and Lualhati drew close to their mothers. They continued to walk toward the Crane.

When they came in full sight of the Great Crane of the West, Ikigai realized something was wrong. Everyone in the marketplace hustled about, but it was as if they were going through the motions and not actually doing anything. They were deathly silent. As for the Crane, he was completely still, and when Ikigai and Malaya's family reached him, they saw why.

The Great Crane of the West was in chains.

It occurred to Ikigai that the pretty young woman with the coal-black eyes had not been waving at her in greeting. She had been trying to wave them away.

Shouts and screams broke the silence. A thundering of hooves echoed from behind the Great Crane who remained motionless, chained to the ground. Ten horses appeared, riding out from behind the Crane, and rumbled toward Ikigai and Malaya's family. Masked by bandannas, the riders surrounded Ikigai, Malaya, Tala and the children, pointing their swords and knives and arrows at them.

Ikigai gritted her teeth and positioned her body in front of Malaya and her family, protecting them as best as she could against the Brothers of the Keepers of the Key. "It was a little less dramatic than that in real life," Geri says.

"That was real though?" I say.

"Crazies found out when she was leaving. They paid someone off, snuck on board the plane, and surrounded Ikigai and Malaya's family. They were gonna kill her."

"I thought she made this part up for a more dramatic climax."

"I mean, there is some exaggeration."

"Like?"

"It was only a few New People's Army guys, like three of four. They were very quiet about it. The other passengers didn't even know what was going on."

"What else was exaggerated?"

Geri thinks. "It was a plane, not a Great Crane of the West."

"Well shit, Geri, I know that."

"Did she tell you who was there?"

"You could have warned us!" Ikigai shouted at the Great Crane of the West as she faced the contingent of Brothers.

The Crane sighed loudly. "There are many things I could have done little warrior. I could have stayed on the other side of the ocean and eaten more fish from the waters of your homeland. I could have called in sick and written a new symphony. That is my true passion, after all. This job is crushing my soul. If this situation resolves itself in a satisfactory manner, I kid you not, I am done, I'm quitting. I just want to eat fish and focus on my music…"

"Shut up!" one of the Brothers shouted and when Ikigai looked at this Brother, she saw a thin young man, his head and lower face covered by two separate bandannas. Ikigai could tell it was the same Brother she and her companions had taken with them on the rowboat they'd used to escape the Island of the Keepers of the Key. The Brother dismounted his horse and stepped up to Ikigai, nose to nose. He removed the bandanna covering his head, revealing long black hair dyed with streaks of red. Then he removed his other bandanna, and Ikigai found herself staring into the angry face of Bayani Matapang.

Meanwhile in prison, as Tagagawas spit out teeth and blood, he smiled. The guards had managed to pull the other prisoners off him. If they had not done so, Tagagawas would surely have died. He was battered and broken. The guards had to call in doctors to make sure his damaged body did not get worse.

But as Tagagawas lay in the prison's hospital, in pain, he could not help but laugh.

★★★

"It's pretty," Lily said as we looked at the tiger eye stone in my palm. "It *does* look like your eyes."

We sat in Columbia Park one weekend day, she and I, on the benches near the soccer field where this all started, for me at least. Where the spoiled girls, led by Ms. Pigtail, tried to force a beautiful soul down their path: a path that denied how small, how frail, how weak, we truly are; how lonely and how afraid to face the poison and trauma in our own veins. They called her weird. They bullied her, and I believed that I saved her. I did not. She was there to save me and to destroy me; to destroy the identity I had so carefully put together: my Junior, my athlete, my tough, my cool. Lily touched a finger to the tiger eye I held. "Can you remember anything else?" she asked.

"She had the other one," I muttered. "Two tiger eyes." I closed my fist around the stone and asked a question of my own. "How come you won't talk to me?"

"I'm talking to you now? I talk to you every day."

"You talk around stuff, and everything always means something else."

"Then you have to listen."

"I *do* listen. I thought I understood, but I don't."

"What do you want to understand?"

"You."

She whirled on me. Her blue eyes went ice cold and her nostrils flared and she smiled a haughty smile: the smile of a Destroyer and a Queen. She demanded, "What was her name, Junior?"

"I can't remember," I whispered, feeling small and not liking it.

"Why can't you remember?"

I beat my head with my fists and groaned. Lily grabbed me by the wrists. "Stop," she said, harshly. But I was still stronger than her and I kept going, smacking my fists into my head over and over again. She had to stand and put all her weight into holding my arms down. "Stop!" she demanded again. Then she let me go and threw her arms around me, wrapping me into the cocoon that was her. I buried my face into her coat and sobbed. It hurt so much and I didn't even know why. "You can't hurt yourself," she whispered.

Something clicked open again.

"A car crash," I mumbled. "They told me it was a car crash."

★★★

Ikigai stared at the Brother with steel in her eyes. "So what now, Bayani?" she asked, while Malaya interpreted. "Is this meant to be some grand reveal? You think I didn't recognize you on the Island of the Keepers of the Key? Why do you think I didn't kill you?"

Bayani stood silent, his face contorted with rage, his brothers on horseback grimly looking down on Ikigai and Malaya's family. Bayani slowly pulled his knife from the sheath on his hip. Datu and Kidlat shouted at their old friend in the Language of Traders and their mothers fought to hold them back. Lualhati clutched the fabric of Ikigai's pants. Ikigai pushed the girl behind her.

"And what will you do with your little knife?" she asked. "I am doing everything I can to find Justice. You're going to get in the way of that? You want to stop Justice so that piece of dung can keep hurting children the way he hurt you? The way he hurt your friends? Then go ahead, cut my throat."

Bayani brought the blade to Ikigai's face. Malaya and Tala and the children shouted at Bayani. Ikigai did not flinch. She held his gaze. Then Bayani brought the blade down to his side. Trembling, he opened his mouth.

And he screamed.

He screamed long and hard and at first it sounded like the scream of a beast in pain, then it sounded like that of a man in rage. But as Ikigai listened carefully, she heard it for what it truly was — a scream not much different than what she'd hear when her daughter was an infant, howling in her crib.

So Ikigai listened as this scream died down, and before Bayani could take another breath, she grabbed him. She grabbed him and hugged him and forced his head to her shoulder. She closed her eyes and held him with all her strength as he struggled and she spoke as Malaya interpreted. "Let me go and I will never leave you."

Bayani tried to pull away but Ikigai's strength at that moment came not from her arms but from her conviction. "I know there are so many others," she went on, "just like you. For whom Justice was never attained. I have nothing left, Bayani. Nothing left of what I thought made me, *me*. I have only this."

And with that, she let him go and pulled forth her Purpose and held it in her hand. "This is all I have left: my very Purpose, the reason for which I get up in the morning." She held it out to him. "I give this to you. Do you understand? I give this to you as my promise. Let us go. Let us seek Justice against Tagagawas. And when we are done, I will return. I will come back here, to this land. To fight for Justice for all the children that all the outsiders have hurt here. Let us go, and I will come back and I will never leave."

Bayani reached out cautiously and took Ikigai's Purpose. He held it between thumb and forefinger and gazed at it. It was a stone.

But not just any stone.

I pulled the tiger eye from behind my pillow. "Was it like this one?" I whispered.

Mom nodded.

"You had the other one."

"I did."

"Where did these come from?"

"We're getting there."

The Brothers of the Keepers of the Key looked at Bayani, awaiting a decision. He closed his fist around the tiger eye stone and looked once more at Ikigai. Then he turned his back on her, walked over to his horse and mounted it.

The Brothers followed Bayani as he silently led them away from the Southern shore of the Island of Traders, leaving Ikigai, Malaya and her family alone. One of the Brothers shouted something in the Language of the Keepers of the Key as they faded into the distance.

"What did he say?" Ikigai asked Malaya.

"He said to tell the fool who insulted his mother that if he sees him again he will play soccer with his decapitated head." Malaya shivered. "That guy is really gruesome."

"Mickey didn't even insult his mom," Ikigai remembered. She and Malaya chuckled. Tala was not amused. The children looked about warily, wondering if it was safe to relax now.

Ikigai took in the importance of what had just happened.

She had given up everything now. She felt free. She felt panic. She felt light. She felt afraid. She looked at Malaya, taking in every detail of her friend's face.

"Are you okay?" Malaya asked.

"Yes. Let's get this silly Crane free."

"She updated me on all this over email," Geri says and makes a hand motion like she's typing on a smartphone. "Hey. It's Ikigai. Just convinced a bunch of NPA fighters to get off my plane. Taking off. See you in 15 hours." I laugh as Geri shakes her head. "Yeah," she says. "A bit understated."

"I think it was her humility," I say.

"See, she'd be humble with big shit like that, right? But with little things? Arrogant as all hell. Made no sense."

I laugh. It's funny because it's true.

"I grab Nate, we head out to the airport the next morning," Geri goes on. "I know she's beyond exhausted, we gotta make sure she's got help as soon as she lands. But of course, on our, literally, on our way there, I get a call from Martel. With some more disturbing news."

Ikigai did her best to sleep through the flight, but that blasted Crane could not keep his mouth shut. "Little warrior," he said. "You have given me a new lease on life. We simply cannot waste our days wallowing in misery as our souls are not fulfilled. This is my last ride, I swear. I will focus every ounce of my existence on the production of my next symphony. And I will name it after you. I will call it *The Tale of Ikigai* and *The Land of 7,000 Islands*. It will be a heroic piece. Your name will be made immortal."

"I don't want to be immortal," Ikigai told him, disgruntled, as Datu and Kidlat and Lualhati giggled at the interaction between her and the Crane, understanding enough from Ikigai's body language to find it rather funny. "Just get us to my homeland safely and we'll call it even."

"I most certainly will, little warrior."

"And maybe let me sleep too?"

So, the Crane quieted down, and Ikigai once again found herself drifting in and out of consciousness, until she was jarred awake by the air currents of descent. She peeked out over the Crane's wings and saw the welcome and familiar sight of her own land.

The Great Crane of the West landed gently on the Pacific Northwestern shore of Ikigai's homeland and let his passengers off. Datu, Kidlat, and Lualhati gazed about in awe. Malaya and Tala, more fearful of the unknown as adults often are, drew close to Ikigai as she led them. Ikigai turned to the Crane and said, "Take care, my friend. If you are serious in the pursuit of your passion, this may be the last time we see each other."

The Crane raised a huge wing and the air bellowed around him. "Goodbye, little warrior. May you succeed in the completion of your adventure."

Ikigai smiled. "Thank you," she replied. "But I think this adventure is just about done."

The Crane's mood changed. "Never let your guard down until the fight is over."

Ikigai narrowed her eyes. The Crane simply ignored her after this. Ikigai led Malaya, Tala and the children away from the shore until she saw a fellow warrior. She didn't expect her heart to leap with joy when she saw the Amazon, but it did. They rushed toward each other and hugged and Ikigai introduced the Amazon to Malaya and her family.

The Amazon smiled at everyone, but Ikigai could tell something was wrong. The Amazon asked Ikigai, "Can I talk to you over here?" and pulled Ikigai aside.

"What's the problem now?" Ikigai asked.

"I don't have the greatest news," the Amazon replied.

"Get to it, so we can figure out how to deal with it."

"Tagagawas. He was severely injured. The Judge said he's not in good enough shape to stand trial."

"How did that happen?"

"Apparently, Tagagawas openly shared his crimes with his prison mates."

"Ah," Ikigai sighed sarcastically. "He didn't do that on purpose, at all."

"It was a desperate move and it worked. The Judge postponed the trial."

"For how long?"

"Date hasn't been set yet. It'll be a while though, at least a few months, maybe longer."

Ikigai felt the ground drop out from under her as she looked toward Malaya and her family. "That move wasn't desperate, it was smart. They can't stay away from their homeland that long. They have jobs and lives they have to get back to. But if we send them home now after everything they've been through, they won't come back. Tagagawas knew that." Ikigai felt nauseous as the world spun around her. "Tagagawas will never face trial."

CHAPTER 12

"She collapsed," Geri says. "Knees buckled right out from under her. I had to catch her before her head hit the ground. When she came to, she just stared through me, said one thing."

Geri stops talking to pick her teeth with a toothpick. We'd ordered Vietnamese. I make a flurrying motion with my hand and raise my eyebrows impatiently.

Geri smiles. "She said, 'I want to see my daughter.'"

We had a free period in math class which most of the kids spent chatting away. We all liked talking so much back then. Lily and I retreated to our bubble. By then, the other children had accepted us as the two weird recluses and left us alone.

"Was she a friend?" Lily asked.

"More like a sister."

"I'm like your sister."

"You're not my sister," I said adamantly. For reasons I just could not deal with at that point in my life, I especially felt the need to make that clear right then and there.

"Junior?" Ms. Broner the stoner tried to shout my name above the chatty roar. I looked up. She beckoned. When I stood, I saw Dad enter the room. "Hi," I said as I approached him, confused. He forced a smile. "You should get your coat sweety."

It was still the middle of the day. Traffic was light. It didn't take long for Dad to drive to the airport. He pulled into the passenger pick-up area for flight arrivals and muttered, "Don't see her." Then we saw a Greek statue come to life and jog toward us, waving. Dad put the car in park and nodded toward the statue who approached. Dad rolled down his window. "Greg?" the statue leaned over and asked.

"Yeah, sorry, I forget your name."

"No worries. Geri Bradford. Pull in there, in police parking. I got you covered."

He did so and we got out of the car. I couldn't take my eyes off this statue-woman who was almost as big as Dad. She smiled at me. "Hey, Ikigai."

"It's Junior," I said shyly.

"Hi, Junior. You don't remember me, do you?"

I narrowed my eyes and shook my head. Dad looked at her as if he wanted to say something but didn't. "Come on," Geri said. "Let's get you to your mom."

Geri led us through the airport with huge strides, but I kept up with her, jogging when I had to. I wanted to see my Mom. Dad lagged behind. Geri took us through a side door, past the security screening line, and directly to the concourse. We walked past a few gates. Then I saw my mother sitting, her head in her hands. I exploded into a sprint.

Mom raised her head as she heard me coming and the sight of her almost made me stop. She was a thin woman to begin with but she'd lost even more weight. She was also prematurely gray and she usually dyed her hair, but her natural color had grown out and it was almost completely gray now. The past few months had aged her years.

Still, she was Mom. She stood and I ran into her arms. It was like running into a brick wall. There was no softness on her, anywhere. She wrapped me in what felt like the branches of a tree and let out a noise from her chest through her throat that sounded like it would have been a sob if she hadn't caught it and forced it back down. She smelled different too, as if she had been living underwater. It was a little frightening. She wasn't the same Mom.

Apparently, she thought the same of me. She cupped my face with her hands. "I leave three months and you grow up on me. Did you get even taller?"

"I don't know," I smiled shyly at this tree-woman who used to be my mother.

Geri the Amazon joined us. "Thank you," my mother said to her. Geri smiled and squeezed Mom's shoulder. Then Mom looked about wildly. "Where's Malaya and…"

"Nate's with them," Geri explained calmly. "He took them to get something to eat."

"Who's Malaya?" I asked.

"I'll explain later," she told me.

"You did promise," I replied.

"I know," she agreed. Dad walked up and nodded at my mother. She nodded back and smiled.

"Oh, oh," I said. "You have to meet my friend. Can she come over later?"

"Not today, baby."

"Why not?" I held myself back from a full out whine.

"I needed to see you." She stroked my cheek. "But I need you to stay with your dad a few more days."

"Hey," Dad pointed out, "she hasn't seen you in months."

"I know," she said to him. "Do you mind?"

"I don't mind, Ikigai, it's not about minding. It's about she hasn't seen you in months."

"There are a few more things I need to take care of," she told us both.

"There are a lot of things you need to take care of. Where's your priority?" Dad asked.

Geri stepped away, knowing this family discussion needed space. I expected Mom's eyes to glow red and her to fly off the handle. She didn't. She looked at my father and smiled. "I love you, Greg," she said.

Dad stared at her, open-mouthed. It shocked me too. "I just need a few more days," she said. "This little adventure isn't quite over yet."

"Ikigai," Dad said, his tone quieter and calmer, "did you get my texts?"

"I did." She grabbed my hands. "I know you've been going through a lot while I've been gone. But I'm going to explain every-thing, okay? I promised you, and I'm going to keep my promise. I just need a little more time."

I nodded and fell into her arms. Those long, strong arms. She kissed my cheek and whispered into my ear. "I love you baby girl. My little Ikigai. Always. Always. Always."

Joy was not a word that came close to describing what Ikigai felt as she was reunited with her daughter, but the reunion was unfortu-nately short-lived, for her work was not yet complete.

Ikigai and the Amazon met with the Prosecutor, the bookish warrior who would use the word of the Law to argue against Tagagawas' Defender in the Judge's Court. The three of them nodded at each other, then entered the Judge's chambers.

The Judge peered at them and held back a sigh. "Now why," the Judge began, in a voice that seemed to issue forth from infinite leather-bound books, "can we not delay this matter until Tagagawas has healed and is fit to stand in Court before his Accusers?"

"His Accusers cannot wait here indefinitely," Ikigai explained, fighting through her exhaustion and forcing patience into her words, for the Judge had great power and was not one to offend.

"Then let them go back home, to return here at a more suitable time," suggested the Judge.

"There will never be a more suitable time than now," Ikigai replied.

And with that, Ikigai launched into the story of everything I have told you these past nights. She provided the Judge a much shorter version of course, perhaps also with less embellishment.

When she was done, she stated, "You see, your Honor, the obstacles we overcame to bring the Accusers here were arduous. If they go back home now, they will lose all trust in us. They will not return. And Tagagawas will never stand trial for that of which he was accused."

The Judge leaned back in his chair with half-closed eyes and pondered silently for what felt like an eternity. When he finally opened his eyes and parted his lips to speak, Ikigai, the Amazon, and the Prosecutor, tensed at what he would say.

"I will let you know tomorrow," the Judge pronounced.

Ikigai hid her anger. At least he had not outright refused her request. Yet. "Thank you, your Honor," she said. And they left his chambers.

★★★

"Come on," Lily pressed. "What was her name?"

"I can't remember. I can't remember," I said, trembling as we stood outside her home in the winter chill. Lily grabbed my hand and we sat on the curb of the sidewalk. I buried my head into her shoulder and squeezed my eyes shut then opened them again.

"She died in a car accident. That's what they told me."

"Mom is home now, right?"

"Yeah, mom is home. Momma's…"

"'Kay, then maybe she knows."

"Momma 'kay,'" I mumbled, something clicking again. "Momma ka. Just pedal, just go."

Lily brushed the hair from my eyes. I stared at the ground and shivered.

★★★

Geri was helping Martel with trial prep in his office when Zach Weddle walked in, holding a manila folder. Geri peered at Weddle with the usual caution.

"How can I help you Zach?" Martel asked.

"You get the call from the judge?" Weddle asked in return.

"Yes sir, we did. Sounds like the trial's on after all."

"You got what you wanted."

"Best of luck in court, Zach."

Weddle nodded. "Where's Agent Johnson?"

"Getting some much deserved rest."

Weddle dropped the manila folder on Martel's desk. "Show that to her," he said, then quickly left. Martel and Geri traded a look. Martel opened the folder and thumbed through its contents.

"Shit," he exclaimed.

The next day, after much anxiety, Ikigai was informed that her request had been granted by the Judge. Tagagawas would stand trial for his crimes in The Land of 7,000 Islands.

That was a triumph. But now there was another problem.

Ikigai and the Amazon were summoned before the Prosecutor. Remember the packet provided to Tagagawas and his Defender by the Shadow Warriors? Well, the Defender had provided the Prosecutor with a copy of its contents.

"This," the Prosecutor announced, as he held up the packet the Defender had given him, "will make the Jury of Tagagawas' peers question if you were biased in the course of your actions, Ikigai."

"There was never any bias," Ikigai replied hotly. "I didn't know…"

"You'll have to convince the Judge and Jury of that. The Defender is going to make this very, very difficult for you. And you know what else he's going to bring up. Last chance. Are you sure you want to go through with this?"

"I have never hesitated," Ikigai said. "I will not do so now."

The Prosecutor traded a look with the Amazon and nodded. "Okay, then. This will be a hard fight. But we are in it. Together."

The tears flowed down my face. I knew what was in the packet. I still could not bring myself to say it. My mother stroked my hair. "I need you to keep being very brave," she said.

"Keep going," I whispered, and clutched her hand.

Lady Justice, to whom Ikigai the Warrior had sworn her life, stood blind and silent above the gathering of the Court. The Judge, Justice's avatar, sat directly below her. On the Judge's left sat a Jury of twelve of Tagagawas' peers. Below the Judge, the Prosecutor and Defender stood, each prepared with their respective arguments. Tagagawas sat beside his Defender, grim, emotionless, still bearing the wounds of the attack he suffered from his fellow inmates.

The Prosecutor first called Datu to the stand. Afterwards, he called Kidlat. The boys provided their Testimony of Deepest Secrets through an interpreter who understood the Language of Traders. The Jury listened, impartial. Then the Defender cross-examined both boys, giving neither any quarter. He attacked the Testimony of each, attempting to poke holes in their accusations. The boys, though warned this would occur, were still shocked at the treatment they received. They glanced over at Ikigai and she stared back, hurting because she could do nothing to help.

But the boys held their own. Their stories stayed consistent, as Ikigai knew they would. After all, they were telling the truth...

Then the Prosecutor called Lualhati to the stand.

As Lualhati provided her Testimony, her voice was small, but her eyes flashed with the smoldering heat of the mouth of the Beautiful Lady. The Defender attacked her as well. Lualhati remained unmoved. Her story was simple and her story was true. Ikigai and the Amazon and the Prosecutor allowed themselves to breathe just a little. For they could tell that after listening to Lualhati, most of the Jury were fighting back tears.

Ikigai marveled at the spirit of the children. She prayed that the Heavens would grant her but a fraction of their courage. She knew she was going to need it.

The Prosecutor called Ikigai to the stand.

Ikigai stood and approached the Judge and felt as if she moved through Time the way her oars moved through the sea when she and her companions escaped the Island of the Keepers of the Key. She did her best to control her breathing as she sat between the Judge and the Jury.

The Prosecutor asked her simple questions, designed to prompt Ikigai into telling the tale I have just shared with you and presenting the evidence she had found of Tagagawas' transgressions.

When the Prosecutor was done, he sat, and the Defender stood, focused and smug. He knew how he would attack Ikigai. But, like any good fighter, he would not chase the knockout blow quite yet. He needed to soften his enemy first, weaken her defenses and her spirit.

"You spent a lot of resources helping these people attain their Freedom," the Defender said.

"Objection," the Prosecutor proclaimed. "Argumentative."

"What resources did you spend to help these people attain their Freedom?" the Defender demanded.

"I've documented all resources spent," Ikigai answered. "We needed to spend money for travel and for inns when navigating about The Land of 7,000 Islands."

"And what of the money your team provided to Tala that went above and beyond travel expenses? Why did you provide her with such funds?"

Ikigai knew this question was coming. She answered without hesitation. "My compatriot Mickey provided Tala with this money, to make up for the wages she lost not working the day they retrieved her Freedom."

"Is it the responsibility of you and your fellow warriors to assist those in need with lost wages?"

"It is our responsibility to seek Justice. We could not do so without acquiring Tala's Freedom. Tala could not acquire her Freedom and afford to lose a day's wages."

"Just seems like you and your compatriots went quite a bit out of your way."

Ikigai did not respond. There was no question to answer. Her pulse quickened, she knew what was coming next.

"How did you first get involved in this case?" the Defender asked.

"I was asked to examine artifacts belonging to Tagagawas."

"How were these artifacts acquired?"

"During a search of his home."

"And why was his home searched?"

"He was accused of raping a child."

"A child in The Land of 7,000 Islands?"

"No."

"Where was this child from?"

"Here. Our land."

I was hyperventilating. Mom put her hand on my back, watching me carefully. She did not ask again if I wanted to continue. We were far past the point of no return.

The Defender picked up a packet from his desk. From this packet he pulled forth a photograph. He showed this photograph to the Judge and the Jury. "This photo was taken mere weeks ago," he told them and showed it to Ikigai. "Who is in this photo?" he asked.

The photo was of two little girls, sitting on a sofa on a front lawn.

"That girl," Ikigai said pointing to the one on the left, her voice softening, "is my daughter."

"And who is this girl with your daughter?"

"Her best friend."

"And is this friend not the very child who Tagagawas was accused of raping?"

"Yes, she is."

"And what happened to the accusations this child brought against Tagagawas?"

"They were dropped."

"So, your daughter is friends with the very girl who first accused Tagagawas of stealing her Innocence? Accusations which were dropped, but which nonetheless, led you to go all the way to The Land of 7,000 Islands to find more accusers?"

"The evidence I found amongst Tagagawas' artifacts is what led me to go to The Land of 7,000 Islands."

"But you found this evidence because of a search that was supported by the accusations of your daughter's best friend?"

Ikigai gritted her teeth. "Yes."

"And you had no bias in this matter?"

"I did not."

"Were you seeking Justice for your daughter's friend?"

"I honestly did not know they were friends until right before this trial."

"You expect us to believe that?"

"I don't expect anything. I can only tell the truth."

My face was buried in my hands, my knees scrunched up to my head. Mom sat behind me, her arms and legs wrapping me into a tree-like cocoon. I sobbed. I knew it that day in front of Lily's house: the old-school car, a Lincoln or a Buick, the old-school camera, flashing twice, Lily muttering about the cloud that shouldn't be there. It was Tagagawas' Shadow Warriors. And Lily mumbling about the babies of the heavy or the light. Heavy. No baby. Tagagawas had raped her, my Lily. Heavy. No baby. She was afraid she would get pregnant.

Mom put her chin on the top of my head. "This is about to get a lot harder."

"Keep going," I whispered.

"I don't know Ikigai," the Defender said. "Maybe it is the truth."

"It is. There's no maybe," Ikigai said, knowing the worst was still yet to come.

"You were completely unbiased in the course of your investigation?"

"I was."

"Do you normally work cases that involve crimes against children?"

"No."

"Did you ever normally work such matters?" he pressed.

"Yes."

"How long ago did you stop working these cases?"

"About six years ago."

"Why?"

"I requested that I no longer work them."

"Why?"

"Personal reasons."

"And what were those personal reasons, Ikigai?" Ikigai glared at the Defender, who smiled smugly. "You need to answer the question. It brings your impartiality under review."

"A family affair," she answered.

"Please explain."

"I had a niece…"

"What happened to your niece, Ikigai?"

Ikigai fought not to tremble. "She killed herself."

"Why did she kill herself?"

"She was also a victim of sexual abuse."

"I'm sorry. How old was she when this happened?"

"Eleven."

"Who abused her?"

Ikigai tried to make her mouth move.

"Who abused her, Ikigai?"

"Her father."

"Was her father your brother?"

"He was."

"What was his name?"

"Tenno."

"And what happened to Tenno?"

"He died in prison."

"Monica," I sobbed. The name had finally come back to me. Monica, who had the same tiger eyes as me. My cousin, my big sister, who helped me ride my bike. Just pedal, just go. "You said it was a car crash," I screamed.

Mom held me tighter, distraught. "What else do you remember?"

"You said it was a car crash," I repeated. "But it wasn't and…"

The memory return was a punch to my chest.

Monica with the tiger eyes was in the bathtub, the dark red pouring down her arms, her tiger eyes going pale. I tugged at her fingers. I cried. I begged her, *please don't go to sleep*. I told her, *wake up. Why did you hurt yourself?* I asked. The mucus was dribbling down my chin as I told her, *come back.*

"I was there," I said, shivering violently. "I was there when she did it."

★★★

Eleven years later, in the spring of 2021, I read through the transcript of the trial *United States v. Campbell*. I read it comfortably at home on my tablet, having had it delivered to me via email, subsequent to my submission of an ordering form to the us District Court for the District of Oregon.

I wish I'd been brave enough to finish hearing Mom's story in the spring of 2010. But I wasn't. I screamed as all the memories flooded back at once, Mom holding me as I panicked and convulsed. Then I didn't go to school for four days.

On the first day, I stayed in bed and could not stop crying. Mom stayed home, alternating between coddling me and giving me the space I needed.

On the second day, I was wrath and fury. I hated my mother and I made sure she knew it. She said she would tell me the truth, but she didn't. She made a spectacle out of it all, out of people's lives, their horror and their pain, feeding me bullshit about great cranes and giant turtles and baby garudas. She'd turned it all into a fucking Disney movie.

But that was the second day. On the third day I calmed down and had a clearer understanding. How could she possibly break these facts to an eleven-year-old with suppressed memories? If she had come straight out and told me what was going on, I would have snapped. She knew that. She did the best she could with what she had. And what she had were stories.

On the fourth day, I decided to cut the crap and stop feeling sorry for myself. I was not even the victim here. And my Monica was gone, but in a way she was back in my life: the memory of her voice, her smell, how much she loved me. And now there was someone else who meant the world to me, and I hadn't seen her in four days.

On the morning of the fifth day, I told Mom very unambig-uously I was ready to return to school. "Are you sure?" she asked hesitantly.

"I need to see Lily," I said. Mom did not argue.

Later, I entered homeroom, swam through the roar of all those children, and walked straight to Lily.

Her eyes lit up. "Where were you?" she asked.

"My mom is here."

"Oh."

"She's outside."

"Okay."

I grabbed Lily's hand and led her to the door. Ms. Broner smiled gently at us, she already knew what was going on. We stepped out into the hallway where Mom was waiting.

"Hi, baby," Mom said, and she wasn't talking to me.

"Hi," Lily said shyly.

I could tell Mom was fighting back tears as she spoke to Lily. "Thank you for having dinner with us last week." (It had actually been two weeks ago, I'll come back to that.)

"Thank you," Lily said, looking at her shoes.

"You never have to thank me," Mom said and reached for Lily who instinctively gave in to Mom's hug. As Lily hugged her back, Mom looked at me and smiled. "Take care of each other. Always take care of each other."

As an adult, reading *United States v. Campbell,* I remembered these things. I read through my mother's final response to defense attorney Zach Weddle. I wasn't brave enough to finish the story when I was eleven.

So, I'll have to finish it now.

The Defender smiled. Ikigai the Warrior was tired. A sense of something with which she was all too familiar crept into her gut.

It was that panicky feeling you get when you're losing a fight. She tried to breathe through it. How dare this man. How dare he bring her life into this court of Law, smile smugly at it, tear it up, spit on it to distract the Jury from the issue at hand. She did not know Lily Phelps was her daughter's best friend. She was not Wonder Woman. Between work and raising a child, yes, she dropped a ball somewhere and did not realize exactly who her child was spending all that time with. She breathed through those thoughts too, watched them carefully, did not engage them. For they were the thoughts of a victim, not a warrior.

And a warrior, in the moment of truth, does not think. A warrior acts. And so, without thought, Ikigai stood and growled. "Perhaps I am biased. That's the point you think you've made, correct? That because of my daughter's friendship with a victim…"

"Alleged victim," the Defender corrected, "whose accusations were dropped. And your statements were not elicited by any question."

"…and because of my own personal tragedy," Ikigai talked over him, "I have a particular bone to pick with Tagagawas. I do not. I have a bone to pick with anyone who does what he did to any child."

"*Allegedly* did. I have no further questions," the Defender told the Judge.

"You hurt a child, any child," Ikigai continued, "and you cross my path? I will do whatever it takes. Nothing, absolutely nothing, will stop me."

"No further questions, your Honor," the Defender repeated.

"Ikigai…" the Judge said.

But Ikigai continued, her voice growing louder and softer at the same time. For underneath her words were the roar of a tigress, a Beautiful Lady's eruption, the laughter of boys playing patintero, the screaming of a little girl's eyes, the promise made to a fighting rooster. "I do not care about geography," she growled. "I do not care about terrorists. I do not care about Shadow Warriors. I do not care about any and all things you or anyone else could possibly throw in my way. I *will* find the facts. I *will* find the truth. And if you are guilty, I will ensure you never, ever hurt another child again."

"Ikigai…" the Judge warned again.

She sat back down, took a breath, and looked at the Jury. "And that's what I did for this case, and that's what I'd do for any child, anywhere, mine, or yours," she pointed at the Defender, then at the members of the Jury one by one, "or yours, or yours, or yours."

The Jury stared at this gray-haired tree-woman with the voice of a tigress and did their best to appear impartial. But a few of the jurors could not fight back smiles of admiration.

(Mom actually did say most of those things, but she stated them in the context of AUSA Martel eliciting them during his redirect examination. It'd be boring if I wrote it that way.)

"Step down, Ikigai," the Judge told her. "The Jury will be instructed to ignore your remarks as they were not elicited by any specific question. Especially since the Defender rested."

Ikigai knew that didn't matter. Spoken words heard cannot be unheard. Even the Judge did not have that power. She stepped down, fighting back a smile herself.

But the Judge had other power. After the Defender and the Prosecutor wrapped up their closing arguments, the Judge instructed the Jury to deliberate and to provide their decision.

Hours later they returned.

The representative of the Jury spoke:

"For Count one of Coercion and Enticement, we find Tagagawas, guilty. For Count two of Coercion and Enticement, not guilty. For Count three of Coercion and Enticement, not guilty. For Count one of Travel with Intent to Engage in Illicit

Sexual Conduct, guilty. Count two of Travel with Intent to Engage in Illicit Sexual Conduct, guilty. Count three of Travel with Intent to Engage in Illicit Sexual Conduct, guilty. Count one of Engaging in Illicit Sexual Conduct in a Foreign Place, guilty. Count two of Engaging in Illicit Sexual Conduct in a Foreign Place, guilty. Count three of Engaging in Illicit Sexual Conduct in a Foreign Place, guilty. Count four of Engaging in Illicit Sexual Conduct in a Foreign Place, not guilty."

The not guilty verdicts were for the counts pertaining to Bayani Matapang, but this did not diminish the victory at hand. Ikigai watched Malaya, Tala, Datu, Kidlat and Lualhati hug each other as the court-assigned interpreter explained to them what was going on. The Prosecutor and the Amazon kept themselves under control. Tagagawas looked at his Defender, and finally, finally, crumpled into his chair, defeated.

Seven counts, guilty as charged. They had done it. They had won.

The Judge had the power of sentencing punishment. But he would not execute it yet. "We will reconvene three months from now," he said.

★★★

When the trial ended, toward the end of winter, I hadn't yet known any of this. All I knew was Mom was back home and spending as much time with me as possible. Dad even gave up some of his custody days and let her keep me a full week when she was done with the trial. Things went back to normal. Sort of.

When we paddled on the Willamette River, before the rising sun, something had changed. She would often stop in the middle of the water, stare off into space, and shiver. And the first morning I got ready to jump into the river and swim, she gripped my

shoulder and held me back. "It's okay, baby, let's just keep paddling in." She never made me swim to shore again.

In some ways she was harder. Her hands felt like knotted wood
when she touched or cuddled me. But I noticed this because she
was touching and cuddling me a lot more than she used to. It was
as if her body had grown harder to protect whatever had grown
softer inside.

But things had changed inside me as well. The mist was still
there, particles of disjointed memories blurring my vision. I knew
she could help, but I did not know how to bring it up. So one
morning, as winter was transitioning to spring, instinctively
knowing that what we were each going through was somehow
connected, I said, "You still haven't told me why you were in the
Philippines."

"When the time is right, sweety."

"You promised. That was our deal."

"And I will tell you the whole story. When the time is right."

Another morning, watching the sun rise on the banks of the
river, I said, "You need to meet my friend…"

"Lily," she interrupted. "Yes, I do."

I paused as it occurred to me that at that point I had never actually told her Lily's name. I shrugged it off, mothers knew everything after all.

"We can have her over for dinner, if you like. Maybe at your
father's house? He has a real kitchen table," she chuckled. I nodded
excitedly.

Dinner with my parents was quiet. This didn't surprise me as Lily
was painfully shy. Mom and Dad seemed to respect the silence of
my friend, and they acquiesced to it, talking in low voices about
bills and mutual friends, while Lily chewed Dad's spaghetti and
meatballs and looked at them with a blank expression. Once in a

while, Mom would catch Lily's eye and she would smile and Lily would smile back. This made me happy, I could tell Lily felt safe with my mother there.

After dinner, on the front porch of Dad's house, as Lily and I breathed in the spring evening and waited for Mom to come out so we could walk Lily back home, Lily grabbed my hand.

"Will you go somewhere with me?" she asked.

"Where?"

"In two weeks. Something's going to happen."

I squinted.

"I have to go to court," she said.

"Are you in trouble?"

"Someone else is. I have to see what happens. Please go with me?"

My loyalty outweighed my lack of comprehension. "I'll go."

When Mom returned me to Dad's house, after dropping Lily off, she wrapped her arms around me. "Just wanted to hug you one more time," she said.

"I have to go somewhere with Lily."

"Right now?"

"In two weeks, she said. A court. She needs me to be there with her."

A dark look crossed Mom's features. "I'll need to talk to your father about that." She went upstairs. I heard her knock on Dad's bedroom door. Then I heard muffled shouts. They were fighting again. I could make out sentences here and there.

"She'll have to face it eventually," I heard Mom say.

"Better ways to go about this," Dad said. "Like take her to a professional."

I walked upstairs, stood outside the door to Dad's bedroom, and added to the shouts. "I *am* going! I don't fucking care what either of you say! My friend needs me and I'm going!"

Mom looked at me in shock. Dad rubbed his head and nodded. "That's what you've been missing out on," he told her. "That's what I've been dealing with. Alone."

I tensed as my mother approached me, worried she'd smack me or worse, tear into me verbally. She didn't. She turned and looked at my Dad with pleading eyes. And in a moment from what they probably once were years ago, Dad read her look and responded, "Yeah, Ikigai. You should take her to yours. It's time."

My mother faced me again, steel in her gaze. "You will go with your friend to court. This is your decision?" she asked.

I choked down the fear, returned the steel in her gaze with my own, and spoke through clenched teeth. "My friend needs me. I'm going."

My mother nodded. "Then I will respect your decision. Go pack your stuff. You're staying at my place for a while."

Later, at her condo, Mom entered the living room where I lay in bed. Holding a small towel and a paper fan, she stood over me. "I'm sorry I screamed at you and Dad," I said.

"You cursed too."

"I'm sorry. It's just, my friend needs me."

Mom sat at the foot of my bed and took in a deep breath. "If you can hold yourself in the silent space of this coming dawn, you will see, my love, that I do not want your apologies. I want your accountability."

My eyelids shot open and I caught a sharp intake of my own breath. She was finally keeping her promise.

"Always remember daughter, warriors do not apologize," she said, watching my anticipation. "It was the Great Crane of the West who had posed for Ikigai the Warrior the first of her many challenges…"

I sat up and leaned against my headboard. My heart pounded.

"I will tell you that story," she continued, "of the things you must know."

My mother and I looked at each other, knowing our world was about to change forever.

"There exists a land which takes the crossing of several oceans to reach…"

CHAPTER. XX

EPILOGUE

Lily buried her face in my neck. She could not bring herself to look at him. The Judge spoke and it became clearer why Mom had revealed everything to me the way she had. This was hard to listen to. Evan Campbell stood in his orange jumpsuit and looked straight ahead.

Lily and I sat in a pew near the back of the courtroom and listened to the Judge's remarks. We were not alone. Next to me was another girl, a girl with dark eyes whose quiet strength was exactly as Mom had described. It was Lualhati. And next to Lualhati was her brother, Datu, then her cousin, Kidlat, and their mothers Malaya and Tala.

(Of course, out of respect for their privacy, these were never their real names. In reality, "Malaya" *had* lied about the death of her daughter. However, Mom had, in fact, determined that "Malaya" was lying by noticing she never referred to her daughter in the past tense.)

Beside our pew stood a group of adults, forming a protective shell around us. PPB Detective Geri Bradford, who caught my eye and fought back a tear as I stroked Lily's hair. PPB Detective Nate Schwinn, who clenched his jaw and looked at the ceiling. And FBI ALAT Mickey Sheptinsky, who was a lot rougher-looking in real life than the way I imagined him. He honestly looked like a professional killer. He had escorted Malaya and Tala and their children back to the states to listen to the Judge's sentencing of Evan Campbell. My mother, who stood with the grown-ups, rarely took her eyes off me and the rest of the children. But when she did, I couldn't help but notice the strange and faraway look in her eyes.

The Judge spoke of compassion. He spoke, in fact, of the compassion that he had for Evan Campbell. That took me by surprise.

He spoke of the compassion he had for the fact that Evan Campbell was a sick man. And he apologized to Evan Campbell. I did not understand this at the time. It wouldn't be until I was much, much older that I would see the wisdom in these words. The Judge expressed that he was sorry he could do nothing to help Evan Campbell overcome his sickness. Then the Judge spoke of balance. He needed to balance this compassion toward Evan's sickness with the need to protect — to protect the vulnerable, to protect Lily and Lualhati and Datu and Kidlat, to protect me, to protect Monica, to protect Bayani. I wished I had gotten to meet Bayani, and Hari, who couldn't make it. When I thought this, Lualhati caught the look on my face. We could not converse, her English was not very good and I spoke nothing of Cebuano. But when I thought of Bayani and Hari, she saw my face, and creased her eyebrows. Then she hugged me, and she and I and Lily sat there, protecting each other.

For the seven counts of which he was found guilty, the Judge sentenced Evan Campbell to 63 years of incarceration. Evan Campbell was already in his forties. He would effectively spend the rest of his life in prison.

Afterwards, we all met in the hall outside the courtroom. There was a lot of hugging and congratulations. And when I caught the glint in Mickey's eye as he looked at my mother, he grinned like a little boy. Then I understood what Mom saw in him.

I stood by Mom as she and Mickey spoke, fighting back smiles from being near each other again.

"Good job, lady," he told her.

"Shut up," she replied. "Apparently, I had a little help."

"We got your application at the Legat."

"I know."

"Won't be official for a few weeks. But it's pretty obvious who's getting the job."

I tugged at Mom's hand. "You're going back now?" I asked, panicky.

"Not yet," she told me. "Let's talk about it later, okay?"

Mom had made a promise to Bayani Matapang, the promise that convinced him to let her go. She gave him her very Purpose and promised to return to The Land of 7,000 Islands. There were too many children there for whom Justice had never been found. She knew she could only do so much, but she knew that she was built for such work. She could not deny this any longer.

I was upset at first. But then it became fun. I would visit her in the Philippines all the time. And as me and Lily grew older and entered our teens, we would visit my mother together. In fact, it was in Manila, at sixteen and fifteen years old, in the privacy of our own hotel room, that Lily and I first held hands, for a really, really, long time.

I was so happy when that happened. We were childhood sweethearts; we'd loved each other since the sixth grade. When the waves of our high school years came crashing against our shore it had come time for us to acknowledge and understand this. It helped that everyone around us was so supportive. Mom said there was no surprise on her part, she knew we were soul mates the first time she saw us together as kids.

But the joy of exploring that new phase in our relationship in the summer of 2014 was overshadowed when, a few months later, we learned Mom had disappeared.

It's time to leave Geri's office. We've been here all night. The sun is starting to rise outside. Geri rubs her eyes and puts her glasses on. "I found the other interview."

"What other interview?" I ask.

Geri takes a breath. "The one with Monica."

I stare at the wall behind her.

"You know I was the one who interviewed her right? Before she... That was my case. I interviewed you too. You still don't remember? That's why me and Ikigai didn't get along so well at first. I'm the one who put Tenno away."

The mist comes back. But I'm used to it. I stand. "I remember what I need to remember for what I have to do right now."

"Sweety," she says gently, but firmly. "Sit down."

"It'll work, Geri."

"You think so, huh?"

"It will. I'm sure she's keeping tabs on the news here. She'll see this obituary and the business about the cremation and she'll stop dicking around and come back home."

"Junior..."

"It'll work."

"Junior," Geri holds my gaze with those wolf eyes. "Did you really believe Mickey's account?"

I deflate and crumple back in my chair and put my head in my hands. "No."

Geri gets up, walks around her desk and puts her arms around me. "Me neither."

"I still don't understand," I say, unable to fight back the tears. "I still don't understand why she..."

Geri rubs my back. "You know, me and her would talk long-distance once in a while after she left for the Philippines. Really talk." Geri looks out of her office window at the slowly rising dawn. "Even before everything that happened with Tenno and Monica, your mom was a lady carrying a lot of ghosts. It sounds like she told you about her father."

I nod and wipe the snot from my nose.

"So imagine, this poor girl's dad gets killed by two officers who apparently thought he was someone else. And this is Brooklyn in the 70s, so you know those two pieces of shit never faced any consequences." Geri sighs. "Sounds like she never really told you the effect this had on her mother."

"She said grandma was hospitalized."

"That's part of it," Geri nods. "But that hospitalization didn't happen immediately, you know. Your grandma, Akai, she already had her own struggles. We're talking about someone who was a young woman in Japan when two atomic bombs were dropped on her country." Geri looks at the floor. "Later, after she went through hell to get to the states, she found love with your grandfather Peter, who was then ripped away from her." Geri sighs. "Akai was pretty devastated and pretty angry and... from what Ikigai shared, it sounds like she took it out on her kids. I think there was a lot of abuse there that Ikigai never fully confronted. And I think Tenno was the one who got the brunt of it."

I'm trembling and the tears won't stop. "Mom said she found inner peace," I bawl like I'm eleven years old again. "After the last time she saw the Emperor's Ghost, she said she found inner peace. What, was she full of shit?"

"I don't think she was full of shit," Geri says and cups my face in her hands which makes me feel stupid since, thanks to my father's genes, I'm as big as she is now.

"I think," Geri says, "I think she was trying to tell you that you were the one who needed to move on from all these ghosts."

★★★

Geri tells me I should go home. I take her advice and head to Mom's, now my, condominium complex. The central pathway, lined with canopy forming maple trees, laurel and azalea at my feet, reminds me why Mom liked it here so much. After she drowned herself – there, I said it, I'm finally accepting it

— we weren't sure she wasn't still alive somewhere, puttering around. So Dad took over the mortgage and HOA payments on the property. When I hit eighteen, I moved into it, got a job at Home Depot to make the payments myself and went to Portland Community College. I worked and got my Associate's in Criminal Justice. Then I applied to the Portland Police Bureau. That was not a popular decision among my peers. I onboarded with PPB right after George Floyd was murdered. Most people I was friends with went out on the streets to scream ACAB and smash Starbucks windows. I'd be lying if I didn't say a part of me, a big part, wanted to join them, especially when I thought of my grandfather. But unfortunately, I'm afflicted with an illness I seem to have inherited from my mother. I've got this crazy notion that if I work from the inside I can maybe make things a little bit better. Maybe. We'll see how that turns out. Hopefully it doesn't lead me to the same place it led my mother. I can surmise until I'm blue in the face all the things she would have done and thought of when she was alone. But that's the thing about suicides — you never know, no matter what notes or artifacts or stories they leave behind for the living, what horror or what peace they would have felt when they finally made the irreversible decision to go.

The condo complex is only two levels and I head upstairs to my corner unit. I fumble with the key in the lock. I'm tired and the lock is old and the key always needs to be turned just right. My struggle is all for naught anyway because the door swings open.

Lily stands in the doorway, looking up at me, wearing one of my T-shirts that's somehow become one of her T-shirts.

"How'd it go?" she asks.

"You want to let me in?"

She playfully pushes the door as if she's closing it.

"Come on," I say and pull the key out. "I'm exhausted."

She lets me in. I take off my shoes and head straight for the bedroom, grumbling. "We've got to replace that lock already."

"Yeah, you do," she says. "Breadwinner."

She's all chipper and it's something I've been trying to practice patience with. She's a morning person. I am not. "You'll be getting bread soon," I say and hit the bed still wearing my clothes. She sits beside me and shrugs. "Not my motivation, but sure." A few months ago she finished her Bachelor's in Psychology with a minor in Child, Youth and Family Studies. Now she's getting her Master's. She wants to be a Child Therapist. I'm so damn proud of her.

Now if only she would learn to leave me alone in the mornings.

"How'd it go?" she asks again.

"That's still my shirt."

"I don't know what you're talking about," she says, crawling up on top of me and bouncing like she's still a kid. As aggravating as this is, I'm glad she's in a better mood. A week ago she woke up in the middle of the night sobbing and muttering about the clouds and the babies of the heavy and the light. That still happens every now and then. Luckily it was my night off and I was able to hold her.

"It's nice outside," she says. "Let's go—"

"Nuh uh," I say. "I'm not going out on the water." But even as I say it we both know I'm full of shit. We've only been married a few months, but Lily Phelps has had me wrapped around her finger since the sixth grade.

★★★

Once we've paddled into the middle of the river I'm semi-glad she dragged me out. The Willamette's waves slap gently against the kayak's hull and the calls of crows echo over the water from the trails surrounding the river and Sucker Creek. It's not raining even though fall is transitioning to winter. Someone's dog barks as it plays by the shore. Lily sits behind me. Our kayak's a little more high-end than the one I used to come out in with Mom. Aluminum frame. A wedding gift from Dad. For all that man's faults he's been nothing but supportive in every aspect of my life. The kayak rocks and I feel Lily shifting her weight behind me, getting out of her seat. "Hey," I say, "what are you, you're gonna fall." Then I feel her arms wrap around me and I hear her voice, soft and warm, in my ear.

"How'd it go?"

"It went, Lily. I don't know what you want me to say."

She squeezes me gently. "Are you still going to pretend there's a cremation?"

I sigh and rest my paddle on the deck. "No."

Lily grips me tighter. She knows as tough as I'm pretending to be I need her right now and if she lets me go I'll be the one who falls.

"Ikigai," she says, and the sound of my name, my real name, makes me crumble. But I'm all cried out and I have no more tears. She kisses my neck. "What do we do in the morning?"

I force the words out. "We get up."

"And then?"

I turn to where the sun is rising over the pine trees on the east bank of the river. As I do a cloud clears and for a moment I'm blinded. A bird calls strongly above and when I look up there's a flash of red and gold – one of the red-tailed hawks in the area. It makes me smile. "That," I say and point to the rising sun. "We face that."

We giggle like we're still in middle school and Lily says, "Then what?"

"We do our best," I whisper. "Our very best."

"At the end of the day," Lily says and I rest in the strength of her arms, "that's all a warrior can do."

Zephaniah Sole is a Martha's Vineyard Institute of Creative Writing Author Fellow as well as an alum of VONA and Tin House. His fiction has appeared in *Epiphany*, *Gargoyle Magazine*, *Collateral Journal* and *Vestal Review*, among other publications. A graduate of New York University, he's been a filmmaker, a public school teacher, and is an FBI agent. Born and raised in Brooklyn, he now lives in the Pacific Northwest.